LET US PREY

Bill Branon

HarperPaperbacks
A Division of HarperCollins*Publishers*

This is a work of fiction. The characters, incidents, and dialogues are products of the author's imagination and are not to be construed as real. Any resemblance to actual events or persons, living or dead, is entirely coincidental.

HarperPaperbacks *A Division of* HarperCollins*Publishers*
                  10 East 53rd Street, New York, N.Y. 10022

Copyright © 1994 by Bill Branon
All rights reserved. No part of this book may be used or reproduced in any manner whatsoever without written permission of the publisher, except in the case of brief quotations embodied in critical articles and reviews. For information address HarperCollins*Publishers,*
10 East 53rd Street, New York, N.Y. 10022.

A hardcover edition of this book was published in 1994 by HarperCollins*Publishers.*

Cover illustration by Danilo Ducak

First HarperPaperbacks printing: January 1995

Printed in the United States of America

HarperPaperbacks and colophon are trademarks of HarperCollins*Publishers*

❖ 10 9 8 7 6 5 4 3 2 1

For Bob Howie
. . . now get off my back

The Devil isn't hate, isn't evil;
The Devil is doubt.
And God is neither love nor goodness;
God is realization.
Keep your eyes open.

—LAS VEGAS, NEVADA
Twilight zone, 4 A.M., 1990—

There are three kinds of people, bro.
Those who don't know,
Those who don't care,
And survivors.

—BINH DINH PROVINCE
Vietnam, 1969—

1

The Hit

The bullet came in 2.5 centimeters low. It refracted upward from the point of impact with the windshield where the lead began to mushroom, but the slug continued in the correct vertical plane and carried into the maxillary midline suture with robust authority. Olento's upper front teeth, palate, and titanium partial denture exploded downward, blowing away his entire lower jaw and ramming shredded tongue debris down his throat. His cheeks detonated out at right angles to the projectile path and smashed against the side windows. As the bullet pitched up and began to yaw slightly, it initiated contact with the posterior wall of the pharynx and drove the maximum possible cross-section of its splitting copper jacket through the area of the foramen magnum. The fragmenting base of the skull and the boisterous bursting of the top three cervical vertebrae created a blizzard of bone that instantly turned Olento's cocaine-saturated lower brain and upper spinal cord into something that closely resembled hominy grits in texture, color, and temperature.

Mitch had been on Olento's tail since they popped through Cajon Pass at seven that morning. After the stop in Barstow, he shadowed the BMW back onto I-15 and tailed behind. As the two vehicles closed the Field Road exit, the Blazer accelerated and passed the BMW. Mitch eased up two hundred meters ahead and held the new position. Olento was on cruise control; it was an easy spot. The bridge at Afton was next. Ram would be coiled in the blue shadow . . . waiting . . . watching . . . touching the metal . . . setting his left knee and right heel firmly into the north-facing slope under the bridge. Mitch had noticed the hard kill-light in his brother's eyes at the setup. Ram wanted this one.

In the gray light of the highway overpass, up near the crossbeams in the hot angle where old sand endured the insolent press of young cement, Ram watched the eastbound traffic snake toward him across the desert. The morning sunlight slanted at the wind-shields of the oncoming cars; he was undetectable. The warm stock of the HK-91 ghosted up and gently kissed his hard cheek as he centered an approaching driver in the Leupold glass. Two hundred meters from the over-pass the shape hovered. The face appeared large, unnatural, flat in the lens. At fifty meters he squeezed off an imaginary round as the rifle axis dropped five degrees to compensate for the closing angle.

Click!

Metal on metal. Satisfying. Solid. Visceral.

At two minutes to zero, he snapped a five-round magazine into the receiver. From a dark burrow near the edge of the shade an inquisitive ground squirrel flickered to a sitting position to study the intruder. The smaller animal froze in place, focused a side-looking eye on the larger one, and waited for something to happen.

The Blazer would run just ahead of Olento's BMW. In the thin morning traffic, picking out the car would not be difficult. Ram pictured Olento moving at him through the crystalline indifference of the Mojave. He thought about the square pug face with the wavy pompadour that could be made in a fog of whale sneeze on a bad day. He saw the lying eyes. He thought about the cocky attitude, the assumed immortality of the con man. He smiled. He was about to correct a serious biological mistake.

And Ram saw them. In the summer distance. Twenty minutes late. The Blazer was coming fast, eighty, eighty-five. As the adrenaline pumped through his system he could feel his testicles crawl; then the rush backed off, became part of his blood, and a familiar steadiness iced down his arms.

He eased Olento's face into the scope. The image floated on the lens in the detached manner of magnified things. It hung and rippled like a thin memory in the heat rising off the blacktop. Ram feasted on the moment. Then, in that eternal second of the squeezing down, the drifting visage of faded brown skin vanished from the scope, to be replaced, in one atom of time, by a spiderweb of fractured glass as the windshield of the BMW was violated by the spinning 7.62mm product of Winchester's meticulous sons and daughters.

Olento had been motoring along on cruise control

with his right leg extended casually across the center console. Only his right index finger rested on the steering wheel at the six o'clock position. The bullet caused the finger to slip off the wheel with no force at all, and the BMW continued in a straight line. Ram had fired once. As the car flashed past he could see the sinking ooze that covered the side window and he knew he had exploded the skull. It was a "clean" shot.

Ram shifted position to watch the BMW continue down the freeway. The car ran on for almost a quarter mile before it started to drift right at the urging of the road's camber. Then the front right wheel caught the soft earth at the shoulder, and the car cut toward a shallow drainage ditch that ran along the roadway. The vehicle bottomed in the ditch and hurtled skyward as it rebounded out of the depression. The BMW seemed to float for a long time with its front end pointing straight up. Then it came to earth rearfirst and commenced to change itself into scrap. There had been no other traffic nearby to witness the event, but that would not have mattered to Ram. They had reasoned that the highway would be lightly traveled.

Ram slipped the HK into a fishing rod carry, glanced east then west down the freeway, and climbed out from under the bridge onto the overpass. The Yamaha cracked to life at the first kick, and as he wheeled left down the ramp he snapped up the chin strap on the black full-face helmet. He accelerated to sixty-five and moved onto I-15 heading west.

Mitch had watched in the rearview mirror as the BMW passed under the Afton bridge. It came back into the sunlight after blinking out of sight in the bridge shadow. When more seconds passed and the

BMW continued to hold station behind him, Mitch could feel his pulse tighten. Something had gone wrong. He felt a hundred tiny ants start to scratch across his forearms. Then he noticed the silver car begin to drift. It gently floated to the right in the glass. In the next moment the image blossomed into a billowing explosion of sand. Violent. Soundless. He lit a cigarette and exhaled. The nicotine and the surge of the kill got to him at the same time.

Three sensations swept through him in the next minute as he relaxed, as the concentration of the task fell away.

He became physically aware of the sense of speed and motion that came up from the road through tires, stiff shocks, and frame; he became intellectually aware of the quick anger that accompanied a death that was too quick and simple for such as Olento; and he became emotionally aware of something coiling back to sleep in his soul. And he didn't know what it was.

2

Rebeca

Rebeca was messed up, but coherent. At ten o'clock in the morning, the midweek *turistas* in the video poker area of the Sands Casino were outnumbered by the employees. A few inveterate slot warriors gambled tentatively at the blinking machines. The change girls circulated at half speed. Except for these desperadoes working off the last of their traveling funds in glassy-eyed disbelief, there didn't seem to be any potential marks. She adjusted her sunglasses and thanked fate for the subdued light of the place. She had the bite of a hangover from too much blow and much too much booze. Her eyes hurt even in the scant light; the sunglasses hurt the bridge of her nose; her legs ached from lack of sleep; and the ribs on her right side were still sore from the scripture-screaming evangelist who had tried to screw her sideways on the coffee table three hours ago. Her eyelids felt like rusty Brillo pads, and the roof of her mouth seemed to be coated with a layer of asphalt. About par for a six-trick day. She inventoried her abused parts and told herself she needed another cigarette about as much as she needed another pair of balls resting on her chin, but she was flat out and the need for nicotine was putting ugly little scratches on her brain.

The trick sat alone at one of the tabletop video poker machines. She looked him over. He wore a loose gray pullover and a pair of tan stretch-polyester pants. *Short-cropped blond hair, receding somewhat. Average to small dick. Would tire easily. Probably a rug-eater. About forty years old. Twenty pounds overweight under those baggy threads. Didn't seem too bad ... certainly not down and out ... but hard to classify. Definitely not local, yet not standard-issue tourist. Could have been one of the clipboard crowd laying off for some East Coast book, but he didn't look arrogant enough. Clean hands and nails.* She thought he was non-cop, but the Man was tough to finger these days with all the dime-narcs around. A gym bag nested on the floor between his legs, and a silver farm of quarters was fanned out on the glass in front of him. He inserted the coins slowly, with a playful rhythm. To her way of thinking, that meant one of three things—he had won big in the last few days, he was thinking of something else, or he was a goddamn idiot. No matter what, he was smoking a cigarette. And she needed a cigarette. She aimed her enterprising crotch at him and walked over.

She eased onto the seat next to Polyester.

"How ya doin'?" In her semideep slur.

"Not too bad. Win a few, lose a few," said the

mark after a small pause that indicated he hadn't seen her coming. He could smell the booze.

"Are ya winnin' anything?" *Fuck,* she thought, *I can't talk. I just asked him that.*

"I'm a couple of bucks down. Just feeding the machine."

He did a double take. The first look left him in doubt. He figured her quick on the second look. Hooker. Either still high on something or slightly brain-dead, a real good possibility considering the junk these folks scored on the street these days. Young, maybe twenty, twenty-one at most. Dressed like a boy: short hair, jeans, T-shirt, wallet in hand, nice tits, good shape, about 5'5", a wide but pretty face with interesting lips that for some weird reason reminded him of Brooke Shields's forehead.

"Can I get one of those?" She indicated the cigarette with a nod of her head and a little-kid–type point of her finger.

He dug a cigarette out of his shirt pocket and handed it to her. She put it into Brooke Shields's forehead and leaned forward for the match he had struck.

No class, she thought, *doesn't even carry a lighter.*

She sat smoking and watched him run some hands. Neither spoke for a few minutes while she basked in the nicotine. He wondered, in disbelief, why his groin was beginning to tickle. He had been gambling hard over the last four days, the thought of sex dissolved in the rancid twist of overbetting. He had the urge to unzip his fly to see if something with legs had crawled into his skivvies.

"Where ya stayin'?" she said.

"Checked out this morning. Heading back to San Diego in a few hours."

"Wanna party?" Leaning over near his ear.

"What?" Stalling to hear it again.

"Wanna party?"

"Hell. Got no room. Checked out already." Putting it off.

Silence for a minute while he played two more hands. Funny how the quarters never seem to win when you're not concentrating.

"Could have a good party," she slurred. *Jesus,* she thought, *I'm talking like a damn spastic. Work, mouth, work!*

Now he had to decide. There was something different about this girl. She was intriguing in a ridiculous sort of way. Her mind was at the beach, but that might just be temporary. If not, so what? He had to admit he wasn't into jumping imbeciles . . . but he really wanted to see her spread out. She was good-looking like the farmer's daughter was good-looking. She was funny to the point of being a cartoon of this kind of sex. He felt he was in some sort of comedy movie. But his pants were thinking hard thoughts.

"How much?" he asked.

"Fifty dollars."

"Fifty dollars?" he repeated, not really a question. No mention of time, where, or what. This was going to be a rare one. "You got a place?" he asked.

It was her turn to decide. She knew that Ramon would probably be drinking cheap wine on the bed, watching TV. She knew that Carlos would be somewhere around in his dirty diapers, since she had agreed to let Ramon watch him for Rita at her place while Rita worked. Rita gave Ramon three bucks and some Boone's Farm to keep an eye on the kid while she checked groceries at Vons. What she was having trouble figuring out, in her fogged-up condition, was what to do with the month-old puppy she had adopted from Tyrone when he took off to Los Angeles last week. She loved the pup, but he made puppy shit all over the place. And Ramon just stepped over it. The apartment was only an old motel room. One double bed, a dresser, one TV, one hot plate, a refrigerator in the corner, and the bathroom . . . and plenty of dog crap. She could get Ramon and Carlos to disappear for a half hour, but she'd have to keep the pup in the room. This guy's prick would probably fall off when he walked in there. She wondered if puppy shit would rinse out of polyester.

"I've got an apartment," she said, "but it's not fixed up."

"Around here?"

"Not too far. Can I have another one?" Indicating the pack of cigarettes in his pocket. He gave her another.

"What's 'not too far'?" he asked.

"Down past the Sahara."

"You have a car?"

"Can take a cab . . . you got to pay for it."

Down past the Sahara could mean Reno, he thought. He wished his poke would go down. He already had a flight reservation, but he knew he could get a later one. She had him thinking. He continued to play the machine for several minutes, not saying anything. He smoked one with her. She sat there. He noticed that she was not mumbling words as much as before. Maybe the nicotine was getting her brain in gear. It sure wasn't the fucking conversation.

"Well, do you want to party or not?"

He turned his head and looked her over again. Good figure. No fat. Curvy little ass. Medium tits, firm . . . maybe a silk bra . . . nipples pointing, shouting. His tool spearing at the stretch polyester. *Whirr. Click.*

"Why not?" he replied. "What's your name?"

3

Father Kevin Ball

Father Kevin Ball stretched out on the king-size bed in his suite on the twenty-seventh floor of the Aladdin Hotel. He had shed his priestly clothes down to the black cotton pants and had thrown collar, shirt, and coat into a single heap beside the bed. He peered down at his toes over an undershirt that refused to flatten even when he was resting on his back. No need to concern himself with the God suit for the next few days; it had served its purpose. That suit, a few "Bless you's," and the presumption of poverty carried a long way . . . even in this cynical age.

After a few restive moments, he got up and brought his carry-on bag over to the big bed. He snapped it open and inhaled deeply above the four hundred thousand dollars in neatly bundled hundreds. Now here was a smell! The zippy aroma of federal paper was something he could identify with his head stuck in a sack of garlic.

"The Lord provides," he intoned with sermonic volume. He pushed the case shut and headed for the glass-topped bar to lay out a two-inch line of snowy inspiration.

The Lord was providing well.

Two hours later, Kevin of Christ crossed the floor of the casino and manipulated his 270-pound bulk between two players at the rail. He always picked the craps table with the loudest crowd. That was where the dice were passing. That was where the fever was. He loved the lusty excitement of the shoot. Those little red cubes were gods in their own flat Eden, where they ruled the fate of all those straining souls at the table just as surely as God ruled in His heaven. And these gods he could better understand. They created and dissolved fortunes. They could elevate the human psyche to a frantic place. They could paint a depression so black that some lost the light forever. They could inspire unreasonable fantasy and confound the resolve of willpower. They could cause disbelieving men to cry in dark rooms at night, and they could move beautiful women to scream with more intensity than the best nitrate orgasm lovers could buy. To Kevin, the sound of a dice table in full howl had a life all its own. It didn't happen every hour or even every day, but when it did . . . Kevin felt the excitement zing into his gut as he plugged into the rail.

"How's the table been?" he asked the tweed jacket to his left.

"It was just chopping back and forth till about ten minutes ago. That guy down there just made . . . what, his eighth pass, Barney?" said Tweed with a quick glance at a friend on his other side.

"Numbers or coming out?" Kevin asked.

The energy was already transfusing into his chest

beneath his garish, big-flowered, yellow and red, good luck, Hawaiian, starting-to-fade, extra-large shooting shirt.

"A little of each," said Tweed, not taking his eyes off the shooter who with slow deliberation was fingering the dice at the far end of the table. Kevin took a black chip from his pocket and placed it on the come section as the shooter, satisfied with his surfaces, placed one die gently on top of the other. The dealer across from Kevin, seeing the black chip on the come, looked up for the first time since Kevin had taken a place at the rail.

"Hey, Mr. K., how's it going?"

"Pretty good, my man, pretty good. Just got in a few hours ago. How are you doing, Louis?"

The dice bounded between them and ricocheted off the end bumper. A three and a two showed.

"Five . . . a no-field five," resonated the stickman.

Some hardy cheers from the five-bettors spread down the table, and the dealers bent to work paying off the fives. The dealers paid the winning players in order, proceeding around the ends of the table to the gamblers standing next to the stick. The pop, slap, and ripple of chips cut through the animated noise of the players and the friendly chatter of the crew. Louis moved Kevin's black chip to the five box.

The stickman scanned the action from his midrail position on the players' side of the table. He chanted the game along and pushed the proposition bets to appease the box man hunched in his center seat and the pit boss who had come to stand behind the box.

"Hard eight, hard eight's gonna come, I feel that hard eight a-coming . . . who wants my hard eight?" sang the stick.

Kevin saw the stickman fire off a quick glance at

the two good-looking women next to the shooter. Not actually making eye contact with them. In fact, careful not to make eye contact with them, but following up with an eye-rolling deadpan for the benefit of the box and the two dealers across the table. The dealers both grinned, kept their eyes down, and busied themselves unnecessarily with the pay stacks. The box met the stick's eyes, did not frown, and looked away. That was the box man's way of acknowledging the comment. His reaction was equivalent to a normal person's laugh. If he had been offended by the remark he would have continued to stare at the stick. Either way, the expression would not change. That was how box men communicated. They were the hard link between the powerful owners and the wild-eyed, not-to-be-trusted, sticky-fingered, out-of-control, oversexed, drugged-up, probably-screw-the-dog-when-off-work table crews.

Kevin loved it. He floated on the excitement, the straining of hope, the dramatics, the camaraderie, and the compression of human emotion. He never forgot a dealer's name. He would get special gifts for the bosses as the season wore on—silk shirts, cuff links, oddball souvenirs—and he always toked the crews generously. He shared his good luck and laughed away the bad. After years of plucking pale emotional cobwebs from his plodding parishioners, here was his great escape—this game, these people who risked their composure at the table but who had no claim on his compassion when their effervescent little worlds collapsed. He even enjoyed seeing them lose heavily and get that desperate, angry look, as if they had been betrayed by someone. He would watch them and feel a certain freedom. Not many in this town knew of his vows or his God suit. Not many, not even the dealers, knew he was a papal eardrum saturated with the repetitive ether of the confessional. Nobody ever told him the good stuff in there anyway.

He was tired of unimaginative worries. He wanted to wrestle the devil on his own.

4

The Yucca Moth

The Mojave Desert lies between the Great Basin and the Sonoran deserts. Most of the Mojave is in the southern half of California, but it also extends into the southern tip of Nevada and northwestern Arizona. The Mojave accommodates a great variety of plants, and it shows less temperature extremes than the two deserts that border it to the north and south. An exception would be the area north of Baker, where the Mojave drops to below sea level from its general elevation of two thousand feet; there lies the arid furnace known as Death Valley. On the floor of Death Valley, temperatures can reach 130 degrees, and the rainfall is less than two inches a year. But many parts of the Mojave Desert can boast spectacular wildflower displays and even support a few succulents and trees. The tree that is synonymous with the Mojave is the Joshua tree. It is a giant yucca plant, a treelike member of the lily family. Like all desert yucca plants, it looks harmless, even attractive, until you get involved with it. The broad leaves of yuccas are sturdy and stiff, and each leaf is hellishly spined or tipped with a needle-sharp spike that can cause quick, deep puncture wounds. Like a syringe. A typical member of the species is called Spanish Bayonet. It can be dangerous business on a dark night.

The pollination of a yucca can only be accomplished by one kind of moth. The plant can't exist without the moth, and the moth can't exist without the plant. In sultry symbiosis, the yucca moth must pollinate for both to survive. The adult moth does not eat. Ever. Its mouth parts function only to gather yucca pollen and to form the tiny grains into a small packet, which it carries off to another flower after bug sex. There, the yucca moth injects her eggs into the seed pod of the yucca plant, then climbs to the top of the flower, where she stuffs her nickel bag down inside the pistil. The bag of pollen causes the seeds to grow. When her babies hatch, they live on the seeds formed by the efforts of their tough little mother. The tough little mother goes off to die.

South of Kelso, twenty-five miles down the Kelbaker Road, are the strange formations of Granite Cove. In that place, at the beginning of a red and cool dawn, a variety of eyes lifted to meet the April morning light that burst above the jagged line of Providence Mountain. Among the arid boulders glittered the optic systems of banded gecko and fringe-toed lizard; of Mojave rattler and labyrinth spider; of red-spotted toad and great hairy scorpion; of too many antelope ground squirrels and of a late-returning burrowing owl, drunk on wood rat flesh. The wood rat eyes were present, but not working.

And there, wet against the pale dry air, moved the eyes of something else. Eyes of the newcomer. Eyes that fronted evolution's most intricate compilation of dendrites. Eyes that could harden and grow vacant while the mind behind them conjectured action based on needs that fed no mere biological necessity. These new eyes fronted a brain that understood the concept of revenge; that could verbalize on justice; that could decode the whispers of political impropriety. These new eyes had evolved to feed their brain the stuff of thought . . . and they were therefore different from all the other eyes present, which had evolved to feed an empty stomach. The new eyes fronted a brain that swam in soups of opinion, fantasy, emotion . . . a brain that twisted in the wind of abstractions it called fact.

There was a thinness to the air.

The balanced rocks of the place seemed about to tumble into the colony of eyes.

The man proceeded to the base of a great gray boulder and took from its tiny-footed shadow a dark briefcase. He crouched with his back to the rising sun, dialed numbers into the snap locks, and opened the container. He removed the uppermost sheet of computer printout and saw the list of names matched with dates and places. Some names were grouped, some separate. On the last sheet, inked in below the names and places, was a five-tier organizational flowchart. At the top of the chart was the listing Director, Internal Revenue Service.

5

Tape No. 1

21 MAY 1433 HRS./VOX. ACT. REC. SER. 32449.90
ANGEL/TIMBER WOLF
TELCON ZULU UPLINK/YANKEE DWNLK

"How bad?"

"Mr. President, there is further deterioration in the figures coming from Treasury. The volume of extension forms filed in place of 1040s has exceeded worst-case. IRS scans are in. Thirty-seven percent of taxpayers receipted through Thursday filed Form 4868 applications instead of 1040s. What's critical is that twenty-two percent of those extension forms were not filed with the required check. Looks like they might not pay. The rest of those 4868s are nuisance-filed in place of 1040s. The depth of this move is off the board. The tea-bag boys have done it this time."

"What about the denial clause? Can't we use that?"

"The system's jammed. The 4868 form reads 'automatic extension'; the denial clause requires IRS to notify."

"Jesus Christ Almighty. A public appeal? Can we call a time out, talk it back on-line? Goddamn it all, one-third of the people are getting a goddamned government check. Don't the assholes realize what could happen?"

"A lot of taxpayers don't get that check. They just lit up; all it took was coordination. That was the danger pointed out in '90 by Rintell in the Orange Day paper. He saw the problem in focusing the entire population on the fifteenth of April; wanted to segment the system then. Looks like he was right."

"Why didn't they dump that 4868? Stagger the filing dates? What in hell do we have contingency people for?"

"Our problem is up front, sir."

"I didn't get here by not being able to listen. Are we reading this right? Be straight with me; gut feeling."

"I believe so, sir. The Commission is correct. It's a critical tax revolt. It's past words."

"I want to see that Rintell paper again."

"I'll have a copy sent over from the tank. Anything else, Mr. President?"

"No. Thank you."

"Sir."

"Good-bye, Link."

TERMINATE YANKEE DWN . . . FREQ 162.6875
REOPEN/STNDBY

6

Working Girl

Rebeca and Polyester left the casino and stepped out into the glare of the Nevada noon sun.

"How's it going, Frank?" she said to the doorman who stood guard at the side entrance, ready to prevent players from summoning their own cabs. Frank seemed immune to the heat that radiated off the unshaded glitz of the casino. He wore the obligatory knee-length maroon coat with matching gold-braid hat that some boozed padrino had envisioned with awesome inspiration during a late-night owner's meeting in years gone by. Frank's face was seventy years old, though he himself was probably no more than fifty. Possibly too much sun. But most likely too many drinks, cigarettes, and unpaid markers. Another casino hostage baking in the sun of his own little purgatory.

"Going good, Becky."

Frank looked Polyester up and down with a gaze that said a great deal.

"We'd like a cab, Frank," flicking the ash off bummed cigarette number seven.

"Sure thing, baby. How's Rita doing?"

"Great, Frank, just great."

"The kid doing okay?" His friendly gray eyes betrayed the hard face.

"Yeah. Doing fine, doing fine."

"What's that little spic's name? Fidel? Cerveza?"

"Carlos, Frank, Carlos," she grinned back. She gave him a gentle shot to the shoulder that caused his hat to slide down on his forehead.

"But we'll name the next one after you if he doesn't have a pecker," she added.

They both chuckled while Polyester stood there feeling somewhat disjointed by their familiarity. The doorman and the girl seemed like brother and sister in their give-and-take. He was the outsider, the tourist.

"Hey, Stretch," she said with a grin, "what's your fucking name?"

"Gene."

"Gene, meet Frank; Frank, meet Gene."

They nodded. No handshake. It wasn't a convention. Gene felt less ill at ease. They were, the three of them, just Vegas players after all. Part of the old desert dance. Frank winked at Rebeca and signaled the cab waiting at the front of the line down by the stand marker. As the cab drove up, Frank adjusted his maroon hat. Gene noticed, when he slipped him a buck, that Frank carried not a single drop of sweat on his tanned face. *It must be ninety degrees already and that old bastard's wearing a winter overcoat,* he thought. *Son of a bitch . . . the guy must be full of dust.*

They slid into the back seat of the cab. The arid

casino hostage closed the car door for them and turned back to his penance in the sun. Rebeca took a long drag on the last of butt number seven and stuffed it into the side ashtray. She sat with her denim-sheathed legs spread wide and her hand on Gene's thigh. Possessive. He pushed his gym bag down on the floor between his ankles. Also possessive.

"Harcourt Arms," she said to the driver.

"Harcourt Arms. Where's that?" the cabbie asked. His eyes floated in the rearview mirror as the cab pulled out of the casino drive onto Las Vegas Boulevard.

"Past the Sahara," she replied, "about three blocks on the left."

The cabbie nodded.

Rebeca was thinking that it might be better if she tried to talk Polyester into getting a cheap room rather than risk him heading for the hills when he saw her place. She rarely brought customers there. Then again, he might not want to pay for a room and her, too. Better stick to Plan A. To her it was only a place to sleep. But some of these johns were so picky . . . and after all the shit they tried to pull. Damned if she could figure them out. They were, she told herself, just an endless pile of rubber dicks, always different, always the same.

The cab moved down the Strip with the noon traffic. The casinos seemed to exhaust and inhale little clots of people through the open doors. Gene watched the customers move along the sidewalks with the awkward informality, almost guilt, of day-time players. A few carried the standard paper cup of quarters pressed close against the chest as if protecting something of greater value. Small cup. Big dreams.

The cab pulled into a space under the painted Harcourt Arms sign. Gene looked out at a two-story white-and-yellow–trimmed wreck of a motel with a U-shaped courtyard that faced the hot south sun. Some of the old cars in the motel parking spaces would never move again on their own. A half dozen brown-skinned adults leaned on the railing of the second-story walkway and looked down on about ten preschool kids who played around the cars and trash cans in the courtyard. Mostly Puerto Ricans or Cubans, some blacks. An old newspaper swirled across the asphalt in the dry wind and draped itself over the head of a diapered two-year-old, who promptly wobbled around in a circle and fell on his face. Most of the adult observers laughed. Some just smiled. The other children paid no attention, except for one four-year-old who walked over and tried to stand balanced on the prostrate form. Fleshy screams rose from the newspaper.

"Wait here a sec," said Rebeca. She hopped out of the cab. "I want to check the room. Be right back."

Gene watched her two-step up the wood stairs to the second story. The cabbie put his right arm on the seat back and shot him a wondering glance. No words. Just a do-you-know-what-the-fuck-you're-doing look. Gene was wondering the same thing. Mr. Dick had decided to go to sleep.

As Rebeca led him into the room, Gene caught a glimpse of a skinny old man, a wine bottle in one hand and leading a two-year-old by the other, retreating down the second-story walkway. The kid wore a gray T-shirt and nothing else. The old man flashed a scowl over his shoulder at Gene, and the pair disappeared into a room with no door further down the walkway.

The first thing Gene noticed was a rumpled double bed that sagged wearily at the sides and foot. Then he looked down at the middle of the floor, where a small white puppy squatted and pissed in joy at seeing Rebeca, who was stooping to pat him. Then he noticed two piles of puppy crap over by the battered refrigerator. The room didn't smell real good.

"Cokey! Have you been a bad little doggie? A bad little doggie? Have you? Have you?"

Wag, wag, whine, piss, wag, wag.

"Cokey, Cokey . . . give Mommy a kiss kiss. Pretty baby."

Wag, wag. Lick. Piss . . . wag. Lick on the lips. The price was dropping.

Rebeca stood up. "How about a smoke?" she asked.

She went into the bathroom and emerged with a dustpan and a piece of cardboard. She walked over to the two piles and began scooping the stuff into the pan with the cardboard. She carefully scraped the cardboard on the edge of the dustpan to clean off the residue. She stood in front of him with the evil-looking pan in one hand, the scraper in the other. He wasn't sure where to look and was holding out the pack to her when he realized that she had both hands full. He pulled out a cigarette and moved it toward her mouth. She spread her lips slightly to receive the cigarette. She looked him in the eye as he placed it gently between those chiseled rims that still made him think of Brooke Shields's forehead. The way she kept looking at him as he lit the thing for her made him feel the return of a meddlesome tingle that ran between his legs through his crotch and out into the head of his dissolute renegade. It crossed his mind that she was somehow still quite sexy.

She kept looking into his face as he lit the cigarette. She was remembering that if she followed the match with her eyes they would cross and she would look like an idiot . . . even more of an idiot than she already did by standing there in this dump with a load of dog shit in one hand. She hoped he had the money.

She broke off the look and went into the bathroom to dump the load into the commode. The cigarette tasted good, and it helped smother the smell in the apartment. When she came out he had lit one up and was staring down at the smears of brown that still remained on the carpet. He looked a bit perplexed.

"There's some cold beer in the fridge." She sat on the bed and picked up an ashtray from the floor. She placed the tray next to her on the bed and looked at him.

"Sounds good." He opened the refrigerator and watched three of the four magnetic message holders fall off the door onto the rug.

"Don't mind them," said Rebeca.

He didn't.

She drew her legs up under her and sat Indian-style on the bed while he removed two cans from the ten that huddled on the frost-caked shelf.

"Actually, I only need thirty dollars for the rent. Thirty dollars would cover it if that's okay with you."

He popped the tab on his beer. He handed her the other can without opening it. He was still pondering her last statement. He correctly guessed that she was feeling self-conscious about the way the place looked.

"Hell," he replied, "fifty's okay with me."

"No, I just need thirty for the rent," she said and wondered what her mouth was saying.

He didn't reply.

She popped the top, twisted off the ring, and tossed the tab in the general direction of the wastebasket in the corner. It landed on the rug. She made no move to retrieve it. Nor did he. He thought it added to the informality of the place.

"Where you from?" He leaned his rear against the edge of the chipped dresser.

"Miami. In Florida."

He knew where Miami was.

"I left there with my mom when I was fourteen. She had a friend out here in Vegas. They're both in L.A."

"You like it here better than Miami?" he asked.

"More business here. Maybe not more partygoers, but they have the bucks. The Beach is too locked up for a single girl. You need to be a team player there."

They smoked and sipped for a long minute without saying anything. The silence was not uncomfortable. She felt the beer feed some of its cold energy into her skin. She noticed a pleasant itch in her crotch. She hoped it was the beer.

He sensed a curiosity growing in him about the girl, but he didn't know why. He felt horny for her. But she had an unfamiliar effect on him. Maybe because she was young? Her lips? Her farmer-girl face and country body?

"That your dog?"

"Belongs to a friend of mine. Cute, isn't he?"

"Yeah, cute," he said. "Make a good football."

She frowned. "Don't say that." There was more than a hint of reproval in her voice.

"Just kidding."

"He's only a few weeks old."

He regarded the dog with a noncommittal look as it worried an old golf ball under the dresser.

"I probably won't be able to keep him here more than a few weeks."

He wondered why the hell not. *Couldn't fuck up this place much more if it pissed fire.*

She finished her beer with a deep swallow. He watched her strong throat muscles work as she tilted her head back. She put the empty can down on the floor beside the bed. She propped her arms behind her on the bed and sat there looking at him.

"I'll probably be getting a nicer place next month over by the Palace Station," she said. "I'm going to share it with my girlfriend and her kid. Why don't you get rid of those pants and come over here so I can suck your cock?"

He blinked twice. Otherwise, his expression didn't change. Something about mixing apples and oranges bumped through his brain.

He shucked his loafers and pulled off his pants and shorts in one motion. He hung them over the edge of the dresser. He turned and stood there in his shirt. His thing was soft. She had caught Mr. Dick by surprise.

He walked over and stood in front of her. The last strategic thought that crossed his mind was that she hadn't collected the thirty dollars first. As she sat on the edge of the bed and deftly fingered his shaft with a studied inevitability toward those magnificent country lips, he wondered again if this girl was more or less than he imagined. The electric blood began to smother his rational mind, and he decided she was for real.

Damn, she thought, *I forgot the fucking money.* What the hell. He would be good for it. He was not mean; he talked; he thought her dog was funny. Even though he made that nasty football remark. And he looked healthy, no spots or rash. She had milked him firmly when she first handled him. He smelled okay, didn't pass any drip. Actually, he smelled pretty good ... must have put after-shave on his tummy that morning. Lots of men did that. Nice touch.

He was doing fine. Flying high. He had experienced more expertise in his women, but this one was a witch. He concentrated on blocking the Big Rush. *Jesus, this was good! Hello!* He arched his neck back and tried to stare through the ceiling. If only he could stop seeing those lips on him.

She knew she had him. Whenever she wanted, she could take him off. She liked that feeling. He was fighting to be steady, but she knew she had him. The telltale presperm had come and gone. Mr. Polyester was on the string. Why in hell had she gone thirty dollars? He would have done fifty in a breeze. Maybe even seventy. This guy was in love.

Damn, double damn! She had brushed her fingers around his testicles, gently traced her thumb between his buttocks. His thigh muscles bunched, and his balls ratcheted upward in a tight, hot package against his groin. He pressed his palms firmly against the sides of her head, trying to halt her wet, moving lips from short-circuiting his resolve. His fingers tangled in her short hair. He felt the tanned, cool turns of her ears. She obliged him by slowing her motions. He was sure he felt her lips move in a smile that dissolved the suckling pressures along the circumference of his pleasure. His legs had begun to shake.

She could feel him rock and tremble at the simplest move. *Man, if only they were all this easy,* she thought. Yet it seemed like he had been around. Oh, well. Take it easy. Let him spin awhile. Maybe he'd drop a tip on her for good behavior. She eased off and gently hooked her upper teeth on the ridge of his member and wondered what she'd rustle up for Carlos for dinner. There were a few jars of Gerber lamb at Rita's place. And she'd better pick up some formula in case Rita forgot to bring some home when she got off work. Rita seemed to have a mental block about formula. She'd remember everything else but never remembered the milk. They used to joke that Rita's brain refused to admit there were any other tits or tit substitutes that were good enough for Carlos. She used to watch Rita breast-feed Carlos when he was little and get a warm feeling in her own breasts and stomach. His little noises and the way he cupped his hand alongside Rita's tit gave her a warm, almost sexy ache. Once, when they were both high on a good batch of Red, Rita had straddled her as they sat on Rita's couch, and Rita had unbuttoned her blouse and unhooked her nursing bra, exposing her milk-filled breasts. Rita had stretched up on her knees so that her firm brown nipples were caressing Rebeca's eyelashes. Rita had taken her warm, bulging breasts in her hands and lightly traced the nipples across Rebeca's cheeks. The firm, hot, fluid-leaking tip of one breast finally found its way between Rebeca's waiting lips. She had suckled Rita while Rita strad-dled her there on the couch. They both floated in such an erotic stillness that nothing seemed to move except her own pulling lips and Rita's trembling breast. Neither had known such fiery tenderness. They repeated the scene many times afterward, since Rita's pediatrician thought it best for the baby not to nurse once he learned of Rita's drug use. So they nur-tured this delicate passion for months as Rita kept producing milk for Rebeca and Rebeca kept the sweetness alive with her urgent lips. And they would go further into their passion, but the milking was the source of that deep rapture.

Rebeca felt the insistent flex of him and came back from her daydream. The thoughts of her and Rita had left her very wet, warm, and stimulated. Polyester was certainly in the right place at the right time.

Now he was in control again. He had brought his willpower to bear . . . mind over splatter. She had drawn back but there was smoldering passion in her eyes as she looked up at him. The heat in that look surprised him.

"Will that thing stay up while I get my clothes off?"

"It looks like it will," he replied.

"Take off your shirt and stay awhile." She hopped off the bed and went over to the dressing sink that stood outside the bathroom. She stood with her back to him and removed her clothes in a wink. It took him more time to pull his shirt over his head and remove his courier vest than it took her to completely strip. The first thing he noticed was her breasts in the mirror as she straightened up naked. No doubt about it. She was female, she was young, and she was built. High-standing tan nipples crowning showroom tits. He could have hung his hat on those. Missile tits.

She saw him looking at them in the mirror.

"Not too shabby, are they?" she said with a smile.

He couldn't think of anything to say.

"Gotta take a quick whiz," she said.

She wheeled into the bathroom, where she sat down on the john. He could see her from where he was standing, and she looked back at him with her legs apart. Pissing with ease in his presence. Pissing like a football player in a locker room. She smiled as she looked at him looking at her. She jumped up from the john with a quick turn, pushed the handle, and went back to the sink, where she hoisted a long left leg up onto the counter. She ran some water and quickly soaped and rinsed between her legs. The water ran and spilled onto the rug at her feet. She dried herself with a towel, then dropped the towel on the floor over the wet spot on the rug and bounded across the floor in two giant steps to kiss him in the middle of his chest. She put her left hand on his penis, which had slumped to standby status, and gave a few instructive strokes. With her right hand she gently pushed him onto his back across the bed. She straddled him with her hips at his chest level, her left hand on his erection behind her back.

"Look," she said.

She spread herself with her right hand.

He looked where she wanted him to. Protruding between her pressing fingers was the pink shaft of a clitoris that was an inch and a half long. It was as hard as he was, and he could see it pulse along its tight underside with the beating of her heart.

"It did this while I was sucking you. You made me feel very sexy."

She didn't bother to tell him that her thoughts of Rita had something to do with it. But she did like him. Maybe it was because he was so easy to work. He seemed strangely in awe of her, and she liked that. She rarely had an erection like this with a customer, and she wanted to show off, to shock him a little bit, to see what he would say.

He didn't say anything. He just stared at her there. He had never seen anything quite like it. She could feel herself warming under his gaze. With her knees on either side of his chest, she could feel her sex lips spread apart slightly. She slowly lowered herself a few sultry inches until the heated desire between her legs softly kissed the skin of his lower chest. She moved herself gently back and forth on him with a feather-soft contact that bathed them both, where they touched, in the liquid silk that distilled like honey-dew from deep within her. She placed her palms on either side of his head and slowly lowered her face to his. His eyes closed softly, like those of a small child. She kissed him. They floated in that tender kiss for a delicate moment. Then she backed down, buried him within her heat, and hammered his hips with unshackled fury until he came to a place he had never known.

7

Cold Beer

Ram ordered another Molson when he saw his brother come through the door. The place was dark, and Mitch was standing near the vending machines trying to get his eyes to forget the bright California sunshine. By the time he spotted Ram, a cold beer waited for him on the dark wood of the bar. Mitch hiked his frame onto the West Coast version of a bar stool, a deep red Naugahyde captain's chair on a three-hundred-dollar swivel, and took the bottle in his right hand. He tilted it back slightly and looked at the label for a few seconds as if checking for spelling errors, then drained half of it in one long bubbling swig.

"Nice shot," he said. He looked at Ram in the mirror behind the bar.

"Why the delay?"

"He stopped in Barstow."

"What did it look like coming back?"

"Two CHPs, one local. Maybe fifteen lookers. They hadn't even stopped traffic, in either direction."

"How did it wind up?" asked Ram.

"Upside-down. Top crushed flat. Couldn't see much more. I'll give it two days before they figure what happened. Take at least that much time to scrape the sand off that greasy sucker."

"Any trouble at the checkpoint?"

"In Yermo? No. I skipped it on the service road."

"Where did you make your turn?"

They stopped talking as one of the bartenders crossed in front of them to pour margarita mix into a tin shaker. The barman finished, put the bottle of mix down, and moved away.

"Was going to turn back at Zzyzx, but some dildo was on the ramp with his hood up. Went to Baker and turned there."

The two sat for a few moments. Mitch finished off the bottle of beer and signaled the bartender for two more. The beer tasted good, but not as good as it would have tasted back in the heat of the high desert. He had driven through the Cajon Pass and down to Dana Point without stopping. With no air conditioning in the truck it had been a long hot drive. They worked hard to eliminate potential problems in their business, whether they were taking off marks, moving money cross-country, or running some psycho to earth for any outfit, including the law, that couldn't afford to get caught out of bounds. Air conditioning could be a problem. Throwing a compressor belt or overheating the engine in the desert could screw up their timing, draw undue attention. And they dealt in timing; that was their real product. That was the single critical item in all of this.

"Did you catch any trouble coming through Barstow?" Ram asked. "There was a photo radar working around the Sidewinder exit two weeks ago."

"No. I checked pretty close on the way back. But I was on the beaner this morning and might have missed it going out. There's not much chance they'd set up at that time of morning. The shifts roll over around seven in Barstow. The mounties are usually drinking coffee and signing paper about then. Don't sweat it, bro."

Ram reached over and pulled a cigarette out of the pack that lay on the bar in front of Mitch. He lit up with the house matches placed in the ashtray by the barman, who brought them two fresh bottles of cold brew. Ram shook out the match and placed it in the ashtray with an exaggerated bodybuilder's wrist roll. He watched his biceps bunch up and stretch the elastic edging on his short-sleeved polo shirt. Three years spent pumping iron in the Lompoc pen, if nothing else, had given him the opportunity to put on some outlandish muscle. Of course, it wasn't a "nothing else" kind of deal; the hard time had given him quite a bit more. It had given him a master's degree in criminology, but not the kind you hang on the wall. He made connections there that would have taken years to make on the street.

The barman watched Ram slowly pump the arm.

"Since when you smoking?" asked Mitch.

"I thought I'd celebrate a little," said Ram. He inhaled and screwed up his face. "Damn, how can you take these things?"

The barman, with an unsettled look, moved off to the register to add the drinks to the tab.

"How did you come back?" asked Mitch. He refused to acknowledge the great flexing and twitching of muscles that was under way on the bar stool next to him.

"I came straight in. No problems. Fine day for a bike ride."

"Leave anything at the bridge?"

"Some butts from an ashtray in Riverside, a few curly pubes from my little box of African souvenirs, and a couple of used .223 casings from the pit down in San Marcos. Enough to sidetrack the smartass dick who finds them. If he's real sharp, he might even get some preload prints off the casings."

They sat for a few minutes without speaking. Mitch was a lean six foot one, some two inches shorter but three years older at twenty-nine than his brother. He had the sandy hair, green eyes, flashing smile, and explosive temper common to his Scottish-Irish ancestry. He could sing a beer-lit night away with his strong baritone voice and, to the amazement of those who had seen him cut apart a face with his fists, could sit at a piano and cause professional sounds to caress the smoke out of barroom air. In the single year he was sixteen, in a bar where he stacked liquor stock, he discovered the piano. He learned music on his own, quickly, untaught, and with a mechanical determination that was abandoned as soon as the music was his. When he played, his battle-scarred barmates would pause, look at him and wonder on the incongruity of the way he was, then shake their heads and smile. And the music did wondrous things for females who perceived sensitivity against raw roughness, but it led them into deception. He was like fresh steak dropped in a too-hot skillet; he was never far from the sizzle, and the sizzle could get there quickly, it could burn like hot grease, because there was a fury loose in the genetic protein he shared with Ram. Yet they were different. One of Mitch's friends said, in a late-night cloud of cocaine, " . . . with Mitch you see the lightning coming . . . with Ram you see the smile, then your head is gone." Where Mitch liked to drink, party, and burn grass in his spare time, Ram did serious work with the weights, found it difficult to get past mirrors. Ram had the body, face, energy, and carry of the California surfing icon, perfused with a dark, rugged, almost arrogant confidence that would befit a young New Jersey Mafioso lieutenant—dark hair, tight curl to the center of the forehead; square, chiseled features; piercing, glittering eyes; deep, easy voice; and a smile that, in the words of his first female parole officer, "could dislodge tampons."

Mitch was as puzzled by Ram's flexing in front of mirrors as Ram was by Mitch's bar battles. Mitch would invariably elect to conclude an evening's social by seeking out major confrontation, always with large mouth-breathing bipeds who were accustomed to feeling secure in their bulk. Whether these targets of opportunity were accompanied by numerous friends and relatives was of no importance. Ram had come to realize that Mitch believed these large people only served to heighten the mystery of an evening on the town. This behavior put a strain on Mitch's friends and drinking companions. Some did not like drinking beer through split lips. Some did not like talking to cops. Some did not like shelling out for damages. Some did not like hearing their women call them stupid assholes over an ice bag in the morning. At times, Mitch would wonder why the only real friends he seemed to accumulate over the years were unruly bastards with suture tracks in their faces.

But, as Ram frequently had to remind himself,

Mitch could do a hell of a lot of things a hell of a lot better than a hell of a lot of folks. Ram thought about these matters as he tried to wash away the raspy irritation of the cigarette smoke with cold beer. Mitch was a true renaissance man in this new world of twilights. He could handle a power- or sailboat, at night, on a lee shore; he could drive a truck or car anywhere, in any weather, and fix the son of a bitch if it broke; and he was one of the best pilots in the Southwest at altitudes under one hundred feet, as attested to by some highly paid Customs fixed-wingers who had gracefully elected not to undermine the profits of their insurance companies by trying to slide between border mountains at 5:00 A.M. in IFR visibility. Ram considered Mitch to be one of those inscrutable instruments that fate continued to furnish as a gentle reminder that he, Ram, was destined, indeed expected, to exist beyond the petty fences of less challenged men; and that he should spend his years on earth in a state of pleasured grace, performing occasional good deeds for the oppressed when it should so suit him. Anyhow, that was what his fifth beer seemed to be telling him. He smiled at his thoughts.

Mitch broke in on his pleasant reverie. "You were into this job. Why?"

Ram was quiet for a moment.

"I couldn't believe it when I heard his name was on the board. Some guy down in San Diego mentioned it to me at Anthony's; he knew I had been stiffed by the guy before I did my time. He walked with forty grand. Nothing I could do about it then. Too much going down in those last days. Not much I could do when I got out, either. I was on parole and the beaner had some paper on me that might have put me back. We did some things together in better days. I used to see that little brown face in my dreams up at Lompoc. That and the face of the limpdick who set me up."

"What's different now? If the paper is out there, it's still going to be a problem, isn't it? They probate his stuff, open a safe deposit box or whatever, and you've got trouble."

Ram laughed softly. "That's what made the job so appealing. They were going to hit him anyway. So the bad shit is already a given. Talk about getting the green light. I got it worked out with the Manfredos in a little under four hours. I would have done it gratis. Hell, I would have paid them for the contract."

The bartender came over and mopped around their bottles with a bar towel. Mitch watched him as he fawned around Ram's bottle, even lifting it off the counter to dry the beads of water around the base. He saw the man's thumb rub around the open top of the bottle as he held it. Ram was cocking his head to the side, checking himself in the mirror. He was oblivious to the barkeep.

"How you doing, fellas? Another round?"

"We can handle one more," said Ram.

Mitch stared at the bartender.

"You boys staying around here?"

"No, just passing through," Ram replied.

"What do you fellas do?"

Mitch looked hard at the man. "Mostly, we mind our own motherfucking business."

The man fell back about two feet. He reddened quickly. "Sorry, sorry. Didn't mean anything by it," he mumbled. He stepped back from them and went down the barway to get the beers.

Ram turned and looked at Mitch with a surprised

what-the-hell-was-that-all-about look. Mitch was staring after the retreating barkeep.

"Christ, Mitch, what the hell was that for?" Ram shifted his look from Mitch to the barman and back to Mitch again, annoyed, frowning.

Mitch didn't reply. He kept glaring at the bartender, who was down at the far cooler taking the tops off the beers and trying to screw up enough courage to deliver them. When Mitch started to lose it, he was easy to read, eyes going hard, jaws locking tightly behind what would in any other face pass for a faint smile, head cocking just slightly toward the target, but in that moment, there in the bar, something crossed his mind, and he turned back to Ram, the barkeep put out of focus. "Damn, bro, I almost forgot. That guy from L.A. who called us Wednesday."

Ram thought for a second. "The one who wanted a large piece of our time?"

"Right. He wants a call by 2100 tonight. I think he has something for us."

"Any ideas?"

"He's not saying much. Looks like big chips; hasn't talked money at all. The calls are trapping funny, like they're being double-relayed. Everything's real tight. Smells like a pro operation. I picked up the messages on the tape before I took off this morning."

They took up the beer that had been brought by a waitress while they were talking. *Numb-nuts must have gone on break*, thought Mitch.

"No word on supply?" Ram asked.

"Not yet."

"Anybody we know talked of getting up with this guy? Anything rustling in the bushes?"

"Just some blind courier work. Looks like it's moving toward Vegas. The Padre is out. So is G.P."

"We could get Ronnie in CNA at PacTel to ride tonight's call if you think it's worth it. That phone number has got to land somewhere in L.A."

"Don't think it's a straight link. Not judging by what I'm hearing. I'll bet it's being call-forwarded out to Nevada or Arizona and back. It would be a major ride."

"No reason to check this early, then. But I want to know who we're working for. If it's big and smooth, it's big and dangerous." Ram finished his beer.

"So is elephant dick. Let's hit the road, bro."

8

Jesse and Ruth

Father Ball had shifted colors. Back to basic black. He walked along the gently dipping walkway that led out to the end of C Pier. The sun was fierce, and his black frock sucked up the heat like old fireplace brick. A dry desert breeze skittered across Lake Mead and cooked away the sweat from his upper lip before his tongue felt the need to clear the salty mixture from the skin below his small nose. When he reached the houseboat moored in slip C-23, he paused and shifted the suitcase to his left hand. It always surprised him how heavy money could be when packed in bulk. All those weightless green notes that felt like tissue paper if held individually pulled like blocks of lead on his shoulder sockets. He stepped through the opening in the safety lines onto the deck of the craft, which, despite its forty-two-foot waterline, heeled perceptibly at his boarding. He proceeded down the cabin side to the rear of the boat and peered through the tinted glass of the after doorway. He couldn't make out anything through the darkened glass, so he knocked twice.

"Come in, Padre," from within the cabin.

He opened the door, shifted the suitcase again to his right hand, and stepped into the air-conditioned oasis of the cabin.

"You're on time, Padre. Good for you."

"Jesse, good to see you, my friend." Kevin dropped the suitcase to the floor with a thump that made the cabin reverberate from the impact. He looked at Jesse with a gaining comprehension as his eyes adjusted to the subdued light. Jesse was sitting back on an expensive tooled-leather couch. He wore a white silk bathrobe and was watching a baseball game on a small television screen across the cabin. Between his legs, sitting on the floor and watching the game with the back of her head resting on Jesse's groin, was a well-proportioned middle-aged woman with striking red hair that reached down to her waist. She turned toward Kevin, and a glittering smile sparkled in his direction.

"Hello, Father," she said.

"Hi, Ruth."

The woman nonchalantly removed Jesse's hand from her right breast and drew the front edges of her open robe together. She moved easily, with no trace of embarrassment. With a flip of her head that twirled the beautiful red hair back from her face, she tilted her head back again and looked up at Jesse.

"Are you sure you can make it, honey?" She laughed.

"Crazy broad," from Jesse as he rose from the couch and extended his hand to Kevin with a smile. His member swung back and forth from between the folds of his robe like something from a documentary on cobras. Jesse seemed unconcerned about his swaying appendage. Kevin reached out and took Jesse's hand at chest level.

"Can I get you a drink, Kevin?" said Ruth.

She tied her bathrobe, walked over to him with a smile, and took both his hands in hers. Jesse and his penis had strolled over to the bar. Ruth leaned forward and planted a big kiss full on Kevin's lips. Kevin felt mixed emotions. Ruth's lips were unnaturally warm.

"I'd like a scotch and soda," said Kevin. He paused for a moment and thought about the kiss. "On second thought, make that a straight scotch. No ice."

"You're on," from Jesse at the bar. "How about you, Ruthie?"

"A nice cold gin and tonic, sweetheart."

Jesse dug out the ice from the bucket and proceeded to put the drinks together. He poured himself a shot of white rum and mixed it with pineapple juice. When Jesse squatted down to put the can of juice back onto the lower shelf of the small refrigerator, Kevin could see his balls touch the rug. Kevin felt a curious sympathy for Jesse's tailor.

They sat and drank for an hour. The talk was of the tables, of what was happening in the casino management picture, and of the weather on the lake at that time of year. Kevin felt good about Jesse and Ruth. They had a unique appreciation of reality that touched him.

"Jesse, that's a bigger piece of green than usual."

"It is, Padre."

Kevin sensed that he probably should leave it at that.

"It's not the standard wash job," volunteered Jesse. "It's a different type operation."

"Kevin, let me fix up that glass," said Ruth. She had changed her robe for a pair of sweat pants and a wool sweater. The cool of the air conditioning and the ice of the drinks had chilled her. She wore nothing under the sweater, and Kevin studied the way her nipples, puckered by the cold, managed to push their stubby way through the strands of wool.

Kevin was still curious. "There wasn't much to read on my end. I never hooked into the San Diego source," he ventured. "Just got the drop call, made the catch, and came straight out." He rolled the last of the drink down his throat and handed the glass to Ruth. "It's not queer; it's genuine Grade A government green," he added.

"Let you in on a big secret," said Jesse. "It's blind on this end, too. No idea who's behind this one."

"It's a wad."

"Yes, it is."

They drank in silence.

"Well, my two blessed friends, it's time I was on my way. Do you have my Bibles?"

Ruth set her drink down on the end table.

"I'll fetch them for you, Padre." She walked her nipples out of the cabin toward the front of the boat.

"Please, not so many this time, Ruthie. I dread going out in that ungodly heat again. Just three or four will do."

He drained his glass, tilted his head back, and gargled the last mouthful. Ruth returned from the forward cabin carrying three of the books. She opened Kevin's suitcase and piled the four hundred thousand dollars on the coffee table. She put the three Bibles inside and snapped the case shut.

"We're going out on the lake for a cookout next Monday evening. We want you to come along. We'll have this cash moved off by then," offered Jesse.

"Thank you, my friend. That would please God." He hoisted his bulk from the big chair. He took up his case and went to the door.

"See you here at five," said Ruth. "Don't bring a thing, just a change of clothes for out on the lake."

She leaned over to kiss him. Kevin felt her eraser nipples stick him through his God suit.

Kevin crabbed his way down the side of the boat and stepped up onto the dock.

"Adios, my children," he called.

Kevin walked down the dock and moved into the shade of the marina shops at the head of the pier. He entered the dockmaster's office. "Hello, Ward!"

"Hello yourself, Father."

The dockmaster was talking to a lanky blond boy with pale zit-scarred skin. The man looked up with a wide and ready grin when he saw Kevin.

"And who is this new person?" Kevin said. He used his best salvation attack voice.

"This is Perry. He's learning the ropes. Going to be working the haul-out rig. Perry, this is Father Ball, the world's biggest and pushiest padre."

Kevin popped open his case. "Another sweet sheep for the flock of the Lord." He pulled out a Bible and shoved it into the boy's white gut. "Some dark night between the drugs and the twisted women, the Word will save you," he sermoned in a rolling bass.

The dockmaster smiled.

Kevin smiled and winked at the bewildered teen. The boy didn't know what to say.

"That's all right, my son," said Kevin. He patted

him on the head. "You are saved. Providing you stay far from this evil son of a barnacle."

Kevin shifted his attention to the dockmaster.

"And you, my sinful friend, I suppose you've cast your copy of the Lord's word in amongst the fishes?"

"No, no, Padre. Read it every day. Right by my bed."

"A sorry positioning for the Lord's word! Yet near the bed of whores the word must twice shed its golden light."

The dockmaster laughed and shook his head.

"I must away to the sinners," roared Kevin. The faint smell of scotch drifted over his sheep. "Take care, lad. And beware this lost and sinful man!"

Kevin snapped his case and strode out of the office.

The dockmaster laughed softly. The boy stood with the Bible held to his gut where Kevin had pushed it.

"Takes all kinds. Good ol' boy, though. Always passing out those goddamn Bibles."

Kevin walked back to his car in the heat. "Remember the Alamo . . . and the Padre," he said aloud.

9

Lawyers

The diesel pickup truck moved through the morning fog. The soft mist from the warm Pacific hung like damp gauze, and its weave silenced the noise of rushing cars, barking dogs, and crying kids as those sounds tried to lift into the cool air above the California coastal towns. It made the people abroad in it more aware. It slowed things down; it made one listen because there was less to hear.

Mitch guided the powerful truck over the backcountry road. Ram sat in the passenger seat, one leg propped against the dash, a steaming cup of coffee in his hands.

Mitch spoke over the smooth rumbling of the diesel engine, the diesel engine he had rebuilt with slow care just for the joy of getting inside it.

"Run those numbers by me again, bro."

"He wants us to start in two days," replied Ram. "At twenty grand a week, plus expenses. A twenty grand bonus if they need a shot. No warm targets. The job involves twenty-four-hour visual and probably a long-range takeout on some sort of electronic equipment; sounds like a relay transmitter in a private Comm net. The shot goes on their call. No shot, no bonus."

"Sounds fucking exciting; shooting out light bulbs."

"You don't need any more excitement. Keep your ass out of hock for a while. There's major coin here."

"Where do we go?"

"Don't know. That comes tomorrow."

"Our stuff?"

"All our stuff. We're looking at a long-range shot, maybe five hundred meters daylight, one hundred meters dark. We might be able to use the Thermal for a long-range dark shot. The source is hot; demand-feed generator, close in, so the Robeson should do the trick providing the source is up and radiating. If the source is turned off, we go in to one hundred meters with the night scope, maybe the 520. For a day shot at five hundred meters we use the Steyr."

They rode through soft fog.

"I don't know, bro. For a twenty grand shot, I say we use the A-1. We can both hit dimes with that M40."

"I don't like taking out the A-1 on a stationary. The Steyr is a good stick. More than we need for this. It would be tough to have to ditch the A-1. The Corps is too stingy with those. We can get Steyrs off the shelf."

The fog thinned as they continued inland. At a turn in the road, a small rabbit ran across the blacktop in front of the truck. Mitch swerved to miss it.

"You're losing it, Mitch. I would've got him."

"Right. And got rabbit shit all over my engine."

They turned onto the range road and drove for a mile more until Mitch stopped the truck in front of a cattle gate that stretched across their path. Ram left the cab and unlocked the metal gate. After Mitch drove through, Ram relocked the gate and got back in the truck. As he settled onto the passenger seat, the beeper on his belt sounded its electronic chirp. The noise mixed with that of the songbirds in the trees around the gate. Ram raised his hand so Mitch would keep the truck where it was and picked up the cellular phone from the console. He dialed the number that scrolled across the beeper's window.

"Yes?"

In the long silence that followed as Ram listened to the caller's voice, Mitch watched Ram's face harden to stone. Mitch cut the engine and waited. The sun had warmed away the mist; the light sparkled down through the leaves and patterned the hood of the truck.

"When?" said Ram into the receiver.

Mitch watched his brother.

"Where?"

The sound of the birds raked the still air.

"I'll be there." Ram placed the phone in the cradle.

A long moment unrolled in the noisy silence.

"That was Olento's ex-lawyer."

The diesel engine ticked and clicked as it cooled.

"He thinks we should have a talk. He has some letters he thinks I should see. He doesn't want to make trouble, but he says he needs some advice on what to do with them. He says I might want to make 'arrangements.' "

"Arrangements?"

"Arrangements."

They waited.

Mitch finally spoke. "Do you still want to go to the range?"

"Yes. I'd like to shoot. I'm supposed to meet with this lawyer tonight at his office in La Jolla. No sense wasting the morning. Let's go."

Mitch restarted the engine. They drove without discussing the call.

"You're sneaking up on that scope, Mitch. Get that cheek back two inches or you'll cut some more half moons into that knuckle-suckin' face of yours."

Mitch backed off the scope and threw three more rounds downrange. The pad kicked hard into his right shoulder. It felt good. He enjoyed Ram's enthusiasm. When they started shooting, Ram's mood soared. Mitch liked to be with his brother when it was like this, when there were things to be done together, when they made the rules.

Ram watched the printed human-form targets down in the butts through the spotting scope while Mitch fired.

"Right-side shadow? You're left two and down one."

Mitch reset his body in the cool sand.

Pow! Pow! Pow!

"Better," reported Ram. "One for the eyeball."

They were firing the Steyr at three hundred meters and zeroed the weapon as the freshly penciled pages of the data book fluttered in the breeze moving cross-range from the east. It was a good day.

"You're in the bubble, Mitch. Let me have a few."

Mitch got to his feet with the rifle. Ram dropped to a prone position and muscled through twenty push-ups. The elevated heartbeat generated by the burst of activity would simulate the conditions of a hot shoot. Mitch counted the push-ups. At the twenty mark, Ram rolled on his side and reached up. Mitch snapped the weapon into his hands. Ram rolled, took a moment to align his body with the cross hairs, and fired a controlled sequence downrange. The shots cracked through the morning air. Mitch watched the target through the spotting scope. The left eyeball of the printed form punched out in steps. It became a shredded emptiness. Dust rose in a gentle cloud behind the target.

Ram parked the Camaro at the curb a block away from the office of Octavio Enrique Bustillos, Attorney at Law. Mitch was stopped across the street waiting to cover, if needed. The traffic was light. At ten minutes past nine on a Monday evening, things were under control in this cutesy section of La Jolla. Ram waited for an elderly couple to totter around the far corner. That took three minutes, ten seconds. He left the car. The rich brass door on the side of the two-story building was unlocked. Inside the lighted entrance, silence. The stairs before him led directly to the upper floor. At the second-floor landing, he passed through two heavy glass doors that opened into a deserted modern reception area. The bronze sign directory showed that the office spaces were shared by three lawyers, a financial consultant, and a psychiatrist. *A reasonable combination of professions,* he thought. There was no sound except for the hum of a small water cooler that stood against the far wall. He moved down the hall until he reached a door marked with the attorney's nameplate. The door was closed, but he saw light coming from beneath it. The light brushed through the strands of plush carpet at his feet. He listened again. The sound of the water cooler whined back at him. He knocked twice. No answer. He tried the door. It opened. The office lights were on. He noted an empty secretary's desk. Beyond that, he could see the door to the main office slightly ajar. He crossed the floor of the outer office and pushed the door open. Behind a broad, expensive desk was Octavio Enrique Bustillos, Attorney at Law. He sat in a large red leather chair with his head back. Ram looked into his throat, which gaped open at mid-neck. He had been single-sliced from ear to ear.

10

Mules

Rebeca didn't like the taste of the mayonnaise. She was hooked on Miracle Whip. It had that special tang she liked. It was probably the only food product she could identify blindfolded; that and grape Kool-Aid. *Goddamn Tyrone! I told his black ass three separate times to get Miracle Whip. And what does that goofball bring back? Generic mayonnaise. Snake shit. In a dumb big jar that would take five fucking months to eat. Even the damn label is dumb; plain white with big black letters. Jesus!* And now he wanted her to mule some green down to Mexico again. That scene gave her the willies. Taping all that cash to her gut under her tits with adhesive in all that heat. *Crap!*

"Baby, you know what? This is the positive, final, absolutest last time I'll ever ask you to do this. It's easy cash, baby. Nobody gets checked going in, you know that."

"Why don't you do it, then?"

"Baby, baby."

"I mean it, Tyrone. Just because your shitheaded friends are in a bind, I got to put my ass in glass for three days. Bullshit!"

"It's not just this trip, baby. We got the good reputation. William needs us someday, we got the good reputation. Easy money. He comes to us. We're good people to know, baby."

"It's my ass, Tyrone."

"It's a nice ass, too."

"Crap! It's not going to do either one of us any good if it's sitting on cockroaches down in some Sonoran jail, olive dick!" *Shit!* she thought, *I didn't mean to say that.* She saw Tyrone's face drop. She had promised herself she'd stop calling him that. She thought it was funny when she first thought it up, but he sure didn't. He did have a little dick, and it looked sort of like a black olive to her when it was soft.

"Damn. I'm sorry, honey," she cooed. "It's just you get me pissed sometimes when you go back on your word. You said I didn't have to mule anymore."

Tyrone had turned away to the refrigerator with that crushed look he got; his basset dog look, she called it. He took out a beer. He didn't say anything. His eyes were down and were going to stay down until she got him back to his old bullshitting self. She couldn't let him crumble.

"I'm sorry, honey. I didn't mean to say that. You know what you do for me. Your dick is magic. You know that. You're the only guy who can really knock my socks off."

For the life of her, she couldn't figure why men had such a goddamn hang-up about the size of their cocks. They didn't worry near that much about the size of their muscles; they didn't compare the length of their hair; and they sure never felt concerned about how their brains matched up. Shit, they didn't even get emotional about not having much money, and that really was something. Men were odd, strange things.

She went over to Tyrone. He was standing by the window letting Cokey bite the end of his shoelace.

"Hey, honey, be happy," she offered.

No response.

"You got to give me a break. I'm so silly sometimes."

No response.

"You know I love your black ass. I want you to do me."

No response.

"Come on, baby," with a finger snaking through one of his belt loops, tugging.

No response.

"Please don't be so mean. You're my heat. I'll do anything you want."

His eyes moved a bit toward her. She let her teeth bite gently into his shoulder. She looked at him with her biggest eyes. He was looking at her now.

"Please don't make me beg for it, baby," she whispered.

She leaned up to run her tongue along his neck.

His hand started to move around her waist.

"Anything?" he said.

"What?"

"Anything? You'll do anything I want you to?"

"Yes, baby," slowly grinding her warm mound against his hip.

"Then you'll go to Mexico?"

San Diego Bay stretched out to the west. From their room in the twin towers the girls could see a sleek Navy frigate being nosed under the Coronado Bridge. The rails of the ship were lined with sailors in whites, the summer uniform of the day for crews returning home after overseas deployment. The view from the twenty-third floor was impressive. For Rebeca, the sight of so much water and sun brought her back to those days in Miami. But she had never looked at Biscayne Bay from a vantage point like this.

There were four of them. Two from San Diego, one from Los Angeles, and herself. She had worked with the girl from L.A. before, the black girl called Abbey. The other two, Keri and Allie, were sisters from the money-heavy Rancho section in northern San Diego County. This was their first run. They were excited and not the least bit anxious about what they were going to do. Not yet, thought Rebeca. She sat with Abbey on the couch sharing a joint. The two new girls were out on the balcony pointing every-where at once. She figured they couldn't be more than fourteen and seventeen. She got a kick out of their enthusiasm.

"Abbey, Becky, come out and see this big boat!"

Abbey took a deep hit on the stick. She glanced at Rebeca and nodded at the ship.

"There's one boatload of straining cock. You can bet your runny crotch on that. Six months of no snatch. God Almighty! Can you imagine the sore pussy in this town tomorrow? It's gonna smell like a bucket of pecker-skins in a fish market around here."

"Abbey, you sure have a way with words."

"Fuckin' A."

Rebeca laughed out loud.

"I'll bet a working girl could make two grand an hour giving blow jobs to that raft of swinging dick. All she'd need would be a shit-kickin' motor home parked on the pier and some kneepads. Fuckin' A!"

From the balcony, "Come see all the sailors!"

"Come see all the sailors!" mocked Abbey. "Bless my ass! We're packin' into Mexico with fuckin' Mary Poppins and her flea-cunt sister."

Rebeca took a long drag of weed. *This could turn out to be fun after all.*

"Who sent you down?" she asked Abbey.

"Not the same hamster-dick who sent you, that's for sure."

Poor Tyrone, she thought.

Abbey barreled on, "Mr. William Leroy Majeski. The only nigger ever named after a dickfaced honky Polish snatch-sucking con man. The black bastard said something has fucked up his usual money run. 'It'll be just like old times,' he says. I got to drop my regular job, take motherfuckin' sick leave, put my shit-slinging kids with their fuckin' grandma, who don't know shit from sandpaper, and come down to Crystal City here and ride off into the land of simple fucks with two titless wonders. Fuckin' beautiful!"

Rebeca sat in the pleasant glow of the good weed. Her mind tried to decode Abbey's words. She couldn't decide if Abbey was being completely serious. Rebeca guessed she really was a bit pissed. She remembered how she had reacted when Tyrone told her she had to make the run. No matter how easy it had been before, everyone had heard the ugly stories of what could happen in Mexico, especially if your people didn't take care of things for you. They both had seen George Kern after he got nailed in Baja with a load of Thai on the beach. With no backup or money to grease the skids, he had left both kneecaps and his sex life in a barn down there. She could imagine what fun the Mexicans might have with Mary Poppins and her sister.

"I wish those little bitches would come in off that balcony," said Abbey. "I get all fucked up in my stomach when I see people leaning over like that."

"Let's have some more of this awesome weed, Abbey."

"Awesome? What's this 'awesome' shit? You trying to make like some fiberglass-brained beachie surf-cunt?"

William and Tyrone showed up at ten the next morning with the cash. The older girls had gone over the procedure with the young sisters the evening before. They showed how the cash would be taped across their chests above and below their breasts and down along their ribs. The girls were told about the tight jerseys they would wear under the baggy sweaters and how the Mexican heat could make them itch like hell and that they shouldn't start scratching like they had fleas or it would just get worse. They were told that they should do some deep breathing and stretch around a bit after they were taped to test for tightness and restrictions on their breathing. And if they had to get retaped on the way down to La Paz, they were to be goddamn sure not to put tape all the way around their chests or they'd wind up not being able to breathe after a few minutes.

"And if any hot-crotch cherry-chaser tries to go for your tits on the plane or anywhere else, you just call for ol' Abbey. I'll get over to you and poke a fingernail through his worthless nuts."

William and Tyrone carried the money in two small suitcases. They walked past the girls into one of the bedrooms and unloaded the cash onto the big double bed. The six of them looked down at the stacks of bills spread out on the blanket. The two young girls were staring.

"Jeepers," said Allie, "what a lot of money!"

Tyrone looked over at Allie and then at Rebeca, his eyebrows raised in a questioning look. William paid no attention to the remark. Rebeca looked back at Tyrone and shrugged.

"How was the trip down from L.A.?" said Abbey. She was still looking at the money, too.

"No problem," answered William. "Almost got our black asses tangled in a nest of crabs on the fuckin' East Side this morning. They's settin' up to mess with a few cholos chillin' too near Crip turf, but we dumbshit on through. Dingus here is wearing his motherfuckin' red do-rag like some motherfuckin' sidewalk server. We only carrying three hundred grand, so why worry? Fuckin' walk in the park, right, Tyrone?"

Tyrone didn't reply.

William began to divide the hundreds into four piles. He looked up to survey the shirts on the two young sisters, who were standing there hypnotized by the stacks of cash.

"Christ, couldn't you be diggin' up something with tits? These two tweakers lookin' like motherfuckin' football players time they be taped up with this shit."

"They wouldn't be here if they weren't fuckin' ready," said Abbey. She had taken a liking to the new girls. "And they're a lot more innocent-looking than some of those cow-chest cunts you dig up, William. If we did it your way we'd have those peckerhead pilots back in the motherfuckin' plane tryin' for a handful before we got off the motherfuckin' runway. Don't you worry about them. We'll take care of it."

"You fuckin' better take good care of it," he replied.

William kept up the sorting. He stopped before he completed the job.

"Shit. No use me makin' equal loads with all these different-size tits. You figure it out, ladies."

He tossed a handful of bills to Abbey and went out to the living room. Tyrone followed, leaving the girls with the money. William flopped down on the gray couch.

"Tyrone, my man," he said, "lay a Jonesy on me. Need to soothe these motherfuckin' dog-city nerves. It's been a long fuckin' day."

After a few moments the sweet aroma of the marijuana drifted through the suite. Laced with cocaine and dipped in PCP, the stick started to put a glow on William's world of inadequate tits and wandering cash. Tyrone didn't light up, but he felt relieved at finally passing off the cash to the girls. Money in big bunches made him nervous.

It took forty minutes for the girls to tape the load. Rebeca did Abbey first, then they both did the girls. Then Abbey loaded Rebeca. The broad white adhesive tape zipped off the rolls with a professional sizzle as the stacks of bills on the bed shrunk away. When they were finished, Abbey stepped back to assess the work. The four of them stood there in the bedroom looking at each other and at the way their nipples stuck out between the lines of tape and cash. Abbey went up to Keri and nodded. She put her hands on Keri's shoulders and turned her completely around to check the edges.

"Good job," she said.

She looked down at Keri's chest. Keri's tit tips poked up in the air like pinto beans. With her hands still on Keri's shoulders, Abbey bent down and planted a little kiss on each nipple.

"For luck," she said.

Keri smiled.

Abbey went over to Allie and repeated the action.

"Now remember, fuzz-butt, any problems with anything, you let me know, quick. It should be a piece of cake."

Allie giggled at the kisses and looked over at Keri in obvious delight. "Isn't this too exciting!" she said.

Keri nodded, a liveliness sparkling in her eyes.

The four girls put on the stiff cotton jerseys over the tapes. They pinned the shirts into the tops of their ladies' jockey briefs. They pulled on denim jeans and finally put on the baggy sweaters. They fluffed and stretched and adjusted the sweaters.

"No lump, no bump, we're ready to hump!" said Abbey.

She shot a thumbs-up and slapped Allie on the butt.

"Let's go show those limpdicks out front what a professional operation looks like," she said.

"I need a goddamn drink. How about you, Becky?"

"We're not going to get one here, Abbey. Looks like the damn bar is closed for repairs."

"Fuck."

A warm sea breeze meandered freely through the rough cement terminal building of the La Paz airport. It seemed as if the building had no walls where the wind was concerned. Despite having crossed the small coastal range, the air still carried a hint of salt lifted from the tepid waters of the Gulf of California.

It swirled over the green tiles that were the floor of the airport, and it exhaled the mixed aroma of cooked tortillas, wood smoke, sweet dirt, and hard-working bacteria common to all Mexican settlements with the exception of Mexico City, where the air had been killed long ago by carburetors and politicians. But here in La Paz the damp air whispered of soft, lazy seaside evenings and the sting of lime-laced tequila.

"Listen up, fuzz-butt," Abbey said to Allie. "Corral your big sister when she comes out of the little girls' room and meet me and Rebeca by that newsstand over there under the clock."

Abbey glanced around the terminal as she and Rebeca sifted through a group of taxi drivers. The cabbies hawked for fares among the newly arrived passengers.

"We're supposed to meet a short fat guy by the name of Roberto. That description probably fits half the bean-dicks in this place. Have you met him before?"

Rebeca shook her head. Her ears still hurt from the descent; she was squeezing her nose and swallowing hard in an attempt to pop the pressure.

"If you don't let go of your damn nose, we're going to be up to our little tan tits in cocaine, sweetheart," said Abbey.

They stopped by the newsstand to wait for the girls and Roberto. Abbey lit a cigarette and blew the smoke at Rebeca.

"Too bad your buddy Tyrone ain't here, Becky. He could stick that dick of his in there and spear that ol' bubble with room to spare."

The remark made Rebeca laugh just as she was exhaling hard against her pinched nose. The snort of laughter made her eardrums crack in pain, but the pressure popped. "I'd hate to have you for a nurse." The laughing had pushed quick tears onto her cheeks. "Damn, it feels good to get my ears back. I don't know whether to thank you or kick you in the ass."

"I think I'd rather have you kick me in the nose with a little snow, sugar."

"Damn, Abbey. Give me a break."

After sitting next to her on the plane all morning, Rebeca was at the point where anything Abbey said got her going. Abbey knew it and didn't let up.

"I wonder where that bastard is? I should have told William to have this taco clown stick a mother-fuckin' sparkler in his ass so we could find him, but the useless jerkoff would probably forget to light the son of a bitch."

"Nothing happens fast down here, Abbey."

"It's not like our tits are packed in chopped liver, sweetmeat. We could buy half the town with all this shit. It'd be nice if someone showed a little damned interest."

They saw Keri heading in their direction from the far side of the terminal. The crowd of arriving passengers and cabbies had thinned. "I'm all set, Abbey," Keri said. "Where's Allie?"

Orange Day

CLASSIFICATION: ORANGE DAY / ORANGE DAY
Z 172233Z MAY 90
ZTTUZYUW HOHO RUHHAJA0703
1992233-UUAC

Contingency Document 43556.29 Brookings Inst. #3466900
03 Nov.1988 request. / author: RINTELL, Alan Meineke
EXEC. drive; read/comt/init.

Route to: Inter. Affairs, COMM	03
FBI, DIV. FOREIGN COUNTERINTEL.	21
CIA, DOMESTIC OPERATIONS DIVISION	01

Sen. Clifford Claussen, D-Sen/N.J., staff req.
Rep. Jesse Bates, D-Rep/MASS. staff req.

Excerpted: AEK/dfr code 47A

[Civil revolt]
 . . . to assess the potential for internal revolt

within significant U.S. popular elements. These projections in response to Study Req. 32213/88/Brook.

[Covert action disclosures]
. . . and the subsequent series of disclosures by media elements stretching back to 1954 that dealt with U.S. government covert involvement in developing countries, allied nations, and U.S. domestic/political matters . . .

[Gov't disinformation]
. . . since a large majority of media personnel and a meaningful segment of the U.S. population have seen recurring instances of government lying, there is little inclination to accept official denials of involvement . . .

[Civil anger]
. . . the evolution of national anger . . . tired of being lied to . . .

[Non-party]
. . . the realization that these practices cut across party lines . . .

[1954; Guatemala]
. . . when the Eisenhower administration lied to the American people in 1954 regarding U.S. involvement in the invasion of Guatemala. This large-scale paramilitary operation involving U.S.–built assault bases in Nicaragua and Honduras . . .

[1958; Indonesia]
. . . in the failed attempt to overthrow the Indonesian president in 1958 . . . Secretary of State

Dulles telling the congressional committee that "we are not interested in the internal affairs of this country" . . . President Eisenhower saying, "Our policy is one of careful neutrality . . . not to be taking sides where it is not our business" . . . while the CIA's own B-26's were bombing the constituted government of Sukarno as they spoke . . .

[1960; U-2 incident]
. . . the U-2 incident in 1960 . . . a case in which both the Soviet and U.S. governments knew of the overflights, yet the American people were lied to, not merely kept in the dark . . .

[1961; Bay of Pigs]
. . . 1961 when Kennedy lied about the Bay of Pigs . . .

[1964; Congo]
. . . with the clandestine CIA bombing and mercenary intervention in the Congo in 1964 . . .

[Pre-1964; S.E. Asia raids]
. . . concerning incursions into Laos, China, and North Vietnam prior to the Gulf of Tonkin Resolution passed by Congress in 1964 . . .

[1964; Chile]
. . . with the *Washington Post* exposures by Laurence Stern nine years after the massive CIA effort in the 1964 Chilean election . . . and the existence of Project Camelot in 1965 . . .

[1967; Vietnam]
. . . Operation Phoenix in 1967 . . .

[1970; Chile]

... in 1970 when Nixon lied publicly about the efforts of the U.S. government, in concert with Anaconda Copper and ITT, to subvert the Chilean elections . . .

[1971; Covert theory exposure]

... the discovery, in 1971, of the confidential minutes of the Pratt House meeting of January 8, 1968, by radical students who broke into Harvard University's Center for International Affairs . . .

[1972; Chilean Embassy]

... the American people lied to about the break-in at the Chilean embassy in Washington in May 1972 . . .

[1972; Watergate]

... he lied about the Watergate break-in . . .

[Intelligence losses]

... such as the Tonkin Gulf incident, the *Pueblo* capture, the *Liberty* attack, RB-47 shootdowns by the Russians, and EC-121/U-2 captures by the Chinese . . . representing aggressive, likely incursive, intelligence-gathering ops . . .

[Public realization]

... gradually engendered a corrosive cynicism about their own government despite the former acceptance of the premise that the fight against communism justified any means . . .

[Credibility gap]

... with what facts were available to the public . . .

enough to sow seeds of distrust in government attitude . . . beginning of the "credibility gap" . . .

[Perception of gov't vs citizen]

. . . against this backdrop is the slowly growing public perception of arbitrary, constitutionally suspect actions, undertaken by certain governmental agencies, against the U.S. citizen population . . .

[Constitutional inversion]

. . . runaway autocracy of CIA, DEA, IRS, U.S. Customs, and even the INS, where current legislation allows vehicle seizure from the "little old lady" who picks up an illegal alien to help with the yard work; she is "guilty" unless she can prove she did not know the man was an illegal; "guilty till proven innocent," a concept that . . . to grate hard at the American psyche . . .

[Zero Tolerance Program]

. . . "zero tolerance" programs in practice . . . wherein "connected" people and institutions seem to get boats, cars, and planes returned while the average person . . .

[War on drugs; sequelae]

. . . RICO Act implications . . . wage garnishments . . . random search and seizures . . . "political" gun-control shams . . . cash transaction disclosure laws . . . dissolution of banking secrecy laws . . . computer-driven privacy disintegration . . . mandatory testing . . .

[Gov't shortfall]

. . . frustration with government impotence in

providing even rudimentary protection vs. street violence, corporate trespass, white-collar crime . . . exploding bureaucracy . . . political ethics disclosures . . . judicial paralysis, court overload . . . 1989 HUD scandal . . . savings and loan bailout with the taxpayer taking the multibillion-dollar hit . . . a building resentment vs. IRS intimidation and arrogance . . .

[Flashpoint]
. . . flashpoint . . . some common target . . . flashpoint . . . public communication getting more efficient . . . flashpoint . . . a focusing event: (July 4th? April 15th?) . . .

[Trigger event]
. . . by a precedent-setting incident; e.g. a spontaneous rebellion against a government pay raise, tax, or regulation . . .

[Riot control]
. . . the surprising realization, after the race riots in the late sixties, that a democratic government cannot control a rioting populace, even with troops . . .

[Approach]
. . . total resolve . . . committed contingency planning . . .

[Prevention]
. . . remove flashpoints . . .

[Increase gov't dependency]
. . . greater percentage of population dependent on government checks, programs, retirements, employment . . .

[Disarm the people]

. . . use incident/event to crash-legislate gun control . . . to include locating prior-owned weapons via strict, escalating registration procedures . . . authorities not to be concerned with criminal possession; the ultimate danger lies in the general population . . . criminals can be bought, idealists are more difficult . . .

[Common enemy]

. . . theory of "common enemy"; use of fear . . . Soviets, terrorist action, disease threat, drug wars . . . covert . . . internally generated if necessary . . .

[Opinion control]

. . . media control . . . strong political leadership . . . religious alliances . . . promise reform . . . cosmetic reform . . . reform.

[Self-interest resources]

. . . corporations . . . government employees . . . banking interests . . . foreign allies . . . entertainment figures . . . insurance industry . . .

[Linchpins]

. . . public opinion . . . absolute control of military; preconflict mental conditioning of troops imperative . . .

[Objective]

. . . survival of present government . . .

[Out statement]

. . . the period of years from 1954 to 1974 in which the aforementioned series of media disclosures combined to erase public faith in government, a faith hard won through the idealism of the first half of the century . . . since 1974 . . . at first . . . the vague sense of disbelief, then disappointment . . . evolving into a jaded cynicism . . . in turn, to anger and a peculiar sense of national paranoia.

[Technical invasions of privacy]
. . . electronic eavesdropping: bugs, taps, opticals, laser monitors . . . overheads: Aquila, Pioneer, Sentinel, Sprite, Sky-Eye; Pupil satellites, Vortex, Magnum, Lacrosse, KH-11 . . . data banks; computer track, credit hist. access (TRW), random compliance audits (IRS) . . .

[Inflammatories]
. . . media overreactions . . . book, film, TV emphasis on government corruption/conspiracy . . . IRS "horror story" promulgations . . . radio talk-show instigation . . . fringe-group publicities . . .

[Atmosphere]
. . . a period of frustration/anger . . . potential exists for regional/national reaction . . . containment: probable with contingency planning/forceful execution . . .

V/R AEK

12

Desert Shoot

A tiny rock slide clicked down the gentle slope of the ridge as Ram shifted his position in the loose desert shale. Fine yellow dust rose in the air above the moved stones. The sun lifted over the eastern horizon; heat whispered at the sand.

Mitch handed a cold beer through the dry air to his brother. "Have some breakfast."

On a companion ridge, five hundred meters to the west, stood a parabolic collecting dish on black mounts. They looked at the installation through binoculars.

"Give it a go, bro," said Mitch.

Ram studied the layout, then began to describe what he saw. "I see a dish at five hundred meters, slightly above our position. There are some box shapes on the ground near the dish. The dish and ground equipment are painted a light sand color. There's a five-foot-high fence, looks like some sort of mesh fabric. The fence makes a square around the dish installation. The area inside, where the dish is located, looks to be about eighty square yards. No sound coming from the equipment."

He raised the can of beer to his lips and took a sip; he swallowed, then continued.

"The dish is six feet in diameter; highest point, ten feet; a black collector tower in the center of the dish face, two feet long, perhaps a little less. Beyond the mesh fence, a large square area that saddles the ridge, chain-link fence topped with razor wire. A white pickup truck is parked inside the south edge of the fence. It faces north near some kind of rock bunker. Two white males, mid-forties, sitting on the near rim of the bunker drinking something, probably coffee. Two rifles, barrels up, against the edge of the bunker. One with a scope. No other people inside the fence or inside the truck."

Mitch continued looking at the far ridge. He took up the description. "The truck is a half-ton '84 Ford. It's facing us at forty-five degrees. There's a tarp covering something in the bed of the truck, might be camping gear; some poles sticking over the tailgate. On the ground behind the truck, there's a small black box. Judging from its position, close to the fence, it's probably a perimeter alarm. Maybe a Night Watch. Seems to be a pair of front-and-back flak jackets lying on the hood of the truck. The tires don't look too good on this side, sort of bald; dumb to take a truck with those tires out this far. Couldn't turn with the bikes, even on flat sand."

He paused and settled more comfortably in the shale. He looked through the binoculars again. For the next ten minutes he talked steadily, detail after detail, intense, thorough. Finally he stopped.

"Anything else, wiseass?" said Ram. He was always uncomfortable at how much more Mitch seemed to see.

"Nothing else, chicken legs."

The morning wore on slowly. The summer sun poured through empty blue sky onto the arid hills and out across the shimmering bajada. They watched the opposite ridge from the shadow of their shallow cut. By three in the afternoon the sky was white with heat.

"Nice fuckin' weather," said Mitch.

"You sure that radio can take this heat?" asked Ram.

"Fuck the radio. It's me I'm worried about."

"Make believe you're at the beach."

"If I was at the beach, I could get a cold beer and dip these little roasted nuts of mine in the ocean."

They waited in the hot silence. The two men on the far ridge sprung a tarp from the truck for shade. They were sitting in folding chairs backed against the pickup in the shadow, and Mitch could see them sipping at cold drinks taken from a cooler they pulled from the bunker.

"Look at those fuckers," he said.

Ram didn't respond. He was flexing the muscles on his bare forearm, trying to keep a tumblebug from escaping back into the sand.

"Give me the bag," said Mitch.

Ram pushed the water bag over to Mitch with his free hand. Mitch pulled out the stopper and doused water over the cotton ghillie-cloths that covered his head and neck. The water was warm, but it brought a pleasant cool to his skin as it began to evaporate immediately in the dry heat. Ram flexed his forearm hard. He crushed the beetle into a milky smear.

Mitch looked at the far ridge as Ram took back the bag and wet down his own cover.

"Yeah," Mitch sighed. "Here we are dressed up like a couple of camel-fuckin' sandbangers. Sipping hot water and screwing around with bugs. Shit. I could be facedown in some sweet pink ice-filled pussy."

"Ice-filled pussy?"

"Ice-filled pussy. Right."

The desert night came in quickly. A chill breeze jumped out of the north to meet it. What was left of the brutal heat cooled away in minutes; only the rocks and deep sand held a thermal memory of the desert burn.

Ram moved down behind the crest and slipped into a black cotton shirt with long sleeves. He checked the gun cases to be sure they were zipped tight against the grit that would scour the ridge in the night wind. He pulled a poncho from the pack and flipped it up the hill at Mitch, who was scanning the compound in the steel light of the new night. "I'm going down to check the bikes and get some more water."

"Hold it, Ram. The boys are starting up the truck."

Across the wash, the headlights of the truck swung around to face a gate located just below the crown of the hill. After a pause the lights moved farther up onto the crest of the ridge, then stopped. In the collected light of the binoculars, Mitch could see one of the men walk around the truck after closing the gate. The cab light blinked on, then out; the truck moved along the spine of the ridge and disappeared down the other side.

"Those fuckers only work days," groused Mitch.

Ram lay on his belly and looked impassively at the

abandoned site in the cold starlight. "Maybe they have a base camp down on the flats."

"Mercy! That could mean there are more than just the two of them."

"It could."

"That makes this little sandtrap more interesting."

"Especially if they have a couple of good bikes. I don't want to have to ditch this gear."

They looked across the night.

Mitch broke the quiet. "Fuck 'em all. Just what we need. Twelve guys coming at us over the hill. Just like the goddamn Alamo."

"The contract says no warm targets, only the relay. I get the feeling the buyer feels strong about that."

Midnight passed. The truck had not returned. The heat deserted the rocks and drained into the deep sand.

"I'm going to grab some sleep, bro," Mitch said. "Don't miss the radio call. We get a thirty-minute lead. If we have to hump across this wash for a dark shot, we'll need all of that." He slid back off the ridge and moved down the hill, disappearing into the shadows of the draw to the east. At 3:00 A.M. they switched the watch.

The truck returned at dawn. It clattered over the gray hardpan at the top of the far ridge and went through the gate as the rising sun skimmed flat rays of morning over the desert. Mitch glanced back over his shoulder as Ram came up with two mugs of steaming coffee.

With the hard slanting light of dawn at his back, Ram could see the two occupants of the truck. The men on the far ridge were the same two of the day before. "Anything different?"

"Same, same," answered Mitch. "One guy just looked

under the hood; checked the oil. He's closed it up. Took the two flak jackets out of the cab and threw them on the hood again. The other guy is working in the rocks; looks like he's getting something to eat."

Ram sipped his coffee. The Mojave sun would work on them again today. He thought back to when he and Mitch were kids. Their folks had been killed in a car wreck when he was four; Mitch had just turned eight when it happened. It was the first vivid and complete memory that Ram held. They had been hustled off to live with Grandpa Cash. But he was old and almost blind. They spent more time looking after the old man than the other way around. Ram remembered listening to Mitch cry through the long Montana nights of that first winter. He had been sad and confused hearing Mitch break like that. He wanted to do something for Mitch, wanted to make the hurting stop. But he couldn't do it. He couldn't remember feeling much emotion after that first week. Their parents were just gone. Like they were on a trip. He felt nothing. He remembered the lady from the court who came to see them three weeks after the accident. She talked to the old man and to Mitch. They seemed to think it was wrong that he wasn't concerned about the loss. But he had been neutral about the whole thing. He acted better than the grown-ups, and he sensed a pleasant freedom. He remembered how the court lady put her fat arm around him and held his face against her buxom chest. He remembered the sour smell of her. He felt trapped in all that softness.

"Let it out, let it out, my little man," she said.

"Let what out?" he replied, genuinely confused.

Now he looked at Mitch bellied down on the cool sand, field glasses pressed against his face. He looked at the scar along the right side of his brother's head above the ear. The hair had never come back in that place. Ever since Mitch got busted in the head by a winch handle when he was twelve, Ram had wanted to reach out and touch the scar. But he never did. There was something about seeing Mitch get hurt that had surprised him. Mitch never got hurt. Not by things. For Ram to have touched that scar would have meant giving up something, losing something, and Ram didn't want to do that. Mitch had protected him. Mitch had solved all the lousy problems the world threw at them when they were small and alone; he had smoothed cool oil on the sunburns, he had explained why the animals made those screams in the black hour after midnight, he had taught him how the guns of Grandpa Cash worked and how to take the skin off a squirrel in one piece, and he had explained what a snatch was when Ram was seven and the other boys made fun of him for not knowing. Ram figured that he probably loved Mitch. But he didn't know what love was supposed to be. Grandpa Cash never spoke of it, and he guessed that Mitch hadn't seen enough of love to be able to explain it to him. It was a thing from another place, a woman thing maybe. He put it out of his mind. They learned on their own how to deal with the world. That part had been fun. And still was.

He finished his coffee and looked across the pristine desert. The memories swam up to him in the still air. Images of Mitch, of himself. He felt the gentle ache inside, familiar, uncomfortable. He wanted to ask Mitch a question. It was a question from a long time ago. But he had never asked it. And he didn't ask it now.

The day passed as the one before. The sun went from red to orange to white. The dry wind blotted all traces of moisture from eyes and nose. The fine desert grit went to the corners of the eyes and stayed there. The taste of water, the feel of water, from one group of minutes to the next, became the marker that defined time. Human skin flexed and flaked and wept as it fought the heat with dogged evolutionary persistence. By late afternoon even the arid wind exhaled to a stop in the jagged heat. A red-tailed hawk, usually pinned high in the sky by the desert breeze, labored across the baked air. Nothing moved on the desert, and so the hawk could not hunt. The hawk's fleeting shadow ripped over the sand and startled Mitch as he stared into the heat. For him the day had become a challenge. He was interested in the test of will the desert had forced upon them.

"It's not really so bad," he said more to himself than to Ram, who was stretched on his back beneath a patch of desert camouflage net. They had strung the net between four sticks of mesquite and wedged the ties into cracked shale. The shade was an oasis in the white heat, but now the light ribbons of camouflage hung motionless.

"How long do we play this game, bro?" said Mitch.

"As long as twenty grand seems fair. In this heat, that might not be much longer."

"This ain't bad once you get a feel for it."

"Mitch, it's a hundred and twenty degrees out here."

"Dry heat, though."

They drifted into silence. Ram let his mind play

with the old realization that discomfort acted like some kind of tranquilizer on Mitch.

At 0922 the next morning, the radio buzzed on from its standby mode. Three sharp clicks snapped out of the speaker, followed by the white sound of falling air as the receiver activated.

"About fuckin' time," said Mitch.

He rolled over to the set and yanked the mouthpiece from its clamp. He felt a sweet rush of adrenaline sprinkle through his system. Ram was already reaching for the Steyr case.

The radio spoke to them in a flat metallic voice that was clear and remarkably static-free.

"Cowboy, Cowboy, Cowboy . . . this is Mother Wolf."

Mitch keyed the mike as he adjusted the set.

"Mother Wolf, Mother Wolf . . . this is Cowboy. We have you. Go."

"Cowboy, Cowboy. This is Mother Wolf. You are on at my mark. I have 0922 and forty-five . . . fifty . . . fifty-five, fifty-six, fifty-seven, fifty-eight, fifty-nine, mark!"

Mitch and Ram popped in the stop stems on the watches.

"Mother Wolf. I am 0923 and eight, nine, ten."

"Cowboy. You are green and you are cold . . . I say again, you are cold."

"Mother Wolf. This is Cowboy. We are cold. By your call, we are go and cold. Out."

Mitch keyed back the mike and switched off the radio. Ram was sandbagging the Steyr and smoothing out elbow rests in the shale.

Mitch checked his watch. "The mark was 0923. With a thirty-minute lead, 0923 gives us a shoot at 0953."

Ram spoke back. "I mark 0923, I have 0953 to shoot."

Mitch watched Ram ready the rifle. The night had not been as cold as the one before, and the sun had a good start at roasting the desert. It was ninety degrees. By 0953 it would be over ninety-five. He pictured the first amber icy beer. He allowed himself that one distraction, then put his mind back to work. The shot would be at the gear only. That was what the word "cold" meant. No people shots. "It's going to be close to a hundred, bro."

He reached over and grasped the barrel of the Steyr as Ram uncapped the scope. The rifle had already lost the night chill, and the black metal was awash in the heat of the direct sun. The elevated temperature would expand the metal in the rifle, and the enlarged bore would result in reduced muzzle velocity. At five hundred meters, the shot would come in low if the temperature was ignored.

"This heat is going to make the round soft, Ram. I figure eight centimeters, maybe ten." He got a kick out of jumping Ram on the shot. He knew damn well Ram had the heat clicked in.

"Seven centimeters," absently, from Ram.

Mitch had taught him to shoot. And Ram was the best distance shooter he had ever seen, with the exception of Gunny Havlerod. The Gunny tried to teach Mitch to sniper, but Mitch didn't have the right emotion to go long. He got pumped too much in the final moment, when steadiness was a premium. Besides, he didn't like the ethics of killing from a distance. "Chickenshit."

Ram steadied the rifle on top of the sandbag. They secured the small camp. The nets came down, and the gear was bundled for the run. Ram put out a few misleads: red hairs, female; a tissue with lipstick stains; an empty tin of beans gleaned from a rest stop. Mitch enjoyed watching Ram screw up a shoot site. The act had evolved to a humorous ritual as Ram sowed his miscellaneous seeds with solemn flourish from a small tin carried on his hip.

They concentrated on the two men. Both figures were perched on the edge of the bunker, drinking from silver mugs that reflected the sun. Mitch scanned the site, the truck, the fence line. Everything looked as it had the day before . . . almost. He felt some small thing was out of sync, but couldn't put his finger on it; a vague feeling. Maybe it was the position of the truck. It was turned a bit from where it was parked on the previous day, and the doors were both closed. That might be it. He glanced at the time. It was 0951. Too late to talk their way around the site again. Ram was already lined up. Mitch shifted the glasses to the transceiver and focused down on the silhouette of the collector tower that stuck out from the center. He held the binoculars in front of his face with his right hand and lowered his eyes to his watch.

"I have 0952 and twenty seconds," he said to Ram.

"0952 and twenty," Ram replied softly.

"I have 0952 and thirty."

"And thirty."

"And forty."

"And forty."

"And fifty."

"Fifty."

"Spotting," said Mitch. He raised his eyes from the watch to the binoculars. He framed the tower. Ram would count it in. The desert was quiet.

Crack!

The detonation of sound shattered the hanging

silence, then reverberated into the wash between the two ridges and rebounded back at them. Mitch saw a commotion of powdered paint and aluminum puff away from the suddenly twisted tower of the collector. One shot. Five hundred meters. In the heat. Dead on.

"Nice shot. We're gone, bro."

"Right." Ram smoothly fitted the shoot gear back into the case. He worked without looking up.

Mitch made one last sweep of the far ridge. The two men were indistinct half bumps on the small horizon of bunker rocks.

The vivid rush of speed grabbed them like tin-can gin as they raced the bikes over the shiny hardpan. The desert varnish on the shale made the ground sparkle as the wheels ate up the easy miles. The sweet smell of late-spring sage laced their nostrils as the land rolled away close beneath the pegs. They left the flanks of the Chuckwallas behind to the north and swept southeast through raw, empty desert along the winding edge of the Milpitas Wash. They picked up Route 78 and blasted southwest, tires chewing into the softening asphalt, and made for the squat desert town of Brawley, where the Great-June-Beer lay in wait.

In Brawley they offloaded the shoot gear into the horse trailer that was coupled to the waiting truck. They had parked the rig there at the safe drop ten days ago. The bikes, engines still clicking with heat strain, were rolled into the enclosed trailer and locked out of sight. The brothers broke out clean shirts, put fresh spit in their hair, and headed for El Diablo.

The bar was a ten-stooler—three booths, one jukebox, a pool table that boasted a two-degree tilt toward the left rear corner, two back rooms, and a resident whore named Molly Molina whose tits were as sharp as she was ugly. The place was run by Mama Lin. Mama was a bucket of seventy-three-year-old Chinese vinegar. She could cuss, fight, drink, and break wind with the best of the migrant field hands. She spoke four languages, never gave credit, and had a glass eye as a result of catching a pool cue point-first when she was thirty-two and minding her own business one night behind the very same bar. She gave the worst directions, the coldest beer, and the best back rubs anywhere north of Mexicali. She was known to have sent lost Las Vegas tourists thirty miles into Mexico; and the bar was only one block from the main road going through town. Ram and Mitch, working or not, always stopped at El Diablo to check on Mama Lin and sip that cold sweet desert beer.

Mitch stuck his head carefully around the doorframe and peered in to see where she was. Mama Lin was at the far end of the bar with her back to the door scolding a wasted Mex about something. Her Chinee-Spanee was only up to half volume. Mitch bent over and sneaked along the bar until he was a few feet from her.

"Gobble, gobble, gobble," in his genuine best turkey call.

Mama didn't flinch or hesitate. "Gobble, gobble, gobble," she replied in authentic turkey. "Sit down, Mister Mitch, be right on you," without turning around. She finished scolding the slumping Mex.

"Christ, ain't she beautiful," he said to Ram.

They boarded two center bar stools.

"She is indeed very beautiful," grinned Ram.

"What will it be, white boys?" A smile cut sharp wrinkles into her burnt-wood face.

"Two of your best longnecks, sweetheart," said

Mitch, "from the deepest reaches of your icy heart."

"I get you icy, Mister Mitch. Make little hairy balls go way up in back of round eyes."

"Do your best, Mama. This boy has come from hell."

They savored those first beers in total silence. The beer was special, and the cool shade of the old bar ran a close second. Mama went about her business. She knew how sacred that first brew could be to men who looked as these two looked. The caked dust at the corners of their eyes had cracked and flaked off when they had smiled at her. That meant they hadn't smiled that hard in days; hot, dry days. She left them to wonder at the cold.

When the line of empties reached six, Molly Molina walked through the bead curtain that defined her room in the back. She wore a tight purple jersey. Her breasts jutted straight and true. She could have stuck herself in the wall under the right conditions.

"Hi, boys," as she passed by.

She went out to the street on some mission. They turned and watched her leave.

"Nice tits," from Mitch.

"Great face."

"We sound like a fuckin' beer commercial, bro."

"God, she sure is ugly, though," sighed Ram.

"God has a sense of humor."

Mitch drained his bottle.

"You'd need a flak jacket to make love to that, Mitch. Those tits would cut your heart out."

Mitch stiffened. His fist slammed on the bar.

"That's it!" he said.

"That's what?"

"The fuckin' flak jackets. They weren't on the hood of the truck like the other days. They weren't there when you shot. The bastards had them on!"

13

Varki

Jesse stood at the helm and backed the houseboat out of the slip. Beneath the deck, the twin engines rumbled with an easy power. Suckling whirlpools of turbulent water swirled down both sides of the white fiberglass hull. The craft swung away from the padded cement piling at the end of the pier, then pivoted at the stern as the engines were put ahead; the props took a brawny bite of Lake Mead, and the boat accelerated forward. The fat twilight sun burrowed into the low mountains, and the surface of the lake slowly changed to soft gold.

Kevin braced his bulk against the forward edge of the cocktail bar as the surge of power dropped the stern, and he raised his drink off the wood surface so it wouldn't go sliding down at Ray Varki's conservative white shirt.

Jesse had introduced Kevin to the man a few minutes earlier as Kevin hustled aboard wearing his God outfit. Kevin had been forty minutes late due to the traffic jam on the highway leading out to the marina, and the long delay in the rush-hour traffic had made his uniform seem tight and irritating. Now he wanted to change into his party pants and new pink shirt; he was relieved that they had left the dock quickly. He finished his drink with a noisy guzzle and carefully got off the bar stool as the speed of the boat evened out.

"If you will excuse me, good people, I shall perform a Clark Kent."

He picked up his night bag and, with an ominous tilt, lurched his way forward.

"You can use the front cabin, Father," said Ruth. She was slicing green peppers at the galley counter. "Watch those steps."

"Bless you, my child."

Down in the forward cabin, Kevin maneuvered about and struggled to keep his balance while changing. He tried to sort out his impressions of Mr. Rayburn Edward Varki. The man looked like an oversized accountant. At first Kevin had thought him unremarkable; then he looked again. Varki appeared well-muscled, with a square jaw and a solid, tense neck. Wire-rimmed glasses pinched down on a narrow pointed nose. His thinning gray hair was in wispy retreat above a pale flat forehead, and his tight sharp lips carried a faint bluish cast. The man seemed pleasant, but Kevin could read a coiled energy in him. Maybe it was the eyes. They were a dull green, almost misted over, as though afflicted with cataracts; but in the very centers, so small he would have missed it had he not been looking closely, showed a pinpoint glitter of yellow fire. When Kevin had first noticed it, he had to check himself from staring for too long a time. He had started to turn his head to see if it was a reflection from the setting sun, but then he realized Varki had his back to the west.

There were three other people on board. A sullen, hard man was introduced as Varki's associate, but was clearly not a peer. He was keeping to himself on the rear deck. He wasn't just looking at his surroundings, he was dissecting them. Kevin guessed he was muscle. A second man, one whom Kevin had met before, sat at the bar with Varki. They had been talking over drinks when Kevin boarded, and they had broken off their talk when Jesse made the introductions. The man's name was Gene Plum. Kevin recognized him as a courier who worked the Southwest out of San Diego. They had carried for some of the same people in the past. Gene was good for a free meal ticket and a few laughs, but Kevin hadn't spent much time with him on those rare occasions when they had met in Vegas. Between jobs, Kevin much preferred to do battle with the dice, and Gene didn't show much interest in table games, not unless it was a table that supported the supine form of a young maiden in some convoluted stage of lust. The third person was a striking black-haired Eurasian girl. She looked to be in her early twenties. She had the ease and carriage of a front-line showgirl, and she had flashed a smile at Kevin when Jesse introduced them that made a distinct, if fleeting, zing of awareness pass through a fat-buried part of him. Her name was Aixa. Jesse had taken care to pronounce the name slowly so he would remember it.

"Eye-eeks'-a," he had said.

Jesse hadn't mentioned who she was. Kevin wondered if she belonged to one of the men or whether she was a friend of Ruth's and Jesse's.

Kevin completed his efforts in the forward cabin. He looked down in admiration at his huge pink shirt. It was, he thought, one of his greatest acquisitions. He tried to get an image of himself in the mirror on the bulkhead of the cabin, but the mirror was too small. The shirt had been hanging on a rack in the back of the Big Man's Shop, and he had spotted it from the front of the store as soon as he walked through the door. It was him.

He reconquered the three stairs, squeezed through the narrow hatch, and, with his arms outstretched for effect, made a theatrical leap into the main salon. The thump of his hop drew the attention of all except Mr. Hard, who was still outside checking for predators.

"Ta-daaa," he sang.

"Kevin. That looks super!" laughed Ruth.

"Let me get my sunglasses back on," yelled Jesse. He let go of the wheel and faked fumbling around on the helm console, trying to affect a look of panic. Panic didn't fit on Jesse's face.

Gene and Aixa were laughing, too. Kevin noticed that Gene had begun to migrate toward Aixa. The noise of the engines evidently had defeated his talk with Varki.

Varki sat at the bar with a drink that was as full as it had been when Kevin had gone below to change. He looked at Kevin and the new pink shirt. Varki did not smile.

"Kevin, here's your drink," laughed Ruth.

The tears of her laughter fell like spangles into the catch-basin formed by her breasts, which were half-jacked out of her halter. Kevin could bring Ruth to the brink of hysterics without even trying. Of all the people he knew, he liked Ruth best. She was his perfect congregation. Her closeness with Jesse, so open and total, eliminated, for Kevin, any of the bothersome complexities of sex, however subtle, that could cloud relationships between a man and a woman. Kevin liked Ruth just because she was Ruth. She was relaxed, honest, unpretentious, and uninhibited. Quite the opposite of the women to whom he preached. And Jesse, who was submerged in her adoration, floated in a comfortable confidence that permitted a deep, if odd, friendship to exist between the three of them.

For her part, Ruth thought Kevin was the funniest man she had ever known. The sheer incongruity of his behavior made her rejoice. Though she couldn't put her amusement into words, Kevin had only to stand in front of her to put a smile in her soul. She had told Jesse about a dream she often had in which she and Kevin were walking through the debris of a terrible bus wreck. The road was covered with the mangled bodies of aged tourists who had met their end on a charter trip to Las Vegas. As Kevin shuffled through the carnage, he would give blessings to the corpses, and then he would turn to her and make some outrageously funny comment. In the dream, she would try not to laugh, but she couldn't help it. Finally, as Kevin continued to make the ridiculous remarks, some of the corpses started to smile. Soon the people who had been killed in the wreck were all laughing. They began to help each other up and to walk around the road picking up their body parts. The dream ended with the whole bunch of them walking down the road toward Las Vegas with everyone singing old songs and laughing while she and Kevin led the way.

"Maybe you two will invent a new religion," Jesse had said.

Jesse put the boat to anchor next to a steep rock wall where the Colorado cut down from the Grand Canyon. They were off the main body of the lake, and the dam was out of sight. Jesse dropped the anchor by pushing a button next to his steering position. The hook rattled out of the bow and, after a few seconds of dragging, dug itself into the river bottom thirty feet below.

As the warm evening settled on them, they made small talk and had a round of drinks, again with the exception of Mr. Hard, who was now stationed on the foredeck checking the empty cliff tops.

"This is a beautiful spot, Jesse," said Gene.

"We love the lake at this time of day," said Ruth. "I think Jesse would live right here if there wasn't so much boat traffic on the weekends."

"I'll tell you, folks," said Jesse, "with that little bear of a generator for electricity and these cellular phones for keeping in touch, I intend to spend a lot more time out here. This place is good for the mind."

"How long have you lived in Las Vegas?" Aixa asked.

Gene had watched her cross one long leg over the other sixty seconds ago and was still staring at the slit in her tight turquoise wraparound.

"We've had the boat for two years. I guess we've been in the Las Vegas area for about six years now. Is that right, sweetheart?"

Jesse nodded. He thumbed his balls through the canvas material of his boat shorts. He never got comfortable in the damn things. He liked the salty look, but he just wasn't cut out for shorts.

"You and Mr. Plum know each other, don't you, Father?" said Aixa.

"We do, my child, we do. And, as Ruth will attest,

it is mandatory you call me Kevin when I am garbed in these threads of the masses. That's a small 'm.' "

"Okay, I like the name 'Kevin.' "

"Yes," he continued, "Mr. Plum and I are acquainted with each other's strengths and weaknesses. We both come from San Diego. But tell me about yourself, my child. And try to do it before our Mr. Plum succeeds in staring that beautiful dress off your repentant childlike limbs."

"Sorry, sorry," said Gene, laughing. "I didn't know it was so obvious, Aixa. Beg your pardon. But please don't move your leg. I could die tonight."

Varki looked over at Gene.

"Well, Mr. Kevin," Aixa said, smiling. "I am a friend of Mr. Varki. I am lucky to have a good memory, and I speak a few useless languages. We meet many people from many places, and I help him with his work in my small way."

"What a disappointment," said Kevin. "I was hoping you were a friend of Ruth's whom she had procured to assuage my tired back, which has been sore of late; I am cursed by the sons of vile Beelzebub, god of flies, all of them wealthy members of the American Medical Association. Perhaps, when these simple, common creatures you see about you are fast asleep, you will come to my place of repose and walk upon my unworthy form with your small pagan feet. It would please God."

"I would do anything, if it would please God, but He has to get Mr. Varki's permission first."

They all laughed, even Varki.

"Now wait a minute, Kevin," said Ruth. "You're my man. If there's any late-night walking to be done on your back, it's me that will be doing it. You won't get him away from me without a fight, Aixa!"

"Girls, girls," intoned Kevin. "You have heard the great tale of the loaves and the fishes? Therefore, be not downcast. My capacities are infinite. I can appreciate the longing you must feel, the heated stirrings in your young loins, the tepid lustings that, in my presence, rend your creamy breasts; be not in despair, for the Lord helps those who help themselves. This mighty golden body, sheathed in appropriate pink, will be offered on the half hour, commencing at midnight, to the maiden who first refills this empty cup of spirits that the forces of evil have drained even as I spoke."

"I'll take a piece of that," laughed Ruth. She jumped up and waltzed Kevin's glass to the bar.

"If you're going to walk on Kevin," said Jesse, "don't break anything. On him, I mean. He's got a lot of traveling to do for us." He was looking at Varki as he spoke.

"Yes," said Varki, "he can travel for us."

Jesse looked at Kevin and felt relieved. Kevin had met with Varki's approval, probably even before tonight. The acceptance of Kevin to handle the big pay runs would mean a lot of green for his friend. More important, Kevin was the only carrier in whom Jesse felt complete confidence. Jesse didn't want his balls in the loop in any deal that involved a man like Varki; Varki had asked him to get the best, and he had recommended Kevin. There were others, many with better experience, but he knew Kevin's mind and heart. He had watched Kevin gamble from the pit. He knew discipline when he saw it. He knew about the still-small cocaine habit. He knew about the money Kevin had put away. He knew that Kevin didn't have a weak spot for women in the sweaty world between the sheets, or for men, as was sometimes the case with penguins; he knew because he had checked, not just by asking around, but by trolling some local Grade A meat across his bow. In fact, he had checked all the way back to the beginning on Kevin. He didn't mind digging on a friend when it was business. And it was just as Kevin had said. No bullshit. One day, young Tony Scala goes to confession. He's got cancer. Scared. Only thirty-one years old and a wife, two kids. Tony wants God to know about the shit. Kevin tells young Tony to get it all out, spill everything, even the names, or Jehovah wouldn't be able to get a handle on poor Tony's salvation. Jesse had to smile again just thinking of it. He could see Kevin's wonderful face putting everything together in the darkened booth of the confessional. Tony dies. Kevin knows everybody. He moves in like a bust-out pro in a sawdust joint. Smooth. Superb cover. Some of the old farts in the organization probably had a few sharp chest pains over the idea of a priest, but it wasn't an old man's game anymore. Good ol' Kevin even did the burial.

Jesse chuckled out loud, almost spilling his drink.

"What's so funny, sweetheart?" Ruth gave Kevin his new drink and a kiss on the forehead.

"Just thinking," said Jesse.

"Tell us."

"I can't. It's not suitable for mixed company."

"Well, ladies." It was Varki. "Would you spare us a few minutes for some shop talk?"

Jesse looked at Varki. He wondered how Kevin and Gene would react.

"Come on, Aixa. Fetch your drink and we'll go bother stone-face out there. See if we can get his dander up."

Aixa smiled. "I doubt it." She knew Mr. Loza had had his dander cut off and put down his throat six years ago in Lebanon.

When the men were alone, Jesse freshened the drinks all around. Gene lit a cigarette. Kevin took his boat shoes off; the damn things seemed to shrink at this time of day.

"Gene, Kevin, Mr. Varki here wants you to do some hard work for him, for us. You've been doing some things for him already, but you didn't know it. This pays well. I trust you both. I have recommended you for the project. We can have an excellent relationship here. Mr. Varki?"

"Gentlemen, I am at the head of a group of Americans, real Americans, who are going to put this country back in the hands of the citizens where it belongs. Democracy is killing freedom. The time to clean house has come."

Great, thought Kevin, *we've got another nut here.*

Varki continued.

"Believe me when I say we have the resources. Your part is critical. Mr. Plum will convey the written directives to our action cells. Father Kevin will be transporting the monies necessary to pay operatives and to procure equipment. There are cutouts and safe drops, but speed and timing will be our chief cover. The work must be punctual and will involve contact with impulsive people. You report any difficulties to Jesse at once."

Gene shifted in his chair. The rattan squeaked.

"You both have worked with Jesse. So before you write this off as some misdirected effort by the lunatic fringe, I would like Jesse to say something."

"What Mr. Varki says is right. I've got the blood side of this thing. Kevin, you're money; Gene, you're the letter carrier. I'm not going to beat around the bush."

He paused to look directly at Kevin, then at Gene. Jesse continued.

"Gene, there's one million cash deposited in the Bank of Austria. Kevin, you've got the same. I know it's there because I put it there, courtesy of Mr. Varki. You know me. I don't bullshit my friends. I have the access codes for you. The money is yours. You get the codes on Labor Day, a little more than two months from now. One million for each of you, two months of work. If you're caught, which won't happen, your beef will be with the feds, no death penalty, boys; beats the hell out of being on the bad side of some of the outfits around Vegas."

"What Jesse just said is true. I know you will believe him if you don't believe me," added Varki.

They sat without speaking. Kevin and Gene were using the time and silence to assess what they had heard.

"What target?" said Gene.

"The IRS," replied Varki.

He let the silence come back again. Then he spoke.

"We're going to take out service centers, regional directors, agents, field offices, and more."

"Big," said Gene. His expression wandered somewhere between humor and disbelief.

"Very big," from Jesse.

Varki seemed to drift into himself in the next moments. The look of control, of objectivity, dissolved into what, in another face, would be a cast of sorrow. "I love this country. I love this great try at freedom. But for thirty years I have watched it die. Like watching a child, my child, slowly die. I have to tell them, we have to tell them. They are letting the flame go out." Then a wry smile. "The country will make it through this thing we do. The Constitution is there. But we must tell them we have had enough hypocrisy, enough greed, enough temporizing. We will say to them, 'Fix it . . . or we will fix it.' There's no more time. What we are about to show them has a crushing meanness to it, but it's going to happen. Some who are innocent will pay, but pay they must. The dream is being killed; even the people are changing . . . they think more of how they can take, not what they can build."

Kevin watched the man. He fought off a smile and marveled at Jesse's ability to keep such a serious, sincere look on his face.

"I know you gentlemen have questions, but do you have any problems with what I said? About the target?"

"No," said Gene. "No, I don't have any problems with the target. Not that target."

"And you, Father Kevin?"

"The only problem I have is with my back."

"Good. Mr. Loza will give you the first assignments before you leave this boat. You may or may not see me again. Jesse is to be your point of contact. He will be the source of further information. Mr. Loza will be Jesse's liaison to me. Jesse has built the action cells and can provide details on them."

"Mr. Varki," said Gene.

"Yes?"

"I'd like to step outside with Kevin for a moment. I'd like to sort out my thoughts. There might be some things we want to discuss with you, since we may not be in direct contact after tonight."

"Very well. The women and Mr. Loza are forward. You can use the aft deck. Jesse and I will wait here."

Carefully shutting the door behind them, Kevin followed Gene outside. The night air was clear and warm. They could hear Ruth and Aixa talking with Loza on the foredeck, but the distance was too great to make out what they were saying. Kevin settled into a deck chair that protested against his weight with a loud squeak. Gene lit another cigarette and put one foot up on the safety line.

"What do you think, Kevin?"

"I think 'one million dollars,' Gene."

"Is it my imagination, or is this guy a loony-tune?"

"It's not your imagination. The guy is a loony-tune."

"And?"

"And the money's there. I know Jesse. Trust me, the money abides in Austria."

They were quiet with their thoughts.

"I hope the guy *is* a beanbag," added Kevin. "If you think about it, you can see how that would be the best of all possible worlds."

"How so?"

"If he's on the level and knows what he's doing, it's going to be *Helter Skelter.* There's going to be a lot of scrambling and some major heat. On the other hand, if it turns out he's a dingbat and nothing goes down, we take our money and have a good chuckle. Believe it, Gene, the money is there. It's our money, and it's really there if Jesse says it is."

"I have an even better idea."

They paused. Gene looked into the water. Kevin looked at Gene.

"Don't tell me. Let me guess," said Kevin.

"Well, why the hell not? Give me a good reason."

"Because that would not be Christian."

"Christian, my ass."

"Forgive him, Lord. He knows not what he says."

"Then talk me out of it, Kevin."

"My son, for one thing, Mr. Varki probably has our dear friend Jesse on some sort of consignment deal. You know; some now, some later. Maybe most of it later. Jesse is Varki's insurance on this deal. If someone should let the air out of Mr. Varki, it could stiff Jesse out of his payoff. Do you remember the Maturo brothers? Jesse took those two children of God out in the desert and wrapped fishline around their little pink peters so tight they couldn't make wee-wee. Gave them all the cold beer they wanted. God took it from there. They lasted four days. God moves in mysterious ways. And painfully slow, at times. Those two fellows were not happy campers."

Kevin got up from his deck chair and walked over to stand beside Gene. He lifted Gene's cigarette from his fingers, took a drag on it, and gave it back.

"I didn't know you smoked, Padre."

"And I didn't know you were stupid, my son."

Kevin continued.

"Stop to think about the kind of backing we're looking at here. Two million for us. And what in the name of the Blessed Virgin are we? Glorified Keno runners. Jesse is going to get at least that. And what do you think the hit cells are going to cost? On a federal job? Maybe all over the West Coast? Maybe even bigger than that? Then crank into this fascinating picture the probability that someone has to be feeding Varki from the inside. This operation could not afford to go off on a wing and a prayer; as soon as the first hit goes down, definitely no later than the second, the whole system goes red. If you spend money like Varki is spending it, things better go all at once or your field people begin to have second thoughts. So, to make sure it goes at once, you need inside information. Inside information is expensive. You add it up, my good friend. Much wampum, many beads. I don't think that taking out Mr. Varki is a viable option. He just might have enough money left over to cover his backside against the likes of you." He put a big arm around Gene's shoulders. "Besides . . . it's my considered and divine opinion that Mr. Varki is just another backwoods nut with big ideas. This thing is never going to get off the ground."

Gene looked up at Kevin.

"You're right, Padre."

"I *am* right, my son."

"One million. Pretty nice pickins."

"It is that."

"Guess we shouldn't tempt fate."

"Never bendeth over in the shower of the Lord."

The dinner was Chicken Queen Kapiolani. Kevin and Ruth battled one another for galley space for the better part of an hour. Although it was Ruth's galley, she spent so much time leaning over in hysterics that Kevin could have taken, with justice, equal credit for the meal. The savory aroma of butter-fried chicken baking with apples and cider in the confined space of the houseboat had the guests in a cordial state of mutiny by the time Ruth served. Even the taciturn Loza came inside to surreptitiously scout out the progress of the kitchen crew. His timing was good, and he returned to the outside deck with the first plate served. The evening was a delight. After the meal, which included several bottles of magnificent German Auslese White, Varki toasted the ship's company with a quote from Robert Blair.

"Friendship! Mysterious cement of the soul!

Sweetener of life! And soldier of society!" as he met their eyes.

He spoke from the heart, and the hard light in his eyes had drifted away. The moment caught them by surprise, except for Aixa, who smiled.

Kevin thought to himself that it would have been more appropriate to throw out his one remembered quote from Lord Chesterfield—"After their friendship, there is nothing so dangerous as to have them for enemies"—but he decided against it. That would have required more drink than he had consumed during the evening.

At eleven o'clock, the throaty rumble of a slow-moving powerboat approached through the darkness. The other craft drew alongside the houseboat, and they could feel a gentle bump as the boats contacted.

Varki and Aixa stood at the touch of the hulls.

"We want to thank you for an excellent evening. Aixa and I have been in fine company this night. Ruth, the meal was delicious."

"It was nice meeting all of you," said Aixa, smiling.

Jesse and Ruth escorted Aixa out onto the after-deck. The door closed behind them, momentarily leaving Varki alone with Kevin and Gene.

"Gentlemen, I am happy to have met you at last. You come highly recommended. I know we will work well together and will do what has to be done. You have your packages from Mr. Loza?"

Gene and Kevin nodded.

"Then I will take my leave."

Varki extended his hand to Kevin, then to Gene. Before releasing Gene's hand, Varki looked him in the eye and smiled.

"And please, Mr. Plum, I would appreciate it if

you wouldn't refer to me as a 'loony-tune.' "

The small hairs on Gene's neck began to itch.

Kevin pursed his lips and nodded his head slowly. *Ah yes*, he thought, *the wonderful world of electronics.*

Varki left.

It was after midnight when Jesse retrieved the anchor, darkened the cabin interior, and put the engines back to work. Slowly the boat moved toward the lake. Steep cliffs and sparkling stars took form in the absence of the strong cabin lights, and the darkness dissolved into moonlight. Ruth, Kevin, and Gene stood on the foredeck. They watched the water clip easily under the bows.

"This is dangerous, isn't it?" said Ruth.

Both Kevin and Gene knew she wasn't talking about the boat ride. They didn't reply.

She didn't expect them to.

"Be careful," she said.

Back where they had been anchored, the waves of their leaving had dissipated. The water once again sat flat and black with reflections of stars asleep on its still surface. A small rock bounded down the face of the cliff. It bounced twice off the sheer wall, then hit the water.

In the moonlight, the water stars awoke and shivered on the new ripples.

14

Allegory

"How do you figure it, bro?"

"Could be someone is trying to check us out, Mitch, see what we can do, how we work."

"If it was just the damn desert shot, maybe," Mitch said doubtfully. He was still trying to figure how the dead lawyer fit in.

"That little shot cost our buyer a bundle. Twenty grand for the week on standby, twenty grand for this week, and twenty for the shot. Sixty grand. Major coin."

Ram got up to pour more water on the steaming rocks. The temperature in the little room quickly climbed another ten degrees. Mitch sat naked in the superheated air, the sweat pooling off him. It dripped from the tip of his nose and splashed on the floor of the steam room, making a stain on the wooden deck between his bare feet. He hung his head over and tried to make the drops land on a spider that lay tucked in a wet ball on the hot wood.

"No," Mitch began, "something else is up. Those two guys with the flak jackets knew we were going to shoot and when. I can buy the idea that someone is giving us a test run, but that business in La Jolla, I can't put it together.

Ram sat back down next to his brother. The steam pulled the water from their bodies, and they remained for several minutes without speaking.

"Interesting stuff," said Ram.

"Interesting stuff is right."

Mitch sat back against the wood and pulled a towel over his head, hooding his face. "Well, bro, for one thing, it could mean that someone is on top of our goddamned phones. Or maybe was on top of the lawyer's phones, which I somehow doubt. Someone who knows about your dumb fuckin' deals with the beaner. And that someone either wanted those papers for his own squeeze, or he wanted to keep your useless ass out of hock."

"And?"

"I think you've got a fairy godfather."

"The buyer?"

"The buyer."

"Looks like we'd better find out."

"Looks like you're fuckin' right."

At seven-thirty-five that evening, the call came in from La Paz. Ram disengaged from the wide-eyed blonde real estate agent he had picked up in Diego's.

Pop.

He rolled over and picked up the phone.

"Ram," he said.

The voice on the line was sprinkled with static.

"Our fishing boat, sir. We had a storm. One of the

dinghies got washed overboard, the small one. The captain says we need your help."

"Shit," he swore. And Ram didn't swear often.

"Sir, can you hear me?"

"Yes. I hear you."

"We think we know where it is. Do you want us to try to get it back?"

"I'll take care of it. Did you lose much gear?"

"All that was in the boat. The other stuff is okay."

"The fishing gear can be replaced."

"And the boat?"

"Don't worry about it. I'll make it right."

"We'll wait to hear from you, then. The fish are running; the weather is good. Hope you can get down to do some fishing with us."

"We're a little busy right now. Maybe later."

He put down the phone and sat up on the edge of the bed. The blonde reached out and grabbed his wrist hard from behind his back. For her, the phone had rung about ten seconds too soon.

He didn't look around, but got up and headed for the dresser. "Close 'em up, baby. Next time. Business."

Mitch was in the garage working over the cab of the pickup truck with a spectrum analyzer and tone generator in a sweep for electronic bugs. Ram tapped Mitch on the shoulder. "Let's talk."

They went to the dead room in the back of the house.

"Allie's been scooped. In La Paz. Sweet William used her to run cash."

Mitch stared at his brother. "Fuck."

"It just came in. From Julio. The others are okay."

"Abbey, Keri, and Tyrone's street squeeze Becky, right?"

"Right." He looked hard at Mitch. They had watched Keri and Allie grow up. Neighbors. From the first days in California. Someone had made the backyard connection. Abbey? Rebeca? "We fix this one. We fix it free . . . and if the thing doesn't work out, we teach Sweet William how to breathe through his neck." Ram's eyes blazed with emotion for a dangerous few seconds. Then he put the fire away, put it somewhere inside, put it to work. "We split it this way. I stay here and give whoever is climbing the trees something to watch. You go south. Stay deep, real deep. I don't want the computers to know you're moving over. Is your paper in shape to hop immigration at Brown and Tijuana?"

"No problem."

"Take Tillman. Pick up your hardware in La Paz."

"I don't want Tillman. He's too big. Folks remember Tillman. I'll go myself. I'll get backup down there." He thought for a minute. "What the fuck were they doing on that end? You can cover that fuckin' airport with a couple of fuckin' nuns."

The Cessna slid into the pattern south of La Paz at 3500 feet. He picked out Julio Santina's white Bronco waiting at the north end of the terminal building.

He parked the plane near two of Santina's men who were waiting at the small-plane moorings. One of the men wore the uniform of a Mexican Customs agent. Mitch gave orders to have the plane refueled and went directly to the car.

"Tell me the details."

Julio Santina sat behind the wheel and mouthed the wet end of an expensive cigar. He was a short, soft fat man with deep brown skin and a face full of sun ruts.

"The man Roberto was not good in his choice of companions. He drank two nights ago here in Los Arcos with three men of the village of Lopez Mateo. It is on the other side. It is where the whales go."

"Who are they?"

"They are nobody. No connection with the business. It is a simple . . . how you say? . . . ripoff? They make Roberto very drunk and take him to La Ventana. They tie him in a boat. Perhaps they should have shot him? They would have been very hard to find then."

"How did you find Roberto? He got away?"

"*Sí.* He said those *hombres* were dirty like animals."

"You're sure they took the girl with them?"

"We are sure. We talk to people at the *aeropuerto.* They went in a black car. Roberto heard them talk of Lopez Mateo on the night of the drinking. They speak of the women. Of *putas.* Of *chicas.*"

"Did Roberto tell them how much money?"

"He said he did not. He said the talk was of money. He thinks not how much money. But he was not sure."

"Can we talk with him? About what the *hombres* looked like?"

"We can no longer talk with Roberto."

"Shit, Julio, he had enough balls to come back and tell you."

"*Señor* Mitch, a man needs more than the balls. A man needs a *cabeza* to make the balls work."

Julio reached down and started the engine. He turned on the air conditioner. They rolled up the windows and sat there in the sun as the cool air began to work through the car.

Julio went on.

"We know one of them is Sanchez. He wears the big *mostachio.* The village is a small village. The people are few. He will be easy to find."

"Do you have anyone there now?"

"There is an old man there. We thought it best to wait for you. Your brother said we should wait."

"Is there a strip?"

"Yes. A small one. For the *turistas* who come to see the whales."

"Give me a man."

"You have Pisco. He is good."

"I want some small stuff."

"Pisco has the MAC-10. You can have what you want."

"Good. Get me a Ruger or Hi-Standard with a pipe out front. And a Spas for the plane in case we have trouble backing out."

"We have the MK-1. It has the *silencio*. And the Spas. In the back. Pisco will put them in the plane."

"Thank you, Julio. Get Pisco here. We'll leave as soon as the plane is ready."

"Good luck, *amigo*. A bad thing, this. There should have been more care."

Allie churned between pain and fear, between real and dream. She remembered how, in the dream, the man had appeared in front of her at the air terminal as she waited for Keri outside the rest rooms. He told her not to be afraid and showed her a gun pointing at her from a cloth bag he was carrying. She had gone in front of him to the car where the others were. In the dream, she was in the car and the gun kept sticking into her between her legs, over and over again. And it had been pushed into her mouth, making her hurt in her throat. Sometimes the gun looked different, was different, softer. But she couldn't get the images sorted out in her mind. She remembered the pain on her skin when they ripped off the tape to take the money away. But Abbey said the tape should be soaked off. Her skin still burned where the hard leather thing was pressing into her stomach.

She was tied over a fish apron that was draped across a rail in the dark shed. Her legs were on one side, her arms and head on the other. She looked down at the dirt close below her face and saw a line of ants going along the damp earth to some place she couldn't see. The ants didn't seem to care about her. They just kept moving in a thin column as though nothing was wrong. The noose dug into the skin at the back of her neck when she moved. The rope went down and under a second rail near the ground close to the ants. It wrapped around the lower rail in a pretty knot and then went to hurt her left ankle. Her hands were free but she couldn't work the big knots to make the hurt go away. She could only slip her fingers under the noose and tug it away from her throat so she could breathe more easily. When she pulled the rope to stop the choking, the rope hurt the back of her neck, but she had to let the air come in. She felt hot and dizzy from the heat and from the pain. She didn't understand how she could feel so warm when all her clothes were gone.

In her upside-down world, she could hear the sounds of glasses and bottles . . . and men's voices . . . and their deep laughing. But they were not in the same place with her. They seemed outside, away and in some other room. With her head forced down, she could see the insides of her legs up to where the leather was. She could see dark smears of dirt and small lines of red, as though someone had spilled a red juice on her backside. And the juice had run down her legs. Her legs were numb. The thought of the juice made her realize that she was thirsty. Her throat hurt so much. She wanted some water to drink. As her mind began to clear a bit at the recognition of her hard thirst, she felt a small tinge of embarrassment at how she was. What if someone should see her? She pulled harder at the rope on her neck.

The plane roared low over the terrible land of the middle Baja. The light glared fiercely at them through the windscreen as the sun settled down to meet the pale ocean ahead of them to the west.

They talked only at the start. Mitch had drawn as much as he could from Pisco about the town and how it lay on the shores of the bay of the whales. Pisco had sketched the way the village sat between the airstrip and the shoreline. Pisco was cold and efficient; he didn't say more than he knew. Mitch liked that. A rare trait down here.

"Is that receiver in good condition?" he had asked Pisco, nodding at the MAC-10. He knew how the overrated weapon was prone to suffer feed-jamming after a few bursts at its twenty-rounds-per-second rate of fire. The weapon could produce some awkwardly quiet moments when the shit hit the fan.

Pisco had turned his head to look straight at Mitch with a pair of flat snakelike eyes and said nothing; his angry look answered for him.

"Good," Mitch replied.

Swaying on the edge of serious imbalance, the big man, Sanchez, stood up from the littered table. Empty brown beer bottles rolled against the butter-soaked debris of pink cracked *langosta* tails. It was getting dark. His fellow *pescaderos* were facedown in the slop, one making bubbles of briny butter pop and foam in the big dish on which his greasy head lay. The big man surveyed the two unconscious diners and wiped the goo from his hands into his stained shirt. Everything smelled like the fish.

Now I can go see the chica *one more time,* he thought. He could feel the heavy swelling start between his legs. Even with all the beer and the food, even with the big excitements of the day, he would go into her again. He basked in the lusty push of his virility. *El Toro.* He felt proud of his many times with her. Even as the others passed out on the food, he was ready to keep on holing the tight *gringa.* He reached down and touched the filling flesh. He was the biggest of all men, he told himself. This time he would go into her where he had been afraid to before; not because he was afraid of going into her there, but because his *compañeros* might think him some kind of yard beast.

He stumbled away from the table.

The sun disappeared below the horizon as the small plane dropped into line with the eastern end of the dirt landing strip. The late-afternoon wind was strong from the west, and the sound of the plane drifted away, a sleepy murmur back to the mountains.

Sanchez stalked across the small space between the house and the shed. A high wood fence kept the yard from the view of the other shacks in the town. He staggered through the doorless entrance to the shed. The opening to the place faced the direction of the retired sun, and soft twilight diffused over the girl, her white buttocks facing him as she lay tied over the wooden rail. He moved to her nakedness and looked at the long *gringa* legs, one of which was tied into the rope. He gazed down at the woman part of her and reached out and moved her free leg aside so he could look between her legs at the female swellings where the fine hair thinned and disappeared as it left the curves of her sex. Still looking at the girl, he stood back and undid the top of his pants. He wanted nothing between himself and her white skin this time. He removed the pants and stood naked except for his stained, fish-smelling shirt. He would go into her sex first, to make himself wet with her if there was any wet left. He forced an entrance to the bruised flesh. Despite all the holing, she was still tight around him, and he had to use his fingers to support his passage.

The Cessna paused to debark a passenger as it turned around at the western end of the runway. The passenger ran easily across the grass and began talking to an older man waiting in the shadows of the early evening. While the two men talked, the plane taxied back down the length of the dirt strip as if to take off again, but instead came to a stop and parked at the edge of the far terminus. The pilot left the plane and jogged over to the spot where the two men waited.

"Amargo will show us the house of the black car," said Pisco. "It is not far, but we should walk slowly. This man must continue to live here. He would prefer we follow him at a distance."

Pisco took the cloth package that Mitch handed him, and the three men started off in the deepening darkness.

*   *   *

Allie felt the hurtful pushing start all over again. She
had hoped they would leave her alone when the night
came. She had heard them laughing and talking drunk,
and she thought they would go to sleep. The blood
pounded in her head from the position she was in,
and the pounding had become instantly worse when she
saw the inverted figure of the big man coming into
the shed, the pale twilight sky blotted by his shape. She
ground her teeth and held her breath as the hurt was
forced in. It seemed to tear and stretch and set off a
painful fire that burned through her legs. After pressing
deep inside, the thing stopped, embedded brutally
within her. In the fading light, she looked down at the
man's legs braced behind her own, bare except for his
damaged leather half boots and the sheath with his fish-
filleting knife strapped around the dirty brown shin. She
looked blankly at the knife from her head-down position
and saw the long, freshly scabbed scar that half circled
the lower leg. She was glad something had hurt him.
She felt the man's fingers slide from her back. She heard
him spit heavily into his hands.

"It is not much further," said Pisco. He had seen
the man pause at a bend in the dirt street, as if waiting for them to catch up.

For a confusing moment, Allie didn't understand
what the man was doing. He was putting his fingers
somewhere else, smearing something slippery and
warm there. *It must be the spit,* she thought. She
winced as a grimy finger pushed its way into her. It
moved around and sparks of pain bit at her. Then the
man backed his hurtful penis out of her sex. She felt

the finger leave her anus and, for tiny, hopeful moments, she was her own person again. Then she felt the firm push of the bigger thing at the new place. He would split her in two. *It couldn't happen this way.*

Her mind boiled. The pain was so pure it had no meaning; it existed like a thing apart and was far beyond her ability to understand; it burned over and through her in a sear of careless fire. The man moved and her insides moved. He tried to pump at her, and the torture rasped at the small part of her that still thought. His rugged hands vised her waist, and she couldn't breathe. The man arched his head back, his eyes blank in a mindless trance.

Allie reached outside her right leg and lifted out the sharp, delicate knife. She put her right hand against her own right leg so that the long blade rested horizontally behind the back of her knee. The razored cutter pointed across the gap at her left leg like the shining steel rung on a living ladder. It hovered in the space between the thin white legs and the muscular brown legs; the cutting edge faced up. She kept the blade flat against her leg as she slid it up the back of her thigh. At the base of her buttocks she paused for a second as the man's scrotum slapped into her fingers, fingers that held hard to the knife handle. His testicles swung back away from the knife, and she moved the blade higher where the root of his buried penis emerged from her.

Something Ram said once when they watched him lift the weights flashed across her reeling brain. He told them about fighting and showed them how to hit at things. He told them anyone could learn how to move, but the most important thing was to fight one hundred percent. *If you held back, even a little bit, you wouldn't have a chance.*

"Go fast, go hard, and end it," were his words.

*   *   *

The man of Lopez Mateo pointed to a wooden house near the boat ties. He talked softly to Pisco for a moment and was gone. Mitch unwrapped the MK-1, put it into his shirt front, and moved at the house.

She felt a stop as the blade gently contacted the shaft of the man. She paused a split second to breathe in as he rammed all the way into her. She almost let go of the handle at the pain. Then she gathered herself and sliced upward and outward as firmly as she could. She was somewhat surprised at how little resistance there was. She thought for an instant that the handle must have separated from the blade. Then she felt hot liquid spurting onto her back, once, twice, a third time; regular and strong, like a pulse. She felt the hurtful thing, still stuck inside her, shrink away to something small, and with a convulsive contraction she expelled it onto the floor.

The man Sanchez merely stood there looking down. He didn't yell or make a cry; he simply watched the butchered stump of his great pride robustly pumping his life's blood onto the girl's back. When he felt the first black wave of dizziness, he stepped over to the wall and took up the six-foot kelp fork that hung there. With two hands he raised it above his head and lined up the tines over the white back.

Then, with a dull thud, the forehead of Ignacio Raul Sanchez exploded and he fell in a heap on the dirt floor. The column of brown ants began to look for a way around the new impediment.

15

The Beast

Rayburn Varki spun his swivel chair around and stopped with his back to the oak desk. He gazed out the ground-floor window and regarded the broad lawn that fanned away from the Idaho ranch house. The summer heat had not crept up to this part of the state, and the land carried the deep green color and fresh smells that would betoken spring down in the low country. He pressed back against the chair and propped his feet on the low sill of the window box. Smoothing the fabric of his white sports shirt into the waist of his blue slacks, he pushed off the worn gray moccasins, which fell to the russet carpet. With strong fingers meshed together over his flat gut, he closed his eyes. He put his head back and allowed the wash of morning sun to fall upon his face.

"I have not seen you relax like this since the winter snows," said Aixa.

"You may be right," he said.

"I keep trying to think of what might go wrong, but it all seems to flow like the long river."

"Yes, finally it does. In the midst of this complexity it is strange how each thing so easily follows that which proceeds it. It is a tribute to the long planning. You and Loza have worked hard. And we have been fortunate to have discovered Jesse."

"He does not have your fire. I do not think he has an understanding of what we do."

"Aixa, he has his own fire. His skills are not to be filtered through our ideas; his colors do not have to be our colors. He is valuable to the plan as he is; his faith is in the money, he asks no righteous questions. He does not feel the need to justify himself, nor does he seek from us the reason for our actions. His motive is simple. In that simplicity is a purity."

"You are saying avarice can be innocent."

"If it be its own goal. Or has a harmless reason."

"You could make him see our way."

"It is not necessary. And we do not have the time."

"I would like him to understand. I like him. I like the woman Ruth."

"I like them, too. But you would find disappointment with Jesse. He has his own ideal. It is his buttress. It is his singularity. He is not a man to let us clutter up his life with our dreams. That is why he is strong. We are strong for the same reason. The two strengths feed one another."

"He sees no higher good."

"Who is to say which is higher?" he said, smiling. "And we weren't talking of good; we were talking of purity."

Aixa was quiet for a moment. She looked down at the cup she was holding.

"I believe in what we do," she said, "even though many will die. His is only a selfish ideal."

"There are those who believe with much conviction in the goals of the hedonist. They reason that creation gave them nerve endings for a purpose other than survival; that perhaps there is only one of God's creatures truly given over to one's care, that being the self. You call him selfish? We are not as selfish? We are not selfish in our wish to see this decent land get back what it once had? We are not selfish in our desire to want this contagious arrogance of government stopped? To want excised the bureaucratic tumors that are sucking the hope from this once-optimistic people? His simple selfishness can't hold a candle to ours."

He spoke the words with quiet certitude, not with the noisy rise of passion that men use to hide a questioned reason. She knew he could pour out the fever when he had to, when the men before him wanted emotional salt to spice the meal of their frustrations. But it was in this solid, gentle manner that he brought the power down where she could touch it. Aixa felt the words nail down the edges of her mind.

They worked through the morning. The bulk of the task that day involved reworking the master locator, which had been loaded into the computers from the lists Loza had obtained at the Granite Cove drop point in the Mojave Desert. Updates and changes were being fed to them from the man they knew as "Zebra." His appearance had increased the scope of their planned strike by a powerful multiple. Zebra had proven to be, in terms of money and information, the great surge of power they needed to make the attacks more than just a statement. Events had developed beyond their most optimistic hopes. The organization had been motivated, well-financed, and active to begin with, but the timely discovery of a kindred group that could provide this kind of support was a gift from the gods. It didn't matter that the people Zebra represented were long on anger and short on courage; Varki's organization had the resolve to action that the Zebra group lacked. What mattered was that Zebra had appeared when he did, had allowed them to tap with a bolstered vengeance into that great reservoir of discontent that was seething to the surface in this land of corroded freedom.

Late that afternoon they took the ritual break to sip the strong green tea Aixa had brewed. The relationship between the two of them was as intense as it was sterile. Aixa knew she had met the single great person of her time on the day she first beheld Rayburn Varki. It was done in a breath. She knew with the certainty of stone, with the spiraled power of genetic memory, with that cryptic, precognitive flash known only to saints and the dying, that she would stay near him forever. She would hold her poise and elegance, she would effect the relaxed ease of the sophisticate, she would be knowledgeable and witty around the others . . . because she knew that was what he wanted of her. In the blink of an instant she would kill for him if he asked, herself included.

He perceived a deep beauty in Aixa. With his instinctive recognition of human dedication, he had discovered in her this high virtue. He understood the enormity of disfiguring such reality. She was what he had hoped for: someone who mirrored his commitment, someone who could be depended upon, someone who possessed that pristine single line of purpose that got things done.

Aixa served them tea.

She understood exactly what he meant when he spoke of commitment. It was the purity of obsession he admired. And the obsession could be muscle, money, religion, reform, or revolution; it didn't seem to matter. Perhaps the fraud was not so much a fraud then, for he was her obsession.

After tea, they checked Kevin's schedule. The priest would have completed the big money drops in Houston and New Orleans. He should be in Tampa by noon tomorrow. The cell strike leader in each city had been culled from local assets. Jesse's connections with drug distribution nets and organized crime establishments snaked across the country. Cell augmentation was generally in the form of skill-specific operatives recruited from West Coast weapons and demolition people. The cells were small for security reasons, no more than three individuals per team. In each case, Jesse would follow a procedure similar to the one he had with Varki regarding payments. The system worked effectively. It assured loyalty and thoroughness. The strike leaders were set to receive specific target data, which was being transmitted by the man called Gene Plum. Plum was moving in advance of Kevin to instruct the cells. They would incorporate time options to allow for last-minute refinements to precisely coordinate the strikes.

It was on line. After all the work, it was on line.

Varki poured some vintage '47 St.-Emilion as the soft midnight hour came to the still house. They shut down the computers, adjourned to the porch, and raised a toast to the land. The night was smoky with water mist from the mountain.

Aixa savored the first sip. She thought of the man next to her. She thought of his words:

We are beginning to perceive how free world pop-ulations move with a ghostly sixth sense to nurture group survival. Consider a presidential election where the choice is between two second-rate candi-dates. The election of 1988 is a good example. An objective observer is struck by the fact that the people give the Presidency to one party and deliver the Congress to the opposition, thereby rendering to a minimum the damage potential of an incompetent. What causes such political paradox? Is it like the erratic behavior of a single ant that serves a colony logic? Or like the suicidal sting of one bee that con-verts to the survival of the swarm? Does it not appear that the social unit develops its own subtle intelligence? That after reaching a certain critical mass it begins to assume a spectral identity? An identity whose goal is to ensure its own propagation?

Can a bureaucracy become such a beast? I think it can.

Do not mistake our dedication for political, biologi-cal, or religious purity doctrines. We do not subscribe to Nazi racial hygiene schemes. Liberty is the practical recognition of human differences. And it is not enough to state that a free society demands equal opportunity; a truly free society demands variety of opportunity even more. This is a basic tenet in evolution, be it in reference to a species or a society. Freedom feeds vari-ety and variety feeds progress. If you allow your free-dom to be circumscribed, you die as a people; your children choke in the ashes of your lost resolve.

Should we back off in our struggle for individual freedom? If our cause is the right one, shouldn't it be natural for it to evolve on its own merits? Why shouldn't we leave it to the natural process? The rea-son, people, is this: How you think and act IS the process! How you think IS the mill that grinds out the future. And if you don't act, you and your ideas will be quietly crushed by those who do.

Can we be so smug as to think we are the best evolution can accomplish? What if nature, or God if you will, had been a tiny bit more imaginative? Gave us the eyes of the hawk, the hearing of the bat, the tracking ability of the dog? Think of the time saved, the pain avoided. And more. How about three pairs of arms instead of one pair? Make one set of arms into wings? Double the size of the brain? Think of where we could be. The natural process is slow; chance is inefficient. Yet we now have the opportunity to affect our social evolution, to nurture the seeds of freedom. We need to act.

On too many occasions in the history of civilization, people have accepted authority without subjecting that authority to rational examination. A complacent population leaves itself wide open to control. Eventually the abusive bureaucracy demands too much. The end is either revolt or subjugation. Perhaps the problem is not with the power of the abuser; perhaps the problem is with the individual who is willing to submit. Free men and women need not apologize for being enraged by arrogance in government.

Look into your soul. Corner apathy. Root it out. The darkest hours of human history are marked by muted minutes of indifference.

She finished her drink. The soft mountain night had brightened as the moon climbed above the eaves of the old house to light the land before them. Varki had fallen asleep with his head propped against the backrest of the big wooden porch chair, his empty wineglass on the small table next to the railing. She turned her head to look at him as he breathed easily in his slumber. She reached out and timidly rested her hand on the armrest of his chair, her fingers only inches from his. She trembled slightly in the stillness. With a slow, halting movement she raised her hand to linger in the electric air over the back of his hand. She could feel the warmth rising from his skin. Gently she lowered her fingertips until they just brushed the tops of the fair hair that came up from him. Her heart seemed to stop beating, and her breathing stilled as she moved her long, delicate fingers to within an atom of touching the back of his hand. She watched as if in another body as the distance between their flesh slowly closed. With the grace of a falling feather, she touched him.

A single tear wandered down her cheek; she didn't dare move to brush it away.

16

Florida Ladies

A flat tire.

Kevin pulled the big white Lincoln onto the broad shoulder of the freeway. The right rear tire shredded off the rim as everything came to a stop in a cloud of dust. The state of Florida had constructed Interstate 75 with an eye to flat tires. But they still hadn't done anything about the heat. It was high noon. Kevin sat behind the wheel with the big engine idling, afraid to unseal the doors to the inferno outside. He almost delivered a curse of robust proportion, but he recanted in fear that God might snap his fan belt in a fit of retaliation. Kevin and God had an understanding about these things. He looked into the rearview mirror searching for salvation. With six hundred thousand in cash in the trunk, most of it in twenties, he fervently hoped that help would not come in the form of the Highway Patrol. Kevin realized he had underestimated Varki. What had started out as a high-paying joke now looked very much like the real thing, but he was in too deep to back off. And now a blown tire. Maybe getting picked up by the Highway Patrol wasn't such a bad idea.

For some minutes he watched the speeding traffic in the mirror. The oncoming cars were spaced far apart and were few in number. He observed the little gray heads of old people peeping out through the lower two inches of windshield as the cars sped past him. The gritty parade of Florida's septuagenarian legions roared by with steering wheels clutched in the standard two-fisted death grip. He tried to decide whether it would be best to change into his big polyester tourist shirt and change the tire himself, or to maintain his priestly garb and depend on some son of the Blessed Virgin to perform a heated penance in the broiling Florida air. Certainly it would be safer to do the job himself.

He refastened his stiff white collar, wrestled into his black coat, and stepped out into the sun.

He removed the jack from its side-mount in the trunk. He propped it under the edge of the car near the flat tire. He pried off the hubcap with the end of the jack handle, placed the hubcap on the highway side of the car against the good rear wheel, and set it to reflect the sun at the oncoming traffic. Then he smudged a bit of roadside dirt on his cheek, wrapped one fist in his white handkerchief, and commenced to look helpless.

For the next fifteen minutes he fussed and shuffled about in the swirling debris kicked up by careening, atheist-driven cars. Despite his dispirited theatrics, nobody stopped to help with the tire. Finally, in muttering resignation and with a pointed reminder to God that Florida people could use a bit more divine compassion, he set to work.

He removed the two taped-shut cardboard cartons of money and the suitcase that covered the tire well. He wrestled the spare out onto the ground.

The task was his preview of hell.

Sweat ran in salty rivers down his cherubic face and soaked past his white collar to feed the growing stains spreading from his underarms and from the center of his black frock. In the lee of the car, away from the gusts of air generated by passing traffic, Kevin knelt and pushed himself into a realm of physical discomfort quite foreign to his carefully constructed world. He proceeded to work through the disagreeable process. Old tire off, new tire on. He tightened the last lug nut and popped the hubcap onto its stubby prongs. His eyes blinked in the sting of sweat, and he had to stand up to clear his head. Still the heathens thundered past. He felt his knees buckle as he stood there sucking at the tepid tropical air. He steadied himself by clutching the open trunk lid.

A white Oldsmobile Firenza swerved onto the shoulder two hundred yards ahead in a screeching chatter of maladjusted brake shoes. It backed up toward him in a weaving series of spurts and stops, and came to rest after bumping into the front end of his jacked-up vehicle. He watched in horror as his big car crunched its way off the jack and slammed onto the ground. The door on the passenger side of the Firenza opened, and Sally Magdalena Curtain, tall, energetic, sixty-eight years of age, and Catholic, stepped out. As she slammed her door, the driver's door opened and from behind the wheel emerged her companion, tough-looking, steely-eyed, and armed: Gladys Dunlop Winslow, sixty-nine and bent slightly from arthritis, held a black stun gun at the ready in her right hand. She seemed hostile, wary.

"Father, what are you doing out in this heat?" asked Sally.

She wore a light print dress and sneakers. She had a kindly round face and stood about six feet tall, a giant among the wrinkled. Her eyes were clear, brown, and full of concern. Her hair was pulled back in a pioneer bun, her voice solicitous.

"The Lord has set free some of His air from this back tire, my child," said Kevin. He sprinkled a hint of sad humor into his words. "And I've hurt my hand."

Gladys had come to stand next to Sally, stun gun pointed at Kevin's face. She glanced at the shredded tire. He regarded her warily. He had heard stories about these blue-haired people of Florida.

Gladys wore black slacks and a short-sleeved black blouse buttoned to the neck, and carried a black sweater in her weaponless hand. Her gray hair mysteriously danced about her forehead in the still air. Kevin wondered why she was dressed in black in this heat, then realized he was wearing the same combination. At least he had a reason. He stared, fascinated by the hair that moved in the absence of any breeze.

Sally studied the tire, then Kevin. "My dear man! You look a fright. Is there something we can do?"

"I don't know. I confess I'm not good at these mechanical things. My only work is with the Word."

"My stars! You have to rest." She took him by the arm and firmly directed him toward the Firenza. "Sit in here for a few minutes. We have lemonade." He settled into the front seat of their car. The cool air of the interior was a glory.

"Don't you do another thing, you poor man. It's not your job to change tires. We'll put those tools and that terrible tire away. We can at least do that. Gladys, come here and get the man something to drink."

Gladys holstered her stun gun, got back into the driver's seat next to Kevin, and drew off some lemonade from a small cooler. The pale green liquid gurgled into a polystyrene cup that carried a trace of lipstick on the rim. Cubes of ice chuckled against the inside walls of the lemonade jug. A blessed sound. "There's vodka in that. Just a smidge," from Gladys, one hand resting on the belt holster.

Satisfied that Kevin was in good hands, Sally went off to load the old tire into the trunk.

Kevin sipped the lemonade. There was more than "just a smidge" of alcohol in the mix. So what. Delicious.

"Bless you, my child."

Gladys watched him drink. "Cheap tire," she said. "Bet some Florida cracker sold it to you."

Kevin didn't reply. The vodka was tickling his skin. Gladys turned and looked over her left shoulder to see how Sally was doing. When her back was to him, Kevin picked up two envelopes that were stuck in the center console and put them under his frock. Each envelope carried a Social Security return address, and the edges of two checks were visible at the top openings.

Ten minutes later, Sally was back at the window. Her face was flushed from heat and exertion, but Kevin sensed that some of that glow was generated by the munificence of her good deed. He had seen that Good Samaritan aura many times before today.

"God bless you, ladies."

Kevin had two more lemonades and made small talk. Sally took the keys from Gladys and opened the trunk of the Firenza. She fiddled around back there for a few minutes while Gladys sat next to Kevin watching him chug down more juice. Sally returned to the passenger side of the car carrying a big red beach towel that displayed a huge beer can surrounded by furled ribbons in the center. She offered it to him, and he mopped the residual sweat from his face and neck.

"Bless you, good ladies." He unleashed his best faith-laced smile at them. "I am restored! And they say the Spirit of the Lord is lacking in this cynical age. Can I ever thank you?"

"It's a pleasure, Father," glowed Sally.

Kevin beamed and got out of the car. "Thank you again. You are special people. Such generous folks to help this poor servant of the Light." Then he rolled his eyes and slapped his forehead. He removed the Social Security checks still in their envelopes from his frock. A big smile unfolded on his face. "I found these on the side of the road . . . must have fallen out when you got out to help." Sally took the checks, a look of surprise on her face. Kevin nodded and smiled and patted her on the head.

He returned to his car. Before getting in, he walked around to the back of the Lincoln to make sure nothing had been left on the side of he road. He popped open the trunk to check that his cargo was properly stowed. Everything was in its proper place. He got into the spacious front seat, settled gingerly onto the hot fabric, started the engine, and drove off with an exaggerated wave. In the mirror, he could see the ladies wave back, could see their broad, sweet smiles even from that distance.

"Thank you, Lord. You might have sent those dear angels a tad sooner, though. Maybe next time."

17

Teardrops

Allie stared straight ahead. Mitch had cut her free and led her to a corner of the shed away from the body, which he had covered with yards of fishing net found hanging from the overhead racks. He wet some rags in a bucket of water that Pisco had brought from the well in the back yard. He tenderly washed the blood and dirt from the silent girl. She made no move to cover herself. She said nothing. He kept his eyes locked on her eyes as he cleaned her.

"It's all right, baby. Just take it easy. We'll be out of here soon. Do you hurt bad anywhere?"

Allie didn't answer, but slowly raised her hand to the back of her neck where the rope had cut.

"They're gone now. They can't bother you anymore. You were real brave."

He turned her slightly while he rubbed the dripping rags down her back and legs. He tried to keep his eyes on hers as much as possible so she would know it was him, so she would have something to believe in.

He finished with the cleaning, then looked around the darkened shed. He hoped to find her clothes, but could not. He discovered a ragged towel on the netting bench and knotted it around her waist like a sarong after he dried her with it. He stripped off his shirt and put it on her. She seemed so small in the garment; it draped down to the middle of her thighs and she looked like she was wearing a nightshirt.

He knelt before her and gently took her hands in his.

"You'll be okay, Allie. We're going to take a plane ride back to see Keri and Abbey and Becky. It's all right now. They're waiting to help you."

Her eyes flickered and she looked down at him. But she said nothing.

Mitch drew her to him and, still on his knees, softly held her in his arms for a long minute. She put a small, pale arm around his neck.

After a while he was aware of Pisco standing in the shadow by the shed door.

"The others?" he asked quietly.

"They are two," said Pisco. "They are there in the house. Like pigs they sleep in their food."

"I would like to see them."

"I can fix them for you."

"Let me see them first."

Mitch got to his feet and led Allie by the hand out into the small yard.

"Allie, I want you to stay with Pisco for a few minutes. He is your friend. He is strong like your father. Hold his hand. I will be right back."

He started to walk away.

"Mitch."

He stopped. Allie spoke his name again.

"Mitch," and she was looking at him.

He went back to her.

"What is it, honey?"

"Please don't go away."

He looked at Pisco. Pisco was ice.

"*Señor* Mitch, the little one has seen enough."

Mitch glanced at the house, then reached out and took Allie by the hand. He gave Pisco the Ruger he had used on Sanchez so the finishing of the thing would be from the single gun. He nodded at Pisco. He felt tired. He turned and slowly walked out of the yard toward the street that led back to the plane, Allie at his side. Right now, she was more important.

Pisco looked down at the one who slept with his face in the dregs of the deep dish. He reached over and took up the bowl of salt water mixed with melted butter that fed the flies on the table. He poured the greasy fluid into the man's dish, filling it to the rim. He took the hair of the man in his strong hand and rolled the man's head so it was facedown in the thick liquid and held it there. The body began to quiver and jerk as the mouth and nose sucked up the slop. The man seemed to wake from his stupor and struggled to rise from the mess, but Pisco held him in a grip of steel. Pisco watched the level of the mire in the dish decrease as the lungs siphoned it away. It took a full two minutes for the body to go limp.

He went over to the other. The man still slept. He took that one by the hair, pulled the head back, and crushed the larynx with a short strike of his free hand as the man came awake. The eyes of the now voiceless one flashed open in bewildered terror. Grasping the man by the shirt, Pisco pulled the man to his feet and propelled him out of the house, across the yard, and into the shed. In the dim light of the small work shack Pisco went to the body of Sanchez and kicked off the netting. He rolled the body over with his foot so it was faceup. The terrified one was almost docile in his fear and his pain. Pisco took the Ruger that had killed Sanchez and held it in his right hand. With his left, he placed the unprotesting fingers of the mute over his own hand that held the weapon. Pisco pinched the fingers of the man between his own so that the hand of the terrified one would take the fragments of powder from the shot. He fired three rounds into the corpse.

He released the hand of the gurgling man and pushed him to the floor next to the form of Sanchez. Using some pieces of rag to keep off his own prints and to preserve those of Sanchez, he picked up the big kelp fork and went to stand over the trembling form that looked up at him with speechless dread. Pisco looked into the face of fear with his ice-eyes. The man on the floor took one hand from his broken throat and crossed himself. The look of fear suddenly gave way to one of desperation and the form leapt toward Pisco. Pisco caught the man in midair on the fork. The sharp tines popped into and through the chest. One of the tines snapped off in the man's sternum and stuck out of him like a large black needle. The body quivered on the upraised fork. Then Pisco, in his great strength, lowered the skewered one to the floor. That one shuddered to his death.

Pisco wiped the gun, then pressed it into the warm hand flesh of the punctured one to make the prints. He put the gun on the floor. He went away.

Night had come to the small village of Lopez Mateo, the place of the whales.

Santina's home was back in the trees well off the road that led to the bay. The big walls of the house seemed to reflect the thick tension that flowed through the group of people standing in the light of the front porch. The car would be coming soon. The plane had landed a few minutes ago at La Paz. Mitch had said on the radio that Allie had been hurt. Keri's eyes were red, and she was shaking badly. Santina made her take a strong wine to give her courage, but she had gotten worse and had to go into one of the bedrooms with Becky. Santina stood with Abbey and two of the men. They watched the road through the trees.

"The car comes," said Santina.

"Julio, please go tell Keri to come out here," said Abbey. "And take your people away."

Santina and the two men left the porch and disappeared into the house. Keri emerged onto the porch a few moments later as the car turned into the drive.

"You go out there and give your sister a big hug. And stay close to her for a while. Put your arms around her and hold her. Walk with her. Don't let her go from you."

Keri wiped at the tears. "What should I say?"

"Tell her you love her. And don't cry too much. You be a brave girl. Then bring her to me."

Abbey gripped Keri's arm.

"And sweetheart, don't be surprised at what I say to Allie. It may seem wrong to you, but please trust me."

The car stopped in the drive in front of the porch.

Mitch got out and helped Allie from the car. He put his arm around her shoulders, and they walked toward the steps. The man Pisco stood by the vehicle and watched them.

"Allie?" said Keri from the top of the steps.

And then she ran to her sister. Keri tried not to cry hard. Allie raised her arms, and the big shirt made her look very small.

"Oh, Allie." Keri took Allie in her arms and pulled her close. She put her cheek against the side of her sister's head. Keri's tears sparkled down into the Mexican dust.

Mitch stood back and looked up at Abbey. She could see the wet in his eyes, and then he looked away.

"Hello, Keri," in a soft voice, "I'm sorry I got lost."

They walked up the steps.

Abbey stood with her hands on her hips. She put on a smile.

"Hey, twerp, good to see you again. Come give me a squeeze."

"Abbey, they took the money away."

Allie stood looking down at the floor. She went quiet. Abbey reached out and crooked a finger under Allie's chin.

"Come on, short stuff! Get that chin up. Money grows in suitcases around here. That ugly boyfriend of mine has it coming out of his ears. You're the only one I care about; you're the only one we all care about. Knock off that droopy shit and lighten up."

She reached out and gave Allie a long, hard hug. She looked over Allie's head at Mitch. There was a question in her face. He met her eyes and nodded. Abbey swallowed hard.

"Come with me, you little nut. We're going into

that house and I'm going to scrub you raw. When I get through you'll feel like a new penny."

"They did things to me, Abbey."

Abbey looked again at Mitch.

"If I know your buddy Mitch, honey, they won't be doing those things anymore."

Abbey pushed Allie to arm's length and looked directly into her eyes.

"Now look at me, punkin."

Allie looked into Abbey's face.

"Those bastards didn't do anything to you that some of these scroungy bums haven't done to me. Or to Becky. Or to any other poor girl, for that matter. It's the same as happens to most of us one way or another. Maybe you got an early start, but you're not the only one. And you damn well better remember that, or I'm going to get pissed, you hear? Don't think you're such a big shot."

She smiled at Allie.

Allie blinked and some tears finally came.

"Abbey."

"That's okay, punkin." She pulled Allie tightly to her chest. "That's okay."

"Oh, Abbey."

Abbey ground her teeth together and pulled back.

"Look, short stuff. We're not making a goddamn movie here. You ain't going to get me all teary-eyed. You want me to put one upside o' yo' fat head?"

For a small, important moment, the hint of a shy smile flickered at the corner of Allie's bruised lip.

"Now get that busted tail of yours in gear and come with me. Pronto!"

She took Allie by the hand and headed for the door. She yelled ahead into the house.

"Damn it, Becky! Get some goddamn water going

in that goddamn tub. Christ, do I have to do every goddamn thing around here?"

Keri stood with Mitch on the porch as they watched the two go down the hall that led through the house, Abbey muttering and shouting orders all the way.

"Sometimes Abbey seems so mean."

"Sometimes she is, Keri. Not this time."

He looked out at Pisco, who had been watching those on the porch from where he stood by the car. Pisco had been listening. Mitch locked onto the ice-eyes. He thought he saw the hard face soften. Pisco slowly nodded his head at Mitch twice. Then the eyes let go. The ice came back. Pisco turned and got back into the car. He leaned forward, said something to the driver, then sat back out of sight.

The car gently accelerated into the darkness.

Late that night Mitch went out onto the front porch of Santina's house to sit alone with Abbey. She was limp and exhausted. She had no tough left in her. They took turns pulling warm mescal in small sips from a brown bottle in which a white maguey grub ghosted like a bad memory. He told her the whole story. About how Allie emasculated the man by using the fish knife. He wondered how Abbey would react.

Abbey listened to him, and after he told her about it she sat there in silence for a while. Then she cried. Mitch had never known Abbey to cry. It hurt him. He put his arm around her while she wept hard into his chest; she tried to keep her grief from the ears of the others in the house. Earlier, she had said to him that she felt everyone was awake and listening in the night; he thought she was probably right about that.

Abbey didn't speak for a long time. She sat hunched against him, struggling with the sorrow.

"Damn everything," she said, "I wish she hadn't done that."

"I figured you might appreciate her guts."

"You're a good man, Mitch," she finally said. "But why can't you sweet, violent bastards see how sad it is?"

"Hell, I see how sad it is. At least she got in a real shot."

Abbey shook her head.

"Goddamn it, Mitch. Don't you understand? That's the saddest part of all."

Abbey finally got it together, and they finished the bottle. They didn't speak much after Abbey cried. They simply sat and watched the ground fog drift through the low trees of the Baja in the after-midnight hour.

Allie awoke twice while they were sitting there, once with a sharp scream. But they could hear the muffled sound of someone talking to her, soothing her in the darkness.

"We better get some sleep," said Abbey.

Mitch felt cold and strangely alone.

They went to their beds.

18

Ol' Bill

Mitch took the Cessna low over the Sierra de Juarez and swung northeast toward La Puerta. The expansive dunes of the Laguna Salada spread in deep bronze shadows across the arid depression that led from the Gulf of California north to the Salton Sea. The threat of an earthquake would someday jerk at the nerves of the dependent populations of the Southwest. He wanted to be flying when it struck; he wanted to look down on the confusion in the rising dust. *It would be interesting,* he thought, *especially for people who knew about the jungle.*

He crossed the great sand scar and put the small plane into a gentle climb to clear the ridges of the Sierra de los Cucapas. His destination was a short strip of dirt that lay hidden near an isolated pumping station southwest of Jiquilpan. He decided to use the opportunity presented by the trip to La Paz to check the bothersome questions posed by the desert shoot.

He wanted to look from the air at the transmitter site they had taken out. His cover was good; no one to the north, with the exception of Ram, knew where he was.

On the Jiquilpan strip he altered the wing and hull numbers with black mastic; the tape would be stripped off after he returned to Mexico for the legal reentry back into the States.

He passed the dark hours in his sleeping bag, and his thoughts were of the people back in La Paz, especially of Abbey. She was different. All fox. She was still real good at finding things to say to him that he couldn't figure out. Even chewed his ass once or twice in front of everyone. It should have pissed him off, but it didn't. They had met four years ago when he and Ram rode shotgun for Sweet William's South Central Los Angeles operation in a dustup with a local rival. They moved on when Sweet William turned out to be pushing more than weed. Overnight the whole show got top-heavy with kids, crack, and L.A. glass; the easy money couldn't justify that. The customers were in over their heads. The party had turned into a disease, the disease into a horror show.

He fell asleep thinking of Abbey.

He crossed the border at dawn. He drove the plane hard and fast through the shallow valleys, staying below the tops of the low mountains. He thought about the tan one-story building that sat on March Air Force Base up in Riverside, California. Inside that squat, unremarkable structure were eyes tracking across a glowing quilt of multicolored electronic squares. The building belonged to the Customs Air Operations Center West and was part of the electronic screen U.S. authorities constructed to cover the border between San Diego and Brownsville.

Aircraft would appear as small red X's superimposed on the large-scale maps of northern Mexico. Any unidentified target would scramble the UH-60 Blackhawks or Citations to intercept the intruder after it crossed the border. A second part of the screen was Blue Eagle, a modified P-3 antisubmarine plane that Customs used as a down-looking tracker. That plane could have given Mitch trouble, but he knew it was docked. His people inside Customs kept him apprised of its status. He overflew the east end of Brawley and, twenty minutes later, skimmed low over the site where they had crunched the transmitter. He could make out the ruts left by the white pickup truck where it traversed the ridge and could see where the truck had driven down the opposite crest away from their position. The tracks curved north, then east toward the Wiley Well district. The land was empty. Only when the weather cooled in the fall did the rock hounds and shooters run over the area. There was a ranger station well to the north, and they had questioned the ranger two days after the hit, but the man said he had seen nothing in his area. Mitch dropped the Cessna to thirty feet and flew over the campsite. The wind-scoured hardpan was good. He put the plane down into a strong, hot west wind. The morning was beginning to cook.

He searched the camp and the transmitter site. The heat broiled over him, but his determination burned right back. He liked this kind of hunt: looking for the thread that would put it together, looking for the clue that would show the next step. He experienced the thrill that rumpled his psyche when he was about to hunt a predator that didn't know it was being hunted, like the shark coming back up the fish line, like the grizzly coming in downwind of the tracker. It was stimulating to stalk something that had been playing games, games in which he and Ram started out as the quarry. It had happened before. The smart people always underestimated them.

But he found nothing. Only the tracks of unremarkable tires and shoes. No papers, no cigarette butts, no soda cans, no candy wrappers, no paper bags with receipts, no shell casings, no medicine bottles . . . nothing. He decided to spend the night there on the deck. Things were thin. He was getting interested.

At daybreak the Cessna powered off the hard desert, and Mitch circled over the site once more. As he began to gain altitude his eye caught the glitter of sunlight on metal off to the south. When he turned toward the spot, he could make out the outline of a beige car near the agate beds in the Black Hills. He overflew the car and saw a man working the side of a small wash with dry pan and shovel. The man had rigged a large tarpaulin from the back of the car to keep off the sun. A large dog, German shepherd, lay at the edge of the shade worrying something between its paws. The man didn't look up as the plane passed over.

He set down on the shale a half mile south of the car. The man had looked up as Mitch left the plane. The dog was still lying on the shale, but swiveled its head around to fix Mitch with an energetic stare.

"Good morning," said Mitch.

The man stared at him with an unfriendly expression on his sunburned face. He looked about sixty-five, paunchy with short legs, pigeon-toed. He had an orange and white beard trimmed short to match in length the bristled orange hair on his head. He wore tattered green pants and a long-sleeved cotton shirt that had the Corona beer logo written across the front in big blue and gold letters. He stood in a pair of battered gray hiking boots, the kind that closed with Velcro straps rather than laces. The man still hadn't said anything.

The German shepherd appeared simultaneously calm and coiled. Mitch wasn't sure how this thing was going to turn out. The fact that the old man was out here in the middle of summer looking for rocks might be meaningful. The thought crossed his mind that maybe he shouldn't have left his .38 back in the plane.

"Looks like you got some nice agate."

The man continued to look at Mitch.

Mitch could feel his piss level rising. "You hear all right, old man? You're not fuckin' sun crazy, are you?"

The man scrunched up his forehead. "Hear good," the old geezer said. "What you doing out here in thet thing?" The fellow nodded toward the plane.

"Want to ask you something," replied Mitch.

"You know where you are?"

"I'm in the goddamn desert in the middle of summer."

The man didn't say anything for a while. He stroked his short whiskers with a rock-scarred hand.

"And you jes' asked me I was crazy?" He regarded Mitch with a cocked eye. "Ain't one of them sex previts, is you?" he added.

Jesus Christ Almighty, thought Mitch. "Look, old man, it's worth ten bucks if you can help me."

"Reckon you can ask away then, boy." The old man looked up at the sky for no apparent reason, nodded. "Got me some beer in the car. You like beer, boy?"

"Shit, yes, sounds great. Maybe we could start this

conversation over." A cold brew could fix anything, he decided.

They walked together to the old man's car. It was a banged-up early-model diesel Rabbit with only one seat, the driver's seat, in the whole car. The rest of the space was covered with plywood, making one large flat area. Some tools and books lay on a rumpled heap of blankets that covered the wood. A Mini-14 rifle with folding stock was propped against the dash, and a few boxes of .223 shells sat scattered on the blankets near the weapon. Two grocery bags rested inside the rear hatch next to a blue styrofoam cooler.

"Fetch yourself one o' those loominnie seats off the roof, boy."

Mitch pulled down one of two aluminum folding chairs that were wedged into a homemade luggage rack on top of the car. His mind was starting to anticipate the beer. The old man had opened the rear hatch and was rummaging in the cooler as Mitch sat down.

"Here you go, boy. This is real good stuff."

The man handed Mitch a hot, dented can of L.A. beer. Horse piss.

"Reckon I'll light one o' these off myself," said the old rocker. He sat in the sand next to Mitch's chair at the rear of the car, his back resting against the dented bumper.

"Got myself a deal on these fellers. Seven whole cases for five bucks. Load spilled off a truck over to Desert Center six months ago. You got to be in the right place at the right time in this world. Yessiree."

Mitch looked down at the can. He pulled up the tab. No sound came out. Flat. He sipped at the stuff. Worse than horse piss.

"I'm looking for two guys might have been through here a few days ago. Driving a white pickup. They were over west, near the range."

"Two boys in a white truck?"

"Yeah."

"Few days ago?"

"Right. They could have been out here for maybe a week or more."

The old man drank some more beer.

"Friends o' yourn?"

"No."

"You spend a lot of time chasing 'round with folks don't seem to know you."

"That's me." Mitch made himself swallow. "I've checked with the ranger. He hasn't seen them."

"Durn ranger wouldn't hardly know if a durn parade of jay-nekked sportin' women went tootin' by in a bus," said the old man.

Mitch watched him drain the last of the beer and throw the can onto the shale.

"Saw them boys out here 'bout ten days ago. Talkin' to thet durn ranger, too. I was gittin' water there."

"In the white truck?"

"White as ten-day bird shit."

The old man looked up at the sky. "Gummamint folks."

"How could you tell they were government folks?"

"Had a sticker card on the bumper. One o' them cellyphane things."

Mitch hadn't seen any decals on the truck. "You sure about that sticker?"

"Yep."

"Are you real sure? It's important to me."

"Go ask someone else if you don't credit me. Go

ask thet there lyin' ranger. Go ask a durn pump handle, all I care. Tell a durn man what I see'd, but he
don't like what he hears. Go ask someone else, boy."

"Sorry, old man. Keep talking."

The codger was quiet for a moment while he considered Mitch's apology.

"I'm sure on it, 'cause I watched 'em put tape to
thet durn sticker 'fore they left thet camp. Thet good
'nough for you?"

"You saw them tape over the sticker?"

The old man turned and looked at Mitch.
"Goldurn it, boy. You gittin' to be a mighty difficult
man to make talk with."

Mitch made himself stop. He swallowed a mouthful of beer. "Did you see what color the sticker was
before they covered it up?"

The old boy sat and scratched at his beard.
"Colors?"

"Colors. Maybe blue or green on the borders. Or
yellow with red letters. Anything like that?"

"Cain't recall no colors. Got me a bad color eye.
No, reckon I cain't talk on colors."

Mitch had learned to wait.

"Yep. Gittin' onto thet beer wreck was a piece o'
luck. Five dollars fer your whole seven cases.
Anything like thet ever happen to you, boy?"

"Not yet."

"Don't go give up hope on it, boy. Jes' keep your
eyes open up."

"Do you remember anything else?"

"Anything else? 'Bout what?"

"About the sticker. On the bumper."

"Them? No. Jes' the name. Saw it when they drove
on in. Passed right by me at the pump."

"Just the name? Christ! And?"

"And what?"

"What did it say on the sticker?"

"Said 'Nells.' "

"Nells? How about Nellis?"

"Could be. Might could o' missed a letter or so."

Mitch won three more pieces: the truck had California plates, the bumper sticker carried an 0-5 rank tag, and the cab rear window bore a star crack, lower left. The hot frustration that grated while he tried to pry facts from the scrambled brain of the old pack rat melted away to satisfaction. Mitch felt good when he won something through patience. He knew he was not a patient man.

"Old man, you got yourself ten bucks."

"Don't want thet ten bucks."

"Don't want it?"

The old man nodded at the Cessna. "Never had me no ride in one o' those things. Not never."

Mitch got to his feet. An easy smile cracked the dust on his lips. "You're on, partner. Let's go."

He waited while the old boy settled into the right seat and figured out the seat belt buckle. Mitch prepped the engine and prepared to pop the ignition. He looked aft in the ritual of small-plane pilots and yelled, "Clear." The prop jerked over and shuddered the craft with jolting kicks of cold power as the engine started.

"Who you shoutin' at, boy?" over the noise of the engine.

"Just the way it's done, old man."

"Not a whole lot o' folks out here."

"Right."

The engine smoothed, and Mitch eased the plane forward, then pivoted for takeoff. Hard bits of slate and shale snapped under the rolling gear.

"Damn thing rattles a mite, don't she?"

Mitch was deciding who among the Vegas contacts would pay a visit to Nellis. Mouse and Freddie. Freddie had a gate pass as Public Works supplier; it would let him set an easy tail. Freddie and Mouse. That would work.

"Tarnation! This contraption gonna shake plum apart, boy! Feels all rickety. Durn!"

"She's tougher than she feels, old man."

Mitch revved the engine. The big dog sat near the car where she had been posted by the old man. Her head cocked to one side as she watched the plane.

"Shore as hell hope so! Craziest durn thing I ever 'bout rode on. Durn old cellyphane winders flappin' to beat all. Doors a-flappin'! Seats a-flappin'! Durn! Shore she's all right, boy?"

The plane accelerated across the flat-rock surface. The rattles faded in the drum of power. Mitch could feel each piston working deep in the fury of the engine.

"Durn, boy! She's got a bucketful o' go in her, don't she!" yelled the old man over the roar. His eyes were popped wide open.

Mitch smiled. The plane was skimming over the shale.

"Hey, boy. Reckon this here is plenty fast enough."

"Need the speed to get her off."

"What you mean, 'get 'er off'?"

"Get her off . . . up in the air."

"Up in the air? What you mean up in the air, boy? Didn't ask for no up in the air. Jes' ask for a goldurn ride. Nothin' said 'bout no up in the air. Durn!"

Mitch stared straight ahead in surprise. He shook his head. The plane lifted smoothly off the shale.

Mitch glanced at the old rockhound and saw him

looking down at the ground where the car and the dog formed the center of their climbing arc. The old man's right hand was flat against the overhead and his left hand gripped the left seat edge with bloodless intensity.

"Jes' asked for a durn ride! Nothin' said 'bout no goldurn up in the air! Got yerself a powerful problem figgerin' out a man's words, boy. Wonders me more'n a mite how you got this far 'long."

"Come on, pops, you trying to tell me it's not pretty up here?"

"Reckon it's all right. Could be a mite purdy."

They landed back on the shale near the car. The old rocker got out and stood in the rush of the idling prop, baggy green pants whipping in the backwash. Then he planted a hard kick on the right landing gear rubber.

"Didn't no one say nothin' 'bout no durn up in the air." He turned and stomped off toward the car.

19

Mako

Kevin was glad to be heading north. Tampa in summer is not kind to a fat man. On the edge of a tomato field in Ruskin, he transferred one of the two remaining boxes of cash to a trio of slit-eyed Colombians who materialized out of the dust in a black Mercedes. He had been fighting off a tangible sense of unease coming into Tampa. He frequently was the addressee of subtle premonitions that proved remarkably valid. God at work, no doubt.

He pushed the Lincoln into the damp miles of Route 4 through the steam of Orlando on the way to Daytona Beach. The final money drop was in Philadelphia. Then it would be over. Five cities in ten days. He was tired.

He picked up the girl on the ramp coming out of Lake Monroe. He had stopped to feed gasoline to the big car and to relieve his bladder. This pattern of fluid exchange had emerged throughout the course of the last week. The fuel gauge had become an inverted indicator of his bladder capacity. But he still felt out of sorts. The girl would be a good distraction, would get his mind off his unease.

She hopped into the front seat and flipped her green knapsack into the back. Scruffy jeans; brown leather jacket folded over the arm; blue loose-fitting cotton shirt; terminal Reeboks; no socks; short auburn hair; green panther eyes sparkling from an Orphan Annie face. The soft smell of warm leather suffused the interior of the car.

"Okay, big fella, I'm going up to Jacksonville. North Carolina, not Florida. I got no license, but I can help you drive. Appreciate the lift ... far as you're going. I got no money, but I'm great company. Just don't try to mess with me, and we'll get along fine. I don't sing, don't need any advice, and don't want your dope. Keep your hands on the wheel, friend. I carry a knife and I can use it. Let's move this hog."

"Bless you, my child."

They accelerated onto the highway and fell in line with the traffic. After giving the inside of the car a quick inspection, she turned to look at him. "You're not just going to the coast, are you?"

"No, my dear. I hope to get to Philadelphia. If I don't get stabbed first."

"Good. Figured you were going somewhere real. Those California plates. You're from California, you don't need to screw around in Florida."

He thought about that. The logic of the young.

"You a priest?"

He felt the quick slap of her perception. "Yes, I am a humble servant of the Word."

"You don't take it too serious, do you?"

He was silent and wondrous.

They rode through the hot Florida light. He relaxed a bit when he realized that his God shirt and collar hung from the hook behind his seat. But this little lady was sharp. Everything she said had taken him by surprise. He had lucked out.

"I take it as seriously as it needs to be. Depends on the situation. What's your excuse?"

"What does that mean, priest?"

"I think you're too sharp to be hitching rides."

"I'm too sharp not to be."

He couldn't figure that one out. He had the mental image of two rams about to butt horns in a rocky place.

He waited awhile. They were at ease with one another.

"How old are you, my child?"

"Eighteen, priest. How old are you?"

He laughed. "I feel about eighty right now."

"Well, I'm hitchin' because I want to get somewhere. I don't need to do what it takes to get money for bus tickets. I don't have to take some two-bit job to line the pockets of some dickhead capitalist as long as I can think. I get by just fine."

"Spoken like a sinecured Marxist."

"The only Marxist that impresses me is Harpo. And Archie Bunker is a better philosopher than Kant. I like my prejudice with ketchup, thank you. That includes priests. No offense intended." A smile.

"Goodness gracious. None taken, I'm sure."

Silence. Then he looked across at her. "You read. Why aren't you in college beating up on some of your peers instead of defenseless adults?"

"College is just another flashy consumer item for

rich people. They slop it on their kids and park 'em in the street. Hey, look at me. I can pay."

The miles rolled beneath the big white car.

"Why are you going to Jacksonville? Seems sort of mundane for a big world traveler like you."

"My dad is there. He's a medic in the Navy. At Camp Lejeune with the Marines. He's a Senior Chief. I drop by every year or two to give him a little ration. Keeps him on the defensive. They divorced five years ago. That's when I split. They're both good people, but I wasn't going to be the bone in a dogfight. It worked out okay. I like my freedom. They split, I split. Surprised the hell out of them. Bingo. We had some good years."

"That's too bad." Kevin felt some discomfort.

"Wrong. They would have killed each other. Marriage might be a great institution, but it gets screwed up if it has to be an everlasting commitment. That's where people fuck up. Oops! Sorry about the Navy talk."

"Excused, I'm sure."

"A few years ago, the old man shows me this radical bitch . . . a woman Marine . . . can you beat that? He wants to get married all over again. She was something else. She ran the gamut of brains from A to B. I torpedoed that real quick. Took her out like Lawrence Taylor. Ashes. Got her kicked out of the Corps to boot. The old man knows it was for the best. Got her bumping fuzzies with me in the duty room. Made sure we got caught. Too much."

She smiled like a cat at Kevin.

He felt startled again. It took a lot to startle him.

She looked out the window. "Reminded me of what ol' Sam Johnson said. Remember? He said that when a man remarries it represents a triumph of hope over experience. Pretty good line."

"When do you find the time to read?"

"It's the only thing I can do. It's an addiction with me. Got it from my dad. He would read to me when I was a squirt. Whenever he wasn't off on a damn ship. He'd read to me for at least an hour every day. More if Mom didn't stop us. And soon as I could I was reading back to him. He told me that you could read yourself to the best damn education in the world . . . better than you could get at any college . . . long as you had the willpower."

Kevin wondered. He tried to picture the Senior Chief. He couldn't. Kevin realized he didn't know her name.

"What do I call you, my child? My name is Kevin."

"Okay, your name is Kevin. Congratulations."

"And?"

"And what?"

"Who are you?"

"Who do you want me to be?"

"I need to call you something."

"So? Think up something."

"Why do that?"

"Then you'll remember my name. Think up something neat. What do I remind you of?"

"A shark."

She laughed in a burst of animal energy. The white teeth sparkled. "No kidding? That's great."

Kevin cocked his head toward her and squinted.

"A Mako shark," he said. "No. Your teeth are too straight. A Mako is kind of snaggletoothed."

"Hey! I got a snaggletooth. Look here."

She pulled back her cheek to show him a malformed premolar tooth. Her eyes flashed above the mischievous stretched grin.

"Then that's it," he said. "Mako."

She let her cheek go and laughed again.

"Mako! I like that," she said. "Now don't go turnin' it into 'May' or something sweet like that."

"A shark by any other name . . . " he said.

"Mako and the priest."

"So shall it evermore be written, my child."

" 'The great fish moved silently through the night water, propelled by short sweeps of its crescent tail.' I've always wanted a crescent tail." She wriggled her jeans into the white vinyl seat and bared her teeth at the driver they were passing.

"*Jaws*, right?"

"Right. My dad used to scare the hell out of me with that one."

They both laughed. Kevin noticed in the rearview mirror that the driver they had just passed was shooting them the bird. Startled, no doubt. Poor fellow. *I know how you feel*, he thought. And he laughed some more.

They stopped in St. Augustine for some cheeseburgers and a bottle of wine. He thought Mako was the milkshake type, but she insisted he buy a bottle of red wine in the market across from the burger stand.

"Red with meat. It helps the digestion if you're eating all this cheapo fat. You ought to know that, priest. You guys on the Jesus team push this red stuff every Sunday, don't you? Along with the body bits?"

" 'Take, eat, this is my body' does not refer to cheeseburgers, Miss Mako."

"I don't know, those little round jobbers you guys hand out are probably miniburger buns from the Last Supper. Evolutionary precursors to White Castles."

"You use pretty big words for a highway chippie."

"Don't 'chippie' me, widebody, or I'll stuff that cheeseburger where the halos don't shine."

"Lord forgive her twisted and dirty mind."

"A dirty mind is a joy forever. Advocatus diaboli."

They laughed and finished the bottle.

They left the lunch stop and headed back to Route 95 where it stretched north from St. Augustine. Mako had convinced Kevin to invest in a second bottle of red wine. The late-afternoon sun was allowing the Florida air to regain some vestige of circulation. Mako wanted to ride with the car windows open, so Kevin turned off the air conditioning. The moving air from the outside was comfortable and warm . . . like the wine. Mako was insistent that the second bottle not be chilled.

"It tastes richer this way."

"I defer to your research, my child. My experience with three-dollar vintage is limited."

"God, what a snob."

"Don't 'snob' me. This palate has trained on the vineyards of princes. Your ragamuffin prejudice against quality of life falls hollow on the vast range of my superiorities in these matters."

"Vast my ass."

"'Her voice was ever soft, gentle, and low . . . an excellent thing in a woman.'"

"Give me a break!" She laughed and passed the bottle to him.

The pavement slapped easily at the big wheels.

"And what comes next for you, my young companion? Do you intend merely to pass through this life antagonizing others for amusement? Surely you must have some black goal, some scurrilous pact with the devil."

"What happens, happens. Too many things in life are distractions, narcotics to keep a person from thinking. Like a dumbass job, making piles of money, chasing cults, praying for salvation, pushing some mindless cause, drugs, stuff like that. I figure life's too short to grind up and throw away. You look around. You move. You feel. You think. It takes guts to think, priest. Don't give me a cause. I don't need it."

"You're not an optimistic person."

"Optimism sucks. Hope counts for something. Hope can kick the hell out of optimism any day. My life might be a *little* life, but I make my share of discoveries, priest."

"You drink too much cheap wine."

"You *know* it, too. I can see it in your face."

They charged along the smooth road hurling ideas back and forth. Kevin could see the fractious seeds of his own conclusions in her rebellious words. He wondered what some of these ideas, which she framed so sharply, would bring to her as the days of her young life unfolded in the brittle sunlight of a changing world. He felt angry and protective at the same time. Angry at her presumptions, and protective because he liked her.

"Do you have any gum?"

"Gum?"

"Chewing gum. Cleans your teeth after you eat. Gets all the crumbs out."

"I don't have any gum."

"Great."

She leaned over the seat and retrieved her backpack. She unzipped one of the pockets and took out a package of gum. She unwrapped a stick for herself and popped it in her mouth. Then she unwrapped another stick and stuck it into Kevin's mouth.

"Thanks," he mumbled against the piece of gum, which felt hard and stale against his palate.

"It's for your own good."

Kevin glanced at the backpack.

"What do you carry in that thing besides gum?"

"This? Girl stuff . . . and survival gear."

"What's that big lump? Looks like you got a billy club in there."

"This lump?" She knocked on the outside of the backpack at the bulge and laughed. "That's my good right arm."

She unzipped a big zipper that ran across the top of the knapsack. She flashed Kevin her shark grin and, after a bit of shoving and pushing at the contents, she held up a flesh-colored prosthetic limb. A right arm. It was scratched and gouged, and three of the fingers were crushed into splinters.

"Good Lord." He was staring.

"My helping hand," she said proudly. "Got it at one of the dispensaries my old man was working at. Some grunt got it crunched up in a shredder. He must have been a sharp son of a gun. First he gets his real arm stuck in a tank tread, then the VA makes him this one, gives him a cushy discharge, and he goes right out and does this. And they allow those guys to reproduce."

"Why in God's name do you have that thing?"

"Don't actually wear it. Just haul it around shopping centers and airports. Places like that. Keep one arm out of my jacket sleeve, behind my back. Tell the citizens I'm trying to get money to repair the thing. It's a gold mine. Only problem's when some bleeding heart tries to cart me off to a hospital to pay for the whole job. Can't lay it on too thick. Pretty neat, huh?"

She smiled at him and stuffed the arm into the pack.

Kevin didn't reply. He was temporarily out of words. In the silence she thought he might be disapproving.

"Loosen up, priest. Don't you have any secrets?"

Kevin looked over at her. She wasn't challenging him. She had curiosity in her eyes.

"Come on, no secrets, no regrets?"

"Regrets? Not many. I regret I haven't had more kind words for the good people who touched my life."

"What made you be a priest?"

"Optimism."

Mako laughed.

They passed the bottle a few times, pulling at the common teat. Enjoying the hot, dying day.

"To tell the truth, my child, I never really could decide what I wanted to be when I grew up. Now that I'm growing down it's less of a problem."

More miles drifted away.

"You running from something," Mako asked.

"What do you mean?"

"You know. Priests don't travel much. You mess up somewhere? Smoke an altar boy or something?"

"Good Lord."

"Maybe arrange an interest-free loan from God's easy green coffers? Poke the organist?"

"My child, do you need enemies to give meaning to your life?"

"Come on," Mako prodded. "Give me a hint."

"You're telling me a man of God isn't permitted to motor down a highway without being suspect in your skeptical world?"

"Not a highway three thousand miles from home."

"I am on a mission."

"On a mission."

"A pragmatic mission of business."

"Business. Right."

"It's true," Kevin said. "Though it may not meet with your view of the philosophical life. The hard world of business is tangible, authentic, real. It turns its back firmly on the kind of moral speculation that can smother the unwary soul."

"In love, jaded, or bored. Which one?"

"Lord, give me strength."

"Which one, priest?"

"Maybe bored. By smallness."

"Good."

"Maybe curiosity, too."

"A closet hedonist."

Kevin took the last of the bottle in a sweet swallow. He recognized the infrequent and pleasant sensation of letting down his guard. "Now, that makes sense," said Mako. "There may be hope after all."

"A possibility."

"Just think," she said. "You get to experience more of life that way. 'What if, in death, you had only your own life to review, relive, remember, and resee?' Remember who said that?"

"Enlighten me."

"Stonewall Jackson. The ol' general. When he was dying in the shade of the trees. Makes you think a bit, doesn't it?"

Kevin didn't answer.

"Could sort of make for a boring eternity for some folks, don't you think, priest?"

Night came on. Georgia coastal plain became South Carolina pine swamp. The hard vein of Highway 95 rolled out of the humid evening, and taillights began to float in front of and around the big car. The wine, the thinking, and the give-and-take had made them at once upbeat and comfortably weary. The air was heavy with pulp-mill aroma and it mixed with the sweet smell of leather in the car.

"Hey, priest. I got to take a leak."

"We'll turn off near Walterboro and go down to 17 through Summerville. Will your abused kidneys wait till then?"

"Jesus, that's an hour away. You want me to piss out the window? Won't look good on your application for Pope . . . not to mention the side of your car. Just 'cause you got a bladder the size of a dufflebag doesn't mean I do."

"Coarse speech is not an acceptable cover for your lack of willpower."

"Peeing has nothing to do with willpower. Just find me a pot, Mr. Big, or you got a problem."

Kevin laughed. He took the car off the freeway at the exit they were about to pass. Mako disappeared into the service station restroom while Kevin had the attendant top off the tank. He waited until Mako returned before he went in to relieve himself. He wanted to keep in sync with the fuel gauge. He took the car keys with him. He had been in a constant state of surprise since picking her up. He didn't want to come out of the restroom and be even more surprised.

Kevin pulled the car away from the pumps and parked to one side of the service area. He turned off the engine. He wanted to rest. They sat in the fluorescent glare as flickering shadows of summernight moths played across the white hood and across the still-warm pavement of the gas station. Stroboscopic wing blinked in stroboscopic light, and the silence, deepened in the absence of motor hum and wind rush, affirmed the enchantment of their isolation.

"Where are we?" Mako asked.

"Hardeeville, South Carolina, madam. After the great icon of the Hardee Hamburger, for sure."

She deliberated for a moment. "I'm hungry. And I love hamburgers."

"They would be appropriate."

"Let's do it, priest. My treat."

"Well, fan my brow! Didn't know you believed in money, child."

"I'll stand for the burgers. But you pay for the room. I don't want to get to Jacksonville at three in the morning."

Kevin looked at the girl.

"Don't worry about your cherry, Larry. You'll be safe with me. What the Pope don't know won't hurt him."

Kevin heaved his suitcase onto the top of the low dresser that held the TV. The warm night had conspired with the flight of stairs to put beads of sweat across his forehead. Mako pitched her backpack onto one of the chairs by the window and wrinkled her nose.

"This place smells like bug spray."

"It's disinfectant," Kevin said. "I think they call it air freshener. All motel rooms smell like this at first. It goes away as you get used to it."

"I like motel rooms," she said. "I want to sleep near the window."

"Be my guest."

She smiled.

"Hey, priest. I got a friend in Orlando says every time he goes into a motel room, the first thing that happens is he gets a husky. Says it happens every time."

"What, pray tell, is a husky?"

"A hard-on. You know . . . an erection."

"Lord, save us."

"No. I really mean it. That's the truth. He's not the bullshit type."

"If a motel room does that to him he has no need to 'bullshit.'"

"Sure seems funny. Are most men like that? Does it happen to you?"

"No, my child. That does not happen to me. That has never happened to me."

"Don't priests get huskies? Bet they do. Have to."

"Why do we have to?"

"It's natural. You can't do anything about it. Maybe when you're asleep."

"Young lady, why do you persist in things that are none of your business?"

"What does a priest think about when he gets a husky? Try to pray it away? Must be tough to pray with a husky."

"That could depend on what you're praying for."

Mako flopped back onto her bed and laughed with her animal energy. Kevin liked that laugh. It had the best part of life in it.

"You're all right," Mako said, smiling. "I like talking with you. You'll make a damn good priest if you ever want to be one. Guess I shouldn't tease you. No hard feelings?"

She burst out with the laugh again. Even Kevin had to laugh at the words. He shook his head and continued to hang his shirts in the open closet.

They sat on their beds and watched television for awhile. Mako spent most of the half hour raging at the people on "Crossfire." She seemed to disagree with everybody, no matter what position they took. Kevin was filled with wonder at the knowledge she carried. And the opinions. And the echoes in his mind.

She got up once to go to the bathroom.

"Hey, priest. You got any matches?"

"There's some in the ashtray next to the TV. What do you need matches for? Have you decided to burn down the motel, my child?"

"Got to unload, padre."

Kevin looked at her. "You need matches for that?"

"Jesus, Padre. Didn't your mother teach you anything? You strike two matches and drop 'em in the potty when you're through. Sulfur beats up on the smellies. The civilized way to go. A confidence builder. Helps to maintain a sense of class in a crowd."

"I can't remember when I've seen such class."

"You're being sarcastic again, padre," she sang. She closed the door behind her.

Kevin stared blankly at the TV.

An hour later Kevin stood looking out the window at his white car. Mako was busy at the sink washing her underthings. She had bummed one of Kevin's old polyester sport shirts for a nightdress, a pink one, awkwardly translucent. The pale garment came down to her knees.

The car was parked directly below the room, where he could see it. The trunk had been rigged with a triplock, and Jesse had installed an ignition kill switch along with dual alarms that Kevin flipped whenever he left the car. He tried to decide whether to bring the last box of money up to the room for safekeeping. He decided against it. Mako was too smart and too curious to let it pass. She was still full of surprises. And, of course, there were those heart-popping stairs. *Better to preserve the temple of the soul at all costs. Physical exertion must be stoutly avoided to keep the mind as sharp as possible. The money was as safe down there as it would be up here. He had three days to finish the run. Plenty of time.*

Kevin adjusted his big silk purple pajamas.

"God, what an outfit," Mako remarked when he came out of the bathroom after his shower.

"Why, thank you for the compliment, my dear. You are an observer of consummate taste and perception."

"Compliment?"

"Purple is the Lord's color, child. You, of course, with your sweeping grasp of life's subtleties, can appreciate the coordination of the fashionable with the spiritual."

"You look like a bruise."

"Infidel."

Now she stood in front of the TV waiting for the newscaster from Charleston to finish a weak story on the need for tobacco price supports.

"Listen to this stuff," Mako said, shaking her head. "I swear to God, every year the bureaucracy gets bigger and the humanity of it all gets smaller. Orwell was wrong. There's no Big Brother ... there's no one in charge at all. Just the damn system feeding itself."

She snapped off the TV with a vengeance. He heard her rustle beneath the covers of her bed.

"Damn," she said.

"Don't let it bother you," he comforted. "I don't think you can do anything about it tonight. You'll have to wait until tomorrow to change the world."

"Losers," she muttered.

They were silent in the darkness for some minutes. The occasional distant roar of a truck passing by on the freeway drifted into and out of the little room.

"Don't you have even the least bit of faith in the people who run our government?" he asked.

"Does the Pope wear condoms?"

He thought about that for awhile.

"I take it that's a 'no'?"

Another ten minutes went past. Kevin was in the sweet twilight zone of onrushing sleep.

"Hey, priest."

"What?" he mumbled.

"How come you don't say your prayers before you go to bed?"

"I do say my prayers."

"How come you don't kneel down when you say them? I didn't see you kneel down."

"God wants me to save my knees."

"How do you know that?"

"He told me."

"He told you?"

"Yes. It was on a Tuesday. Yes, a Tuesday afternoon. I remember it clearly."

Silence.

"I don't think you're a typical priest."

"You don't like 'typical,' as I recall."

More silence.

"You're okay," she said.

Two minutes went by. Kevin was getting back to the twilight zone.

"I still think priests get huskies."

He didn't answer.

At 6:35 A.M., Kevin awoke. Mako was still out. Down like a flat rock. He went into the bathroom and closed the door. Then he opened the door, stepped out, picked up a book of matches from the dresser, and went back in.

Twenty minutes later he emerged from the bathroom. He felt good. He felt confident. The confidence didn't last long. Mako was gone. So were the car keys he had left on the table next to his suitcase. He experienced a rush of nausea as his adrenal glands unloaded on his bloodstream.

He was at the window in an instant. Car still there. No red light. No alarms. But no Mako, either.

Then he heard footsteps on the stairs that led to the second floor. He couldn't see who it was, but it sounded like the girl. Energetic, light. Then she was there in front of the window, room key in hand. She jumped when she saw his face behind the glass only a foot from her own, and she dropped the key. She regained it and opened the door. She carried the copy of the Tampa paper that had been on the back seat of the car.

"Damn, priest, you gave me a start. You look like you got a bee up your nose."

Kevin didn't say anything. His body was trying to dissipate the sickening chemistry that still swam through his system.

The girl flipped the paper onto her bed and kicked off her beat-up Reeboks. She still wore Kevin's big shirt over her jeans. She dropped the keys on the dresser and launched herself in an arc toward her bed, where she landed sitting against the headboard between the pillows.

"Had to get the crossword puzzle, priest. You weren't going to do it, were you?"

"No."

"Toss me the house pen, will you? It's by the TV."

Kevin looked at her from where he stood by the window.

"Come on," she said, "the pen, the pen."

He made no move to get the pen.

"You're sulking, right? You want to do the crossword yourself. Okay. Flip you for it. Two out of three."

"How did you get that out of the car?"

"What, this?"

"Yes."

"I opened the door and leaned over the seat and took it out. No biggie."

"That car has an alarm system. It didn't go off."

"I shut it off."

"You shut it off."

"Right."

He looked at her.

"Is that what put you on the rag? Because I switched off your hotshot alarm?"

He kept looking at her.

"Hey, priest. I saw you switch the thing off last night when we got out to get the hamburgers. What's the big deal? You think I'm blind?"

"There are two switches to that system."

"Hey! You're our new champ! You've won a trip for two to beautiful downtown Soweto. Toss me the pen."

"You have a unique way of making me angry."

"'He who conquers his wrath overcomes his greatest enemy.' The pen, the pen."

He went over to the dresser, picked up the pen, and tossed it to her.

She started on the puzzle. He picked out some clothes and went into the bathroom to dress. He had just about recovered from the jolt of finding her gone. He marveled anew at her ability to observe. She was sharp.

"Hey, priest," came the voice through the door.

"What?"

"Give me a word for lotto. I figure it should be bingo, but it's only four letters."

"Keno."

"Keno?"

"Keno."

"What the hell's Keno?"

"It's a game played in Las Vegas. Numbers."

"Shit. I'm supposed to know that? This paper sucks."

" 'He who conquers his wrath overcomes his greatest enemy.' "

The voice didn't answer. He finished dressing and came back into the bedroom. Mako was on the bed lying on her stomach with the puzzle down on the floor.

"These damn puzzles should be tough, but they ought to keep them fair. I get torqued when they have a lot of damn foreign words and ethnic crap."

"Keno's not ethnic."

"Sounds like it."

"It's just the name of a game."

"Well, you have to go to Las Vegas to hear about it, so it's not fair to put it in a crossword."

"That's silly. It's a word you ought to know."

"You have to be twenty-one to gamble in Vegas."

"So?"

"So this puzzle is prejudiced against non-adults."

"Poor child."

"Go suck an egg."

She continued filling in the squares. Kevin went to work repacking his shirts. The rush of the shock had worn off. He was himself again. He felt hungry.

They sat across from each other destroying pancakes. The diner was part of the motel. Kevin had moved the car over to the front of the restaurant where he could keep an eye on it. They hadn't checked out of the room yet.

"So you're really into Las Vegas, priest? Sounds funny, a priest bumming around in Las Vegas."

"What's so funny? Give me back the syrup."

"Las Vegas is godless."

"Who says?"

"Everybody."

"Rubbish."

"Rubbish? Rubbish? La-dee-da, here comes the Queen."

"Rubbish is a perfectly good word."

"Nope. Too English."

"Who do you mean by 'everybody'?"

"Just everybody."

"I'll let you in on a little secret," Kevin said.

"What could that be?"

"With your capabilities you could collect a fortune in Las Vegas."

"Gambling?"

"No."

"Hooking?"

"No."

"Good. 'Cause I don't hook. How then?"

"Working for the casinos. You're sharp as an eagle. Operating a casino is about people. About eyes. About speed. You'd own the place in ten years. Start out on the tables to learn the ropes, get into security, then management; they wouldn't know what hit 'em." He laughed. He meant every word. Mako would wear like stainless steel in that environment.

"Thanks for the compliment. Give me back the syrup."

"It's not a compliment. It's an observation."

They continued to ravage pancakes. It was all-you-can-eat; the calories flew.

"What do you gamble at, priest? That Keno thing?"

"I like to shoot craps," he said.

"Boy, that figures."

He didn't reply, didn't rise to the bait.

"I'd like to learn how to shoot craps."

*   *   *

"That's the 'Pass' line. That's where you start."

Kevin had drawn a craps table layout on the bottom of the pizza box Mako found in the motel Dumpster. He told her they needed a piece of cardboard and some dice. The cardboard was easy. The dice were tougher.

"Where did you get these?"

"Around."

"Where's 'around'?"

"Across the street."

"What's across the street?" he said, still puzzled.

"Nothing."

"C'mon, what's across the street?"

"That big bus where the old people are screwing around under the trees. You know. Across the parking lot."

"I don't know."

"You can see it from here."

Kevin went to the window of the motel room and looked out. Mako studied the craps layout.

"That white one over there?"

"Right."

"My child, that bus is from a nursing home. It says so right on the side. Ketcham and Burnham Convalescent Home."

"Parcheesi."

"What about Parcheesi?"

"Got the dice from the Parcheesi game those two old dorks are playing on the picnic table."

"They gave you the dice?"

"Not exactly."

"You took the dice?"

"Priest, are you going to show me how to shoot craps or not?"

"Didn't they say anything to you?"

"No."

"No?"

"No."

Kevin came back and sat down across from Mako at the table where they had set up the makeshift lay-out.

"I went back to the restaurant. I remembered those old-style sugar cubes on the counter, was going to use them. Then I saw those guys fuddy-duddying around on the table. Went over and watched them for awhile. One guy goes off to take a whiz. I switch the sugar cubes for the dice while I was yakking with the other guy. Put them in that lit-tle cup they use."

Kevin sat there looking at her. She chuckled.

"I hung around. Wanted to see what they'd do."

"Good Lord in heaven."

"They shook up the cup and rolled them out. Just sat there and stared at the little bastards. Put them back in the cup and rolled them again. Can you beat that? Like they'd come out with dots the next time. They're probably still rolling the damn things. Are we going to get this show on the road or not?"

Kevin took a long look at Mako, shook his head, and taught Mako how to shoot dice.

"Remember, girl, casino craps looks complicated, but it's only the stupid bets that are confusing. The smartest bet is the simple pass-line bet. Don't forget that. The smartest bet is the simple pass-line bet."

"The smartest bet is the simple pass-line bet. The smartest bet is the simple pass-line bet. Okay, do you want me to write it on my forehead with a knife?"

"The roll starts when the guy with the stick puts the dice in front of a player and says 'new shooter coming out.' That's when you place your chip on the pass line."

"The pass line is this alley around the outside?"

"Right."

"Does it really say 'pass line' like you have it drawn here, or is that just for my benefit?"

"In big letters. Right on every table."

"How considerate."

"The player picks up the dice. One hand only. He can't use two hands to touch the dice."

"Why?"

"Trust me."

"Right."

"The player throws the two dice down to the far end of the table. The far end. The dice have to hit and bounce back off the rubber wall at the far end of the table."

"Hold it."

"What now?" Kevin said.

"Do you have to be the one throwing the dice to put a chip on the pass line?"

"No, my child. Any player can make a pass-line bet when any player starts a roll."

"Democracy lives."

"The dice come to a stop. This is the first roll, remember. If a seven or eleven shows up on this first roll, you win your pass-line bet right away. The dealer will put a chip next to your chip on the pass line. You pick up the chip you have won. You do it right away. If you don't pick it up it's considered a bet on the next roll, and you'd be betting two chips instead of one."

"I love it when you talk like this."

"If a two, three, or twelve shows up on the first roll, you lose right away. Those numbers are called 'craps.' The dealer takes your pass-line bet."

"How rude."

Kevin continued explaining the intricacies of the game.

"And now for the second commandment."

"Which is?"

"Always take full odds."

"Right. Always take full odds. Right. Never heard of it. What the fuck does that mean?"

Kevin looked up at the girl.

"Is it a necessity that you punctuate the learning process with vulgarities?"

"Yes, it is. Continue, priest. Full odds."

"A few years ago, in order to beat other casinos out of a few customers, someone decided to let the customers catch a break. Not a break actually in the customer's favor, mind you, but at least an even-money break that wouldn't hurt the casino one way or the other. They decided to let the customer make a bet in back of his pass-line bet that would pay off at an absolutely flat-money percentage. In most casinos the customer is allowed double odds. Double odds. Say 'double odds.'"

"Double odds."

"That means . . . "

"Double odds. Double odds."

"Are you through?"

"Double odds."

"That means that you can back up your five dollar pass-line bet with double that, or ten dollars. You put it on the table behind your pass-line bet after the point is established. Two times five is ten . . . double odds."

"Amazing."

Kevin patiently took her through the implications, pausing to answer her questions until at last he saw the corners of her mouth turn up in a smile.

"Hey, I think I finally understand it," she said.

"Good, let's play with a bunch of pennies," Kevin replied, reaching into his pocket. "We'll try a few hands to check you out."

"God! The excitement. Are these real pennies?"

"You can make believe they're thousand-dollar chips, my dear. Any more questions?"

"No."

"All set?"

"Is Helen Reddy?"

They rolled dice. At 12:05 the desk called to see when they would be leaving. Kevin told the desk to sign them up for another night. He told the girl on the phone to order a pepperoni and pineapple pizza for them and to procure two bottles of red wine, one cold and one room temperature. He told the girl it would be worth a twenty to her. A twenty in Hardeeville got things done.

At three in the afternoon, one of the two maids on duty came by to make up the beds. She was a black girl of nineteen. She laughed and talked with them. She watched the dice roll. She asked if she could play. In ten minutes they taught her how to shoot the stolen dice. By 5:30 P.M. there were seven people shooting penny craps in room 234 of the Thunderbird Motel. At 7:00 P.M. Kevin donned an appropriately reserved yellow pleated owner's shirt and preened about, offering advice like some Baron of Glitter Gulch. Mako was doing the teaching now. She was instructing how to make hard ways and place bets, but she kept her own bets on the pass line. Kevin could see how she watched her stake relative to the stakes of those who played the junk bets in the middle. He was impressed.

"Hey, priest. This game always do this to people?"

"It can be a dangerous game," Kevin said, his face serious.

He saw her shake her head and go back to the play. He was having a difficult time keeping dollar bills off the table. He was banking the game and had drawn a firm line at quarters. He wanted to keep things social.

"Hey, priest."

"Yes, Miss Mako?" over the heads.

"Have you noticed that nobody closes the door when they take a leak?"

He hadn't noticed.

At 11:30 P.M. someone in another room complained about the noise. Kevin, as the banker, was ahead $114.32, and in a grand gesture of corporate munificence he divided all of the bank's profit and doled it out in equal portions to the eleven souls who were still playing at the end of the game. The happy group departed with animated good-byes, most hauling off empty bottles, cans, and snack debris into the night. Mako was surprised at the profit Kevin had achieved, especially after she counted up her own winnings and found herself to be up twice her stake.

"I didn't realize the bank was making all that money," she said. "It seemed like everybody was winning."

"They may have been winning most of the rolls, my child. But watch how people play. They win a point or two and they start to increase their bets. They bet two and win. Then they bet that four and win again. They bet the eight and let that ride, too. It wins. They go for it again. Then they lose a roll. Just one roll. They've won three out of four times, only lost once, and they're worse off than before the first roll. The casino has a lousy 1.41 percent advantage on the pass-line bet. If you take the double odds, you get the best deal in the casino, not just in the game of craps."

Mako was listening. No clever comebacks.

Kevin leaned back on his bed. "Some people really hang their hat on those numerical odds. And they should. But there's another type of odds. Psychological odds. Those are the odds that say you will lose your discipline. You heard the noise tonight? The excitement? All for pennies, nickels, quarters? It's a social game, child. Everyone is attacking the casino, trying to win together. Hootin' and hollerin'. Make your point, you're a hero. The game has a lot of reinforcement angles. Not to mention the biggest factor common to all the games."

"The desire to win?"

"More accurately, greed."

"You can't say it was just greed tonight, priest. Not for a few lousy pennies."

"You can be greedy for other things, little one."

"Like what?"

"Like excitement. Hope. Like optimism, maybe."

"Maybe people just want to do something different."

"Maybe. Depends on the person. Some people, I think they want to lose."

"Lose?" She scrunched her brow. "You can be deep, priest."

"And I'll tell you something else. If you play long enough, you're going to lose. You can't beat even that little one percent in the long run."

"Never?"

"Never. Not if you can't stop. Maybe not even then."

"I could stop."

"Remains to be seen, Mako."

"I could stop."

"I think there's a good chance you could."

"I could."

"That's the third commandment. Set a loss limit. If you can't keep a promise made to yourself, then you'll know you're a loser. That counts for something. If you have to bet wild, do it when you're ahead. That's when it's fun. Not smart, fun. Fun counts . . . sometimes."

It was after midnight. They lay in their beds in the dark room staring up at the ceiling they couldn't see. The sound of late-night trucks dopplered in and out of the room. Kevin was glad they had stayed the extra day.

"Hey, priest."

"What?"

"You ahead or down for the game?"

"What do you mean?"

"You know. For all the years you been playing, have you won more money or lost more money?"

"For all the years? I've won more money. A lot more, in fact. And they don't tell the tax man if you win."

"You told me you can't win in the long run. Doesn't make sense. Why do you win?"

"If I'm not tired, I can tell when I'm going to win. I can feel it when the dice are going to be right."

"Baloney."

"And I quit fast when I start to lose, when the dice turn around and the feeling goes away. Walking away from the table is the best thing I do."

Silence.

"And I expect to win," he added.

"Everybody expects to win."

"No, they don't."

More silence.

"Damn," she said, "you'd make someone one hell of an old man."

They went to sleep.

In the morning, Kevin awoke to a pressure on his left arm. Mako had crawled into bed with him during the night. She slept with her back to him, on top of his arm. She had taken his hand in her two hands and still held it to her chest like she was hugging a stuffed animal. She looked small in his big sport-shirt nightgown. He stayed for a long time without moving.

He had never thought about what it would be like to have a child of his own, sleeping in his arms like this. A few soft tears ran down his round face, and he tasted the salt of them.

He dropped her off at the old white building that housed the USO in Jacksonville, North Carolina. They parked the car and walked together down to the shore of the New River in the late-afternoon sun. Mako and Kevin stood together beneath the swaying skirts of Spanish moss that slowly two-stepped to the gentle music of a Carolina summer breeze.

They didn't speak and returned to the car. They held hands while they walked. Back in front of the USO he asked if she would be okay, and she said she would. They wished each other luck. She watched him turn the car and drive away.

He drove slowly at first because the setting sun was in his eyes and the road was narrow . . . and because he missed Mako. He didn't stop to eat dinner. Eating alone had no appeal for him that night, and he didn't halt the long drive until he reached Springfield, Virginia, on the outskirts of Washington,

D.C. He was in his motel room by midnight, stretched out in the dark on his bed on top of the covers, still in his clothes, still with his shoes on. He hadn't felt loneliness sink its cold teeth into him like this in twenty years.

He awoke the next morning still in his clothes, still on top of the covers.

One half hour after passing through Baltimore he noticed the chip of red lens glass. It lay next to the edge of the windshield near the small rubber dome of the repeater light. A ray of rising sun flickered through the morning haze, hit the thin glass, and refracted up to catch his eye. His mind began to tumble. For the second time in two days he felt the chemical jump on his blood.

The big car smoked to a halt on the exit ramp. Kevin toggled off the trunk alarm and had the lid open before the dust from the road edge had settled.

The box was still there. The tapes across the top seemed intact. Not lifted. Not cut. He leaned to examine the right side, the left side, the back surface that faced away from him. All intact. He grasped the box and tilted it up to look at the bottom.

It was cut.

A slash twelve inches long smiled at him. He lifted the box and shook it. The remaining money packs bumped around in the space created by the missing blocks of cash. He was sweating. *How much was gone?*

He set the box down in the trunk and tore open the top. A third of the cash was gone. *Were the hundreds taken or just bundles of twenties?* He realized that he shouldn't be standing there on the exit ramp fumbling with what was left of three hundred thousand dollars in cash, with what was left of his composure.

He hefted the box out of the trunk, put it on the

front seat on the passenger side, and got back behind the wheel. A tickling drop of sweat fell from the tip of his nose. He followed the feeder road until he came to a turnout where some banged-up trash cans stood next to a graffiti-scarred historical marker. He began to count.

The cold, still liquid of the martini was so clear that Kevin could have believed the glass empty were it not for the image of the olive, distorted by the icy fluid, wavering in the dim light. *One hundred twenty thousand. Most of the hundreds. Cut any other side and she would have gotten mostly twenties. When did she do it?* It had to have been while he slept. Or even during a break in the dice game. Maybe there had been a partner. Called in from one of the food places, or when they stopped for gas and he thought she was just using the restroom. Maybe even a connection with the Tampa gang that knew he was traveling heavy. No. They couldn't have known that he was going to pick her up at the Orlando ramp. No way.

He tried to find another possibility. Last night at the motel in Springfield? That didn't work either. The alarms were good, you had to get to them both within fifteen seconds. One, maybe. Both? Only if you knew where the cutouts were. And you could only see that from the inside. From the inside.

"From the inside," he said to his martini, "from the inside." That was the operative word, all right. From the inside. From the inside of his car and from the inside of his heart. *God, it hurt to feel like this.*

He tried to picture her going through the car. Hit the switches, into the trunk getting only what she could carry, only what would stow in that damned bag. Then she would see the red repeater light on the dash. With those beautiful laughing eagle eyes of hers. Watching. Back into the car. Break the light.

One twenty big ones. He could call Jesse. He should call Jesse. The cash wouldn't even have to be wired. Just a call to Philly and he could pick it up on the way in. Quick as a whip. But there was something wrong with that. He'd have to tell what happened. He'd look dumb. Amateur night. Conned. Aced. Smoked. Sucker city. A good friend, Jesse, let down, made to look bad. His own reputation compromised. A reputation that meant something to him. He hadn't really admitted it until now.

There was something else. They would go get it back. Even if he tried to cover it, they'd find her. People would remember. God, would they get it back from her.

The fourth martini was smoother than the first three. Time to move. He could think on the drive to Philly. He had a day and a half to play with. The drop time was his call. He could stretch it a day or two.

He went back to his car. As he waited to enter the road from the lounge, he looked across the street at a billboard. The guy from TV. The cop with the lollipop. Pitching an ad for the Player's Club. In Atlantic City.

Atlantic City.

He checked the map.

Two hours, at the most.

20

The Miss

Century 21 was going to give it another try. She had been haunting Diego's for two weeks hoping to find him again. Two damn fantasy-ridden weeks of frustration. She couldn't get that awesome bastard out of her mind. That smile. The way people came on to him. And those arms . . . "guns," he called them. And his shy eyes. And the fact that he had done hard time. And how everyone looked up when he came into a room. And that cock. Damn! Especially that. What in the hell was happening to her?

She kept her blonde hair frizzed up because it had been that way on the night Ram had seen fit to pick her up. Her ends were splitting . . . just like the ends of her nerves. She wore the same bracelets, the same earrings, the same style dress. But, of course, not the same dress. People at the real estate office were looking at her. She kept losing her calculator. She would frequently catch herself staring at the fly area of men's pants, at the bumps behind the zippers. Of coworkers and customers alike. She caught herself doing it even when the prospect's wife was standing there. One guy had grabbed her rear in return as she was showing him a condo agreement. Some sort of male signal, apparently.

She remembered where Ram lived, but he had said not to drop by. He would call her. Period. That night he had received the phone call from that goddamn fisherman in Mexico she was on the edge of something that had never happened before. The big number three. She had floated to climax with her vibrator countless times. She had been nibbled to ecstasy by her dates, by her second husband, and even by the cute little closer fellow who made her come four times on top of the big oak desk down at Cheatham Escrow. But never had she won a real cock-generated orgasm. She had felt it coming on like a white-hot freight train. Despite what her women's magazines told her about cocks placing third behind electronics and tongues, that one was going to send her farther than she'd ever gone before.

And he gets a phone call to talk about *fishing*.

Now she had it again. Right in front of her. They were in his weight room. Sunk in a sea of giant bean-bag cushions. She lay on her tummy between his legs, her head near his knees, her left arm lounging across his thigh, her right hand trembling and trying to encircle that remarkable cock, fingers unable to get all the way around. She was awed. And proud. Proud that she had made it get like this. She knew cocks weren't supposed to be regarded as independent objects. That was the kind of thing that men did when it came to sex. All the magazine articles said so.

But since she had turned thirty-nine, she seemed to have evolved into some sort of female chauvinist.

This certainly was an exceptional object. For the first thirty-eight years of her life, she didn't think of cocks as isolated structures. They were erotic because of the sweet intrigue that went along with getting one into you . . . because of the romance, because of the tenderness, because of the love, because of the referrals.

She could feel the spilling wetness between her legs, and she endured a rushing blush of embarrassment at her lubricity. Reserve and mystery had become lost causes.

She looked down at her nipples as they alternately brushed against the slowly churning skin of his testicles. Her brown tips stiffened and sprouted out hard to meet the moving, rutted skin of him that was so different there. She watched in fascination as her probing nipple played up and over the tight swollen length of him. Everything was diameters and heat. A delicious electricity surged in her hips, and she felt as if the lower half of her body had become detached from the rest of her to float on a sea of animal snarls. She seemed now swept to a distance, looking down at the scene from afar, so full of the moment that her brain grew dizzy as it boiled in the delightful lust. The rush was coming. Not just the thought and imagining of the rush, but the rush of the climax itself. And she was still to mount that hot, throbbing chunk of him. She drew up on her knees, straddled him, then had to go onto one foot to position the roiling center of her between-legs over the pulsing reach of him. Her hand looked small, timorous, greedy as it guided him to the lush, craving softness at her center.

Pushing. Spreading. Pushing more. She rose a bit, moved slightly, then pushed again, moved him to her eagerness. *Make it wet. Make it start.* Heat, waves of vertigo. Rise again. She could feel the top of him saturated with her sleek moisture. *Slippery. So hard.* She pushed down firmly, forced her sex down over him, finally pressured his size to start into her. A quick rub of tissue against tissue and the first resistance yielded. The world spun for a moment, followed by the hot delirium of the filling. Down, down. Rising gently to marry new, sweet differences, then down and down and down some more. She felt the firmness buttress against the inside end of her, and she forced the delightful depravity even further. Possessed. Gloriously possessing. Full, full, and full.

She hung in the sensuality, poised in wonder at the incredible rush that was building. A quivering stillness perfused what was left of her mind, and she prepared to dare the slow thrusting.

That's when the first peanut hit the back of her shoulder.

"Hey, bro."

She became dimly aware of more peanuts being bounced off her shoulders from somewhere behind her.

"Bro. We got something."

Two more peanuts.

"From Freddie."

Another peanut. It was all coming apart again.

"In Vegas. Get your ass up."

The brothers sat in the dead room. Drinking beer. Mitch had brought along an extra can for himself. The last thing they heard as they entered the room was the sound of glass breaking somewhere upstairs.

"Sounds like your girlfriend dropped a glass, bro."

"Nice lady. Seems pretty high-strung. What's up?"

"Freddie and Mouse. They got the truck the second day. Slick. They're good boys."

"Any problems?"

"None. Covered both gates. Saw it going in the back off Nellis Boulevard. Wearing 0-5 bumper stickers."

Mitch paused to pull some beer. They felt the walls rattle as the front door slammed. Ram leaned the chair back against the wall and looked at Mitch.

"Did they follow it in?"

"Right to Operations. Freddie used his Public Works pass. Nosed around checking air conditioners and got chatty with some Airman writer. Got our flyboy's name. A lance colonel type. L. G. Muldrow. He's a JCS briefer on the Inspector General's team from D.C. Has a temporary office in Ops looking at the competition data from the Combat Air Games. And we got lucky."

"How?"

"Saw him talking to a major, Marine type. The writer said they work together. Freddie said it fit one of our descriptions. Sounds like our second boy."

"A Marine major. With the Air Force IG? Unusual."

"Freddie backed off. Didn't want to get too obvious. He left Mouse outside parked near the truck. The major took off and Mouse got his name tag. Major T. T. Evans."

"Any more?"

"More. Freddie has this dental technician on the hook. Sports bettor. Nicely overextended."

"Only in Las Vegas."

They finished the beers. Ram crumpled up the empty can between the fingers and thumb of one hand. Mitch was unimpressed. Mitch opened the extra can.

"The tech couldn't find the colonel's dental jacket. Must be carrying it with him. But the major's was in the file at the dental dispensary. The tech ran a copy and passed it to Freddie. All the work done on this guy is there in the dental record. And all the annual checkups; all the way from OCS, including the location of the clinics where the work was done plus the unit information on the patient that tells where he was assigned at the time. Got the whole career track right there."

"And?"

"The major has an interesting past. Lots of the usual stuff getting his tickets punched. Some Infantry Training Schools time, ITR instructor, some Tank Battalion stuff, and into 1st Recon at San Mateo. Then he pops over to the 2nd Marine Air Wing at Cherry Point. Fucking around with Harriers. Weird. The pattern breaks up. Put in his time in Nam, but mostly staging shit from Camp Hansen for Third Division. Could have been some blank spots there. Maybe over the line with the spooks. Our boy is in and out of Washington from time to time, can't tell who with, then he winds up in a fucking Ordnance Maintenance Company at Camp Pendleton. A fucking Ordnance Maintenance Company! After all the other shit. Can you figure that? Must have fucked one of the JCS wives."

"Marines do funny things."

Mitch drank some more and sat shaking his head.

"And here he is fucking around with a blue IG."

"Not to mention spending his leave time sitting in the Mojave for our benefit."

"Not to mention that."

They sat for a long time. They finished the beer. Ram looked up at Mitch. "What do you have working?"

"I don't like these guys, bro. They're out of place. I told Freddie to go back in. Told him to lift some prints if he could, from papers, coffee cups, a tape dispenser, the truck if it gets safe. Told him to get some voice tapes, too. Good ones. Maybe fuck up the air conditioner in the office, leave it turned off and drop in a VOX recorder. Get a voice we can recognize if we hear it somewhere down the line. And try to get a lead on the colonel's health or dental records. He might have to get some treatment one of these days. It might be a good idea to have Freddie drop a little caustic in the mystery colonel's coffee, burn his fucking gums a bit. That would give the dental tech a shot at the record."

"Just be sure there's no line to us. Freddie is on his own. He'll get paid for it."

"Thanks, bro. I bet I already thought of that."

"Just being careful."

"Fuck."

Ram got up and followed Mitch out of the room. They walked into the kitchen. On the front of the refrigerator was a note impaled on a steak knife. The knife was driven right through the textured green metal of the door.

"Jesus, look at that, bro."

Ram went over and pulled the knife out of the metal.

"What does it say?" asked Mitch.

"It says, 'You are a son of a bitch.'"

"Why would she say something like that about you?"

Ram looked at the note again. "What makes you think it's for me?"

"No reason for her to be pissed at me, bro. I hardly know the lady."

21

Atlantic City

He didn't care for Atlantic City. No feel. No space.
That was the big thing. No space. No space at the
tables. No space to wander outside the casinos. No
sense of the Big Empty . . . of the desert that floated
the city of Las Vegas away from reality. You couldn't
build another Las Vegas without going to Texas or
Alaska. Wouldn't be the same.

Kevin wandered through the noise and elbows of
the Showboat Casino. The inside pockets of his
denim sports jacket were puffed with one hundred
thousand in twenties. In the side pockets of his yellow pants he carried the lean hundred-dollar bundles.
Forty thousand dollars' worth. Twenty thousand to
the inch. Most of what was left in the box. The pants
pockets felt strangely vacant.

He kept turning the memories of Mako in his
mind. He still couldn't digest the whole thing. It distracted him. It distracted him a great deal.

"Now a couple of other items," he remembered his words to her. "Don't gamble when you have to win."

And here he was.

"Don't gamble when you're tired," he told her. "Don't gamble when you're distracted. Don't gamble if you need to win. Don't gamble when you've had too much to drink.

"Got all that?" he had said.

"Got it," she had replied. She got it, all right.

Nuts!

So here he was. He needed to win. He was tired. He was distracted. But he hadn't had too much to drink. Might as well go for the sweep. He looked around for the lounge. The vibes weren't right to gamble anyway.

When the toga-clad waitress brought him the second martini, he reached into his jacket pocket to fish out his wallet. As he did so, the rubber band on a clump of twenties snagged on the edge of his wallet and the bundle fell to the carpet. In the dim light, he didn't see it fall.

"Sir, I think you dropped something."

The cute red-haired waitress balanced her tray in her free hand and stooped to retrieve his money. She looked at the bundle as she straightened up and laughed as she returned it to him.

"Hey, big fella. If you need a date all you've got to do is ask. You don't have to troll."

She laughed again and patted Kevin on the head. She left before he could say anything.

Kevin took the money, stared at it, then put it back in his pocket. He realized it wouldn't be a bad idea to start thinking any time now.

He finished his drink and signaled for one more. He wanted an excuse to get the waitress back to his table. When she delivered the third martini, Kevin passed her a hundred-dollar bill.

"Oh, my," she said.

Kevin placed the martini he had carried away from the lounge on the marble surface of the main cashier's cage. The smooth rock felt solid and cold. He exchanged the tacky bundles of twenties for dignified hundreds and tipped the bored lady who counted the money forty dollars. "Thank you, my good woman."

"Any time," she replied. She picked up the forty-dollar tip and put it in a pocket in her dress. She was bored again and looked away.

Kevin portaged his drink away from the cage toward the scripted neon buffet sign at the far end of the casino. He stopped to drain the martini, but mainly to feel if anything was talking to him . . . luck or God or something like that. Not yet.

He aborted the buffet idea and veered toward the lounge instead to procure another martini from his only friend so far in Atlantic City. It felt good to liberate olives from icy juniper oppression.

Could it be that he was getting drunk?

As he neared the lounge, he froze for a moment on one leg. Some people from Iowa stopped to look at him. He stayed still. No. Not yet. No vibrations at all. He smiled at the Iowas. He went into the lounge.

His friend was gone. The pretty red hair was gone.

Fiddlesticks.

He sat down anyway. A blonde girl with a pink face came to serve him. She had resplendent, obtrusive breasts, three quarters of which she willfully displayed as she bent to take his order. She smiled and seemed very solicitous. Somewhere, in the outback of Kevin's wavering mind, the connection was made that red had talked to blonde. *That's okay,* he thought. *That's okay.* He didn't at all begrudge working girls their obvious conspiracy. Conspiracy was what made the game so curious.

Two more martinis and a twenty-dollar tip.

He wandered over to watch the action at the crap tables. The dice looked slow and heavy. Nothing there.

He watched the roulette wheel. Pretty game. Round and round. Clickety-click. Big stacks moving over the smooth felt. No direction.

Off to the blackjack tables. The numbers were too much. Adding. Remembering. Out of the question.

He meandered through the colorful casino crowd, passed by banks of clanking slot machines, and stopped to watch some Canadians play the big Money Wheel. The four couples were together on some sort of junket. They had big junket badges on their chests. They were from Montreal. The excited group made a fearsome crescendo of noise as the big wheel rotated to its usual agonizing stop between the big payoff numbers.

Kevin fell in with all the excitement. The martinis spun through his system like that big wheel. Kevin found himself smiling, then laughing, then yelling with everyone else as the massive wheel spun in ponderous rotations to magnificent decisions. It was hypnotic, a jubilee. He knew the happy players were bucking some of the worst odds in the house, twenty percent or more, but it looked like it was worth it. He thought of the tight-jawed craps player fighting the tables for a minor 1.41 percent but betting too much money, and he wondered who was smarter.

Kevin was swept into the action of the wheel. He put a few of his own twenties on the one-dollar sec-

tion. The sum was too ostentatious for the junke-
teers. Some of the Canadians looked at him. He realized his mistake, so he cut his bet back to five
dollars. Folks didn't have quite as much fun when
they were made to look like pikers.

Kevin was hoping that the wheel man would give
the group some numbers. He had watched one night
in Las Vegas as two wheel operators practiced hitting
numbers. He had been amazed by their skill. It made
him sad. He didn't think the casinos needed that sort
of malarkey, not when they had twenty percent on
the players to start. He put that thought away also.
He was having too much fun.

One of the bubbly Canadian ladies put a dollar
down on the flag space. Forty to one. Fat chance. It
hit. Good Lord! Up and down and up and down she
went. Howl! Yell! Hoot! Kevin noticed that even the
grizzled wheel operator had a smile. Glad for the
excitement. A Money Wheel never gets much play.
Normally just a quiet station, a lonely old dealer next
to the glassed numbers.

Kevin left the table. He toked the dealer a ten-
spot. He would have toked him more, but it only
would have confused the Canadians. He smiled at the
old bear. He knew those aged muscles could have left
that flag at nine o'clock. Cold.

He checked in and went up to the room. He
stretched out on the big bed. A nice room. It felt
good to get his shoes off. The martinis seemed in
peaceful coexistence with his soul, and he indulged
the pleasant feeling of lightness that seeped through
his brain as he settled into the big softness. Nice.
Very nice. He pondered for a time on the rejuvenat-
ing effect the huge casinos had on him. He mulled it
over to no conclusion.

He fell asleep.

At three o'clock in the morning his toes got too cold, and he woke up. He felt new and strong. It took a few moments for him to remember where he was. He rolled to one side of the bed, grabbed the edge of the fluffy white comforter, and rolled back to the other side, winding himself up in the quilted material. He stayed still in the big tube of blanket while he reconstructed things and got his toes warm. Mako. The driving. Martinis. And the casino. He completed the orientation. He conjured up a big Reuben sandwich, grilled and hot, lots of steamy kraut, French fries on the side. A dill pickle. And flows of thick ketchup to smear on everything. His stomach made believe it was empty and produced a rumble.

After ten minutes he got up and took the elevator down to the casino. He went to the lounge first. To get one Bloody Mary. He enjoyed a Bloody Mary after getting up from a nap. The spicy taste got him awake and moving. He was having a lot of trouble getting the Reuben out of his mind. He knew he could get one in the coffee shop; he had peeked at the menu earlier.

He sat down in the deserted lounge. The waitress came over to his table with an out-of-place energy for that time of night. She wasn't pretty. Graveyard shift.

"Good day, sir. What are we having this morning?"

Kevin didn't like the "we" business right off. He did not like it at all. "We are going to have a Bloody Mary."

"One Bloody Mary. Hot?"

"Not too."

"I'll bring Tabasco and bitters on the side, honey."

"We would appreciate that. We thank you." He was slightly ashamed of himself.

It was an excellent drink. He finished it quickly, not because he was in a hurry to go anywhere, but because it was so good. As he worked with consummate care around the lime slice, trying to draw the last vestige of pepper grain from the bottom of the glass into his small cocktail straw, he noticed two men enter the lounge from the strong light of the casino.

The men were Puerto Rican, young, twenty-five. They talked in a radiant Latin frenzy. Hands flying.

"Fuck'n assHOLES."

"Assholes is RIGHT. Fuck'n hitless WONDERS. Fuck'n screwed up, USEless motherFUCKers."

They crashed down into some chairs. One yelled into the dim light at the "we" person. "TWO CORONAS, LADY."

"Twenty fuck'n BUCKS, man. One fuck'n SINGLE, we got TWENTY MOTHERFUCK'N BUCKS. FUCK."

"Fuck'n story of my fuck'n LIFE, man."

Kevin chased a few more pepper grains. He almost had them all captured.

"How do you fuck'n figure it, Angelo? Best fuck'n bats in the fuck'n National fuck'n League and the fuck'n motherFUCKS can't get a motherfuck'n SINGLE. Against fuck'n San Diego, too."

"So, Roberto, it's just one of those fuck'n nights. Padres can't lose. Padres' time to win, is all."

Kevin nailed the last grain of pepper. He leaned back in his chair and looked at the ceiling with its sparkling chips of light. He smiled.

He headed for the pit. He was enthused. A fine omen, indeed, but he wasn't all that sure of God's relationship with Puerto Ricans. It might be a trick.

He stopped at the center table. A number of players

were gathered there, ignoring the fact that sunrise was racing across the gray ocean toward their pink casino. Kevin looked at the nametag on the dealer directly across from him. The tag said "Louis" . . . the same name as his little dealer buddy at the Aladdin in Vegas. That did it.

"My name is Kevin, boys. I'm a shooter."

The padre was hot.

"My man, my man," howled Louis. The dice had spun to a stop with eleven showing.

"Yo, eleven! Eleven! Pay the yo's, the line, and the boys," barked the stick. He popped an elbow into Kevin's rib cage. "And pay my wife's cruddy alimony while you're at it."

The table was starting to boil. It had been fifteen minutes since Kevin had moved into position next to the stick. Seven straight passes. He was throwing heat. On the last roll, a come-out roll, he had placed a black chip for himself and one for the dealers on number eleven. When the eleven came home at fifteen for one, the dealers were looking at a fifteen-hundred-dollar transfusion into their toke box. Everyone was on the come. Not a "don't" player in sight. None, that is, with the exception of the house in the persons of the box man, the floor man, and the pit boss, who were halfheartedly trying to make like they were excited for everybody. In a way, they were excited. Big Kevin and a high roller from Cleveland, down on the right corner, were into the house for sixty-seven grand, and the roll wasn't over yet. Both Kevin and Cleveland were now working with pink five-hundred-dollar chips. Kevin had massed a sloppy pile of green, black, and pink to go with his four inches of five-dollar reds. He used the reds to tip the great creamy-breasted drink waitress when she brought him another scotch and water, a not infrequent occurrence. The dealers in this situation had to be careful not to get too carried away since they were salaried by the house, and the house was taking it directly in the shorts. The box man was past the stage of showing testiness toward the dealers and players. He sat there, glum, morose, his iridescent lavender necktie growing tighter by the minute, resigned to letting the dice run their course. It was "his" table, and, with voodoo casino illogic, the pit powers would blame the loss on him. Kevin, even in his passion, was mindful of these things. Only the dealers shared in the tokes, and there wasn't anything he could do to cheer up the box. Kevin didn't mind seeing people lose, but he had a soft spot for the gloomy fellow caught between hierarchy and the sinning multitude. It reminded him a lot of the priesthood.

Louis paid the winners on his end of the table, and lastly piled up the fifteen black chips representing the bet made "for the boys" inside the eleven box. He straightened up, clapped his hands once, then leaned back down to the stack and slid it over in front of the box man. The box man looked at Kevin for a moment, picked up the chips, then inserted them, one by one, into the dealer's toke box bolted to the table beside him. Kevin detected the hint of a grudging smile flicker at one corner of the box man's mouth. *Aha, you old grinch,* thought Kevin, *you do remember how it was.*

"The dealers are down and thank you, Mr. K.," heartily from the stick.

The dice were pushed back in front of Kevin. They rode on the front of the thin wooden cane like little bubbles of electricity.

"All bets down. We're a-coming out again," sang the stick. He glowed with new enthusiasm.

"I've got five hundred they do," said Kevin, "and the boys are on the line for twenty-five."

He dropped a pink chip on the pass line. He placed a green chip next to it for the dealers. Thou shalt tip.

He took up the dice. Clickety-click.

"Come on, little ones, come home to father. Work!"

He threw . . .

The stick rumbled the result. "Four. A two and a two. The point is four."

"Odds, Mr. K., odds." Chips moving.

"All right, ladies, the point's four. Any hard ways bets? Let's not forget that easy money in the middle."

Kevin squinted in the direction of the four.

"What do I have on the four, Louis? Just move it over to the five."

Things were hot, and Kevin, like all streak bettors, began to place chips directly on numbers that weren't the point number. He knew the payoff odds weren't quite as good, but one had to pay for privilege in this world. A streak was a streak. It was how God worked.

The place boxes were filling with chips.

"Gotcha covered, Mr. K., gotcha covered. To the five. I'm taking care of you, my man." Then yelling, "Aren't I taking care of this man?" to no one and everyone. The crew was charged. A hot hand with tippers. Salvation!

"Here we go, folks. We need a four. Make that four, shooter."

Clickety-click . . .

No more room at the table. The crowd, three deep

and growing, buzzed in back of the players. Creamy-tits was fighting her way through the lookers with a load of drinks. She was working hard; tips were flying. Her tips were flying.

The other players rooted him on.

"Come on, shooter, keep it going!"

"Do it, big man, do it."

"Keep 'em hot, big Kevin, keep 'em hot."

Kevin scooped up the cubes in his right hand and checked the table. He had all the numbers except the ten. "Buy the ten for five hundred, Louis." He flipped a pink disk at the ten with his left hand. He flipped Louis a green chip to cover the vig.

"We got a deal, Mr. K."

Rattle, rattle. Clickety-click.

"Work!" . . .

"Five, five . . . no field five."

Everybody cheered; everybody was on the five, especially Cleveland, whose heavy play involved only the five and the nine. He had placed both numbers for three thousand each, and he had managed a come bet on the five for a thousand, with double odds. Kevin's five roll had just made Cleveland eighty-two hundred dollars. Cleveland glowed, tense, happy, and startled all at once.

"We got us a shooter!" yahooed the stick.

The sound rolled around the table. The dealers operated all out, paying the full rail. The stick and the box double-checked the payouts, occasionally picking up small errors; sometimes, even, in the player's favor. The floor man signaled the pit boss for a fill. The box was running low on chips. Commotion up and down the rail. Noise. Excitement. Kevin felt himself swelling up to engulf the whole table and all the players. It was one of those special times.

"Ready, folks? We got a point of four, I say again, a point of four. Now let's get some hard-way action. People, you know it's going to happen!"

"Roll 'em, big fella."

"Yo, Kevin, bring it home."

"Take your time. Keep 'em on the table."

"Be there, mister. Please be there."

"Just one more time, Kevin, one more time!"

Clickety-click.

"Work!"

The stick's first call was drowned out in the roar. The second time he turned up the volume, but it wasn't all that necessary: "Four! A winner four . . . the hard way!" yielding to the noise. No need to talk this game up.

The table was rocking. The four winner paid off the double odds at two to one. Kevin had turned the number into a little gold mine for the players. The noise drilled through the casino, and many a gambler turned to look, some with amusement, some with curiosity, but most with sharp envy, in the direction of the joyful mayhem at craps table number three.

Kevin had been a player for five years. He had been a party to runs like this, and he knew it would stop with a crunching disappointment in a few rolls; but this hand would be a winner. He didn't like the dynamics of losing. He loved to walk away when the others couldn't.

"Kevin, Kevin, you had the ten for five hundred. I'll press you up to a thousand."

He flashed a thumbs-up at Louis. "Right on, my man. That's the game."

The stick bubbled the dice back toward Kevin.

"We're coming out, folks. Coming out with a new

point. Hard ways are off unless you call 'em working," shouted the stick through the din.

"Working."

"Off."

"Off."

"Off."

"I'm working. I'm working on the eight."

"Working on the hard six. That's my dime. No, there. That's it, right."

"Off."

The stick dropped away from the dice, and the big hot shooter picked up the cubes.

"Watch those hands," yelled the stick to the far end. "Watch your hands! Coming out!"

Rattle, rattle. Clickety-click . . .

"Seven! Seven winner. Pay the line!"

Chips crackled down onto the felt as the dealers paid the line. Kevin picked up the two newly captured pinks, and let the first two ride.

"Coming out. Watch the hands. Coming out!"

Clickety-click.

"Hustle on home, mama; father's waiting. Work!"

"Seven. A winner seven!" Roar! Roar! "Pay the do's."

Smack, crackle, pop.

"Kevin! Kevin! Kevin!" began the table chant.

Clickety-click . . . Roar!

"Yo! Eleven! Pay the line."

Again the rolling cheer crested through the players and the lookers. The table had become a green island buffeted on three sides by waves of animated casino creatures. The intensity of the innermost wave radiated outward, and its effect was felt all the way across the casino to the clerks at the hotel reservations desks. It was as though the casino had become a beef steer fallen into some South American river and the piranha had found its throat, the throat that was table number three.

Kevin continued rolling, pass after pass.

Finally it stopped.

On a point of five, one die kicked off the cushion, careened off a stack of line chips, and stopped with a three showing. The other die ran like a top back to the middle of the table, where it spun madly on one corner for six seconds before twirling to a stop with a four laughing back at the players. Twenty-two passes. Thirty-nine minutes. So many delicious numbers. The players shook off the seven-out and applauded Kevin, the dice, each other, and life in general. Two players left the rail at once. Kevin stayed for six more rolls. An elderly lady inherited the dice, but they just chopped back and forth for her. She looked afraid to roll. Kevin was a hard act to follow. He made a chip estimate . . . up one hundred and thirty thousand. Cleveland had taken off eighty grand, but was still at the rail betting heavily; the casino would get some back, maybe all of it. That frantic hand cost the casino a quarter million. And it could have been much worse had it been a high-roller weekend.

Kevin cashed out and walked. He walked away when the others couldn't. He preserved his win.

He looked in the eye of greed and he spit.

Mr. Big.

22

Red Meat

Varki looked out over the restless audience to the far corners of the darkened hall. His eyes drilled into the dim shadows at the back limits behind the farthest row of seats. Looking for the government face. The fed face. He knew it was there. Anyone who spoke these days on the subjects of tax resistance, intrusive government, or race relations knew the face. If not the face exactly, then the look. Or the too-unobtrusive jacket. Or the suit that was too appropriate to be appropriate. Or the Ford Taurus in the parking lot. Out on the periphery. With the three-inch circle in the road dust on the trunk edge from the portable antenna base.

They should know his mind by now.

Occasionally he would try to shape his words during the talks, or during the questioning afterward, to debate the face's silent premise, to recruit the agent away from his automatic world of mercenary objectivity . . . using a phrase, an idea, an echo of the complaint that nibbled away at the center of bureaucratic conscience. With his keen eyes he would catch a shifting of feet, a scratch at the collar, a suddenly focused look. Working that face was more challenging than working the minds of his usual listeners, rebels whose souls were predigested for him by their own frustration. At times, Varki could recognize in that face at the back of the hall a fleeting shadow of question.

But the folks, the good ol' boys. And good ol' girls. Varki loved them. Out there listening like so many wild children. Their addictive need for freedom sending them, of its natural consequence, off in all directions at once; sending them chasing after their free ideas; scampering at random across the dry rows of restraint, convention, and comfort; ever-impossible to muster in a philosophical straight line. Radicals, atheists, libertarians, anarchists, conservatives, freemasons, hermits, constitutionalists, freethinkers, left-handers, ranchers, whores, gamblers, libertines, hunters, panthers, horse traders, and survivalists. A panoply of obstinate nonacceptance. Like a vivid, disorderly, vital field of wildflowers. And weeds. With one common love, the sun of freedom.

Doomed to disunion by social genetics.

Except in one area.

"Don't push me."

Varki had kept to the loose schedule of meetings as the time drew near. The thing was now of itself. He hadn't thought much about his own relative vulnerability. He just wanted to slap the system hard. To make it back up. To make it realize there was a limit. To let it know that citizens could still think, could still act, could still care about something other than their *TV Guide* and a full stomach. He had faith in people.

He simply didn't believe the fighters were gone.

"Mr. Varki, you preach against big government, against the efforts of good men to run a big country. But the roads have to be built. Schools are needed. The country needs an army to defend it. These things have to be paid for. You can't tell me different. It's called reality, mister. I think your case is weak, paranoid. Your talk is disruptive and dangerous. Why don't you try to solve some of the problems by working with the system? We can vote, pal. Or isn't that exciting enough for you?"

Varki looked out into the face of the man who stood in the audience, a brave man to voice such opinions in the midst of those disinclined to have their balloons pricked by pins of reason. Varki admired the man silently from the podium, and he allowed the anticipation to build after the smattering of boos and hisses died away.

Varki took a walk to the edge of the stage, lips pursed, hands across his chest, reflecting. He regained the podium. He leaned forward, close to the mike. He waited. He leveled his gaze at the man. He spoke.

"Sir, you are slime."

Some laughter and a few cheers played through the air above the audience. Some people applauded.

Varki stared hard at the questioner. The man was still standing; he looked a bit rattled, but resolute.

"You, sir, are slime." Varki paused. "Slime." He said the word like it was soft grease.

The man stood there. Alone. A few more laughs. But no cheers this time.

Varki broke off from the man and trained his eyes

on the assembled. He locked up with many of the eyes that looked back, piercing into them with his optic fire. He wrinkled his lip; the hint of a sneer played there.

"You're slime. All of you out there. You're ALL slime."

It was quiet now. He said it one more time.

"Slime."

The man who had spoken before, no longer feeling compelled to stand alone, slowly sat back down.

Varki let the silence deepen. He looked down at a folder that lay open on the podium.

"Let me quote the words of an agent working in the Collections Division of the IRS. This is a direct quote, from a recent interview. It goes like this: 'For me, the genuine and destructive part of my job is the way we all started thinking about the public. This incredible attitude is best caught in the single word we often use when referring to the public. That word is "slime." ' End of quotation."

He paused, walked off a few steps, then stopped. He looked down at the people. He slowly put his hands into his pockets and stood there.

"Slime." He said it softly, without the mike.

He walked back to the podium.

"Slime!" Forcefully through the speakers.

He straightened up.

"Note the plural 'we' and 'all.' These words are those of an agent from the IRS southwestern region. Do you wonder at the attitude, the mind-set that might be capable of generating such words? I wonder at it. An interesting quote, isn't it?"

He held aloft the sheath containing newspapers and reprints of reference material. With upraised arm, he moved the bundle in a slow arc above his head. "The *San Jose Mercury-News*, the *Eugene Register-Guard*, Associated Press releases, IRS proceedings transcripts. I want to share some of this with you."

He put the folder back on the podium and looked in the direction of the man who was now seated. He smiled, and his eyes went soft. "But first I would say something to our friend here. You're a good man, neighbor. You have an opinion, you have thoughts on this business. And you defended your opinion in a hostile environment. That is the most important thing that has happened here so far tonight."

He swept the assembly with kinder eyes.

"People, that's what this is about. Don't hide your conclusions, don't bury your ideas. Test them against other ideas. Refine them. Polish them. Believe in them. Act on them. That is what all this biology is for, why all this brain, muscle, and heart is alive. It is what memory and history and pain and love are saying to us."

He shook his head. It seemed he was looking at each of them in the same moment.

"A free nation can't take a generation off, can't skip out on the responsibility of maintaining the fiscal morality that comes with freedom. We can't coast through time making excuses, leaving our political bills unpaid.

"Remember this: The greatest glory of freeborn people is to transmit that freedom to their children."

He waited, cocked his head slightly.

"Slime? Are you listening, slime? You've read the tax codes. Children pay taxes now. Your children. Your slime? Somehow that doesn't sound right."

His attention went back to the papers.

"1987. Shannon Burns. Ten years old, fourth

grade, San Jose, California. Collected aluminum cans. Managed to save $694 in her savings account over the years. Her father, unemployed, owed the IRS back taxes of $1,000. The IRS seizes Shannon's account.

"Carmin Fisher, nine, saves pennies since age three. Her grandfather is alleged to owe back taxes; his name, with hers, is on the account. The IRS seizes Carmin's account. All $70.76 of it. In July 1987. $70.76.

"Same year. Chesapeake, Virginia. Garry D. Keffer. Age twelve. $10.35."

He waited again, held up the papers.

"$10.35." Paused. "Slime?"

The quiet was charged.

He looked at them.

"Come see these for yourself. But I know many of you don't have to . . . you already know.

"Bad men? Born to this madness?"

He leaned forward.

"I don't think so. Just people. But people changed by a system, by a bureaucracy that gets big enough to finally generate its own values. Big enough to begin serving itself, to consider its own survival needs first. Individuals in such an order eventually perceive that the more power the system gathers, so much more will be the security of each part. They begin to serve the monster rather than the people."

He straightened and looked down.

"Why do I talk only of the IRS? Aren't there other ponderous, insensate, self-serving bureaucracies feasting on the body America? You bet! You know the numbers, the names. Big. More wasteful. More inefficient. More insulated. Even more unreasoning."

And he looked up sharply at them.

"But keep this in mind. The IRS is the tentacle that feeds all the others. It is the required arm, unique in its brazen unaccountability. As it functions today, it is critical in the pillage of liberty.

"From 1915 to 1988, the population of the country increased two and a half times. In that same span, individual income taxes went from $28 million paid to the government to a staggering $400 billion. That, good people, is a factor of over fourteen thousand! In 1990 your quiet generosity yielded up more than $465 billion. How does it happen? Complacency! Get the population to accept the concept of government as benevolent warden. The Santa Claus factor.

"The numbers should scare the hell out of you! Now, add on the Social Security tax. $770 million in 1937, $360 billion in 1990! Remember . . . the population has grown less than three times since 1915!

"But there's something more ominous still. The folks in the striped suits are increasing spending even faster than they are raising taxes each year. That translates to interest payments and more debt. In 1991, those interest payments came to $200 billion. Interest only, people, interest only! That is money twice wasted because it was nonproductive money, money that could have been put to work somewhere else.

"Can we afford this insanity much longer?"

He made the hard look go away.

"We could stand around here all night telling each other horror stories, folks. The IRS encourages that. People who are afraid overpay; better safe than sorry, we think. The average person has been made to acknowledge the reality of tax court, a place where one must prove innocence to win. Not to prove guilt, to prove innocence, to prove the absence of intent. A difficult proposition at best. At times, impossible. That is why every reasoning justice system does the opposite. It would be insane to do otherwise."

He drank from the water glass at his right hand.

"But most of you know these things, don't you? That may be why you are here. You can't really believe what has happened, what is happening. You want someone to tell you it's a strange dream, to tell you what to do . . . or to tell you not to do what you'd like to do."

He sipped from the glass again. He put down the glass and smiled at them.

"I think something will happen, sooner or later. When it does, make yourselves heard."

He paused.

"Even slime has its limits."

The talk ranged back and forth, but always returned to the theme of individual freedom. Varki took questions at the end of the hour. He liked the give-and-take in the time after he talked. It was then that bold ideas would take flight from shy runways. Many, of course, had their own narrow agendas, but Varki was good at sidestepping the Recruiters from Hell. He enjoyed their commitment, and he wondered where some of them went to escape the social consequences of their thoughts. But there were certain questions that were important to his theme.

"Mr. Varki. Who's really running the country? I hear talk of a Trilateral Commission. Set up by a Rockefeller. That true?"

"It's true, my friend. By Mr. David Rockefeller. And there's also the Council on Foreign Relations. You might take a long look at that outfit one day. But you risk making a very serious mistake. Why shouldn't there be a Trilateral Commission or something like it? It seems reasonable to build a coalition of wealth and power. The potential for abuse is real, but those people surely have a stake in freedom and free enterprise. Why go off on a hunt for mystery people to accuse? What more abuse of power do you need than what's right in front of you? The beast is bureaucracy! Phantom government? Sure, there's a phantom government. But it forms in the very real soul of bureaucracy. These damn monsters actually think! They are alive! There's your phantom! The idea seems invalid only because of our egos, because we can't digest the premise. The beast generates the Commission for its own good. The beast generates the 'phantom government' for its own survival. It is not the other way around!"

"I don't understand."

"Think on it, my friend. Think about the cell in your body, the leaf on the tree, the tiny coral animal adrift in the ocean soup. Think how these units of life grow to create something so different from its parts. Look at the template that is right before your eyes in nature. Then, for one shining moment, put human ego aside and glimpse the shape of the thing. Could it be that we are like those cells, those leaves?"

"Does it stop?" one asked.

"It can be changed. It is still the collection of our souls. But we must acknowledge the thing first. We must know that it is. We must see it to control it."

"Mr. Varki, are you saying there could be revolution?"

"Miss, you are already in a moral revolution. And it's you younger people who have the most at stake. You are being made to feel guilty . . . guilty of not 'supporting' your government, of not paying your share, of not giving to your homeless, your poor, your lazy. You are being made to feel guilty by a system that knows how much it can harvest for itself when the power of guilt is unleashed at your hopes in the name of sharing. Altruism ... that great mystic philosophy of Kant that tried and still tries to bury reason. That sprawling, mindless body of nonlogic that reached its purest political form in Soviet Russia and Nazi Germany. Sacrifice everything for the state, for the fatherland. The moral imperative.

"Do you know where real shame lies? It lies not in our refusing to sacrifice to the beast and its feeders. It lies in our letting the great system of capitalism come to bankruptcy. It lies in not having the guts and energy to stand up to these resource-eating bureaucracies.

"Reject this feeding monster. Start by getting rid of the guilt he has planted in your heart ... the guilt that throttles a person from saying she is seeking her own happiness, the guilt that crawls over the businessman when he admits he wants to make a profit, the guilt that tries to make thinking citizens feel selfish when claiming their constitutional rights in the face of 'national' consensus.

"Americans are unique. They have an inborn sense of trust. But when this good faith is seen to be betrayed, when trust is raped, beware! The American does not revolt in hope of finding a better master."

He moved to leave. He turned to them one more time.

"Can you see what's happening? Can you see how the system tries to wall us off from one another, how it tries to strangle initiative? How the beast builds tight rooms to keep us silent and divided? How it tempts us with the sweet promise of unearned security? How it threatens us with false enemies? It builds these dark rooms with laws. With endless, numbing laws. With mindless regulations. With corrosive taxes.

With a suckling mire of red tape that kills creative energy and anesthetizes hope. These rooms, these dark rooms. These are the rooms we die in.

"And this thing can't be elbowed gently. If you only stick your head up to complain, you'll get stomped."

He smiled, picked up his papers. "There are more than a few tax protesters sitting in jail tonight because they underestimated the system's ability to protect itself. You don't turn a mad dog with words. You give it one hundred percent or you fail. You take up the knife, go in hard, and slice!"

After speaking, Varki went to an office building two blocks from the meeting hall. In the privacy of a small room he opened a black oblong case that contained a high-security telephone scrambler. He tucked the handset into the pads, secured it with the backing rubbers, and took up the secondary handset.

"Are you ready?" said Varki.

"We're ready," came Jesse's reply, warped by circuits.

"The time is good?" Varki asked.

"It's good. We go at 1615 Eastern Daylight Time. That engages the East Coast offices before quitting time and catches the western sites just after the noon break."

Varki paused, inhaled slowly. There was power in the moment. He spoke. "Red Meat."

"Red Meat," came the reply.

It was under way.

23

Why

"Looks like he wants to talk to us, bro."

Ram racked the heavy bar onto the hooked rests of the weight bench. The posts clanked and groaned as the burden pressed down. Ram's stomach muscles tightened and rolled his hard body forward into a sitting position on the edge of the sweat-darkened leather. He toweled his face as Mitch popped a beer can in his direction. The cold mist drifted onto the heated skin. Annoying.

"How?"

"Pager. Looks like Mr. Secret is about to finally sun his nuts."

He knocked back half the beer.

Ram pulled the towel around his neck. His chest felt a deep relaxation build as the heat of the workout began to radiate through his body.

"What do you think?"

"I think it's our fuckin' colonel friend from Nellis, bro."

"Think you'll be able to match the voice on Freddie's tape?"

"No problem. The tape sounds like the voice we connected with last month. Can't be sure until we make this call tonight. I'll record it and print it if I have to. Bet I won't need to. Not if my memory's any good."

"Contract?" Ram asked. "A warm one?"

"Feels like it. Could be a citizen. A name, maybe. Or some political job. Lots of fuckin' cover. Too sneaky to be anything else. You're probably right about it being major coin. For once."

Ram stood up and wiped down the bench with the towel. He felt the unease and the excitement mix inside. The curiosity was strong. "Are you going to try to fake your way through Central Names and Addresses at PacTel this time?"

"Don't think it would do any good. CNA doesn't give out addresses anymore. Just names. Our boy probably hasn't used his own name since Karl Malden used cash."

"DPAC office?"

"Waste of time. This guy is on the move." Mitch drained the last of the beer. "Besides," he added, "we got what we need for now. We know he holes up at Nellis. We know who he is. We just don't know the why or the when. We get the when tonight. Maybe the why isn't important."

Ram looked at him.

Mitch shrugged. "Sometimes the why just gets in the way, bro."

24

Paper

Mitch and Ram sat in their rented van in the parking
lot at San Diego's Lindbergh Field. They were parked
next to a small tree that partially shaded the front half
of the vehicle. From their location in Lot Three they
had a clear view of the passenger access that served
the West Terminal. Mitch pushed back in the driver's
seat, exhaled a cloud of cigarette smoke out the open
window, and handed two sheets of paper to Ram.

"Here's your homework, bro."

Ram took the papers and began to read.

NAME: Rayburn Edmund Varki
PHYSICAL: 51-year-old WMA; 6 feet 1 inch; 185
   lbs.; gray hair; green eyes; muscular build;
   square face; thin features; no visible scars;

receding hairline; no bald spot; no physical deformities; wears glasses.

PHYSICAL (WEPS): Handgun, right; rifle/shotgun, left; dominant eye, left; ability: handgun/expert, shotgun/expert, rifle: N/OBS; handgun grip: two/cradle; offhand: N/OBS.

DRESS: Conservative/informal; medium black onyx ring (left), no other.

MEDICATIONS: None known.

INTELLIGENCE: IQ 150+

SOPHISTICATION: High.

PROFESSION: Terrorist; former teacher: college level, political science (ret.).

FAMILY: None.

EMOTIONAL: Even temperament; controlled.

SEXUAL HABITS: No aberrant observed; Eurasian female aide/sec.: Aixa Gordot, approx. 26 years, 5 feet 10 inches; black hair/hazel eyes; possible relationship; lives with; no further.

INTERESTS: Activist, political study/discussion; collecting (texts); publisher of political tracts; NRA; Libertarian (nonmember).

RECREATION: Ski; jog; hike; camp; shooting: skeet and target (short, competitive).

EATING HABITS: Moderate; health foods, will frequent stores selling; subj. not overweight; almonds, pecans, apricots, tea.

DRINKING HABITS: Wine, has extensive cellar; dinner liquors only; no beer.

SECURITY: Apparent multiple alarm (Idaho res.), no outside response contract, motion/IR circuit at res., grounds negative; does not carry visible; body armor inferred but not observed; constant personal guard, Loza Bustani, Tuareg/Algerian (see attached).

ECCENTRICITIES: Strong antiauthority; poss. subvers; will not travel air.

RELIGIOUS: Not observed.

PERS. ENEMIES: None observed.

OTHER: Travels surface only, private car, (1) black Ford Taurus, (2) silver over blue Colt Vista van; (1) and (2) Idaho plates; no stickers, no FM/CB aerials; does own driving; moderate to fast road speed; (1) and (2) stock models, no armor.

... Additional Person ...

NAME: Loza Bustani

PHYSICAL: 42-year-old Tuareg (Berber)/Algerian male; 5 feet 9 inches; 150 lbs.; black hair; brown eyes; slight build; wiry; thin face; elong/heavy features; 4" vert. scar (left cheek); 1" vert. scar (rt. upper lip).

PHYSICAL (WEPS): Handgun, right; rifle/shotgun, right; dominant eye, right; ability, expert all; handgun grip, one/two; offhand: yes/expert; other: knife, garrote, unarmed; level: N/OBS all; verified Hx munitions/explosives.

LANGUAGE: English, good; others: N/OBS.

DRESS: Conservative/informal; no jewelry.

ECCENTRICITIES: N/OBS.

OTHER: Threat level: professional/high; history: Middle East, Rhodesia, domestic implied; no domestic wants; no domestic record.

Ram looked up.

"Good paper. How much of this from the buyer?"

"All of it. This guy's better organized than most. A nice piece of work."

"Very nice. Did you get to see our man?"

Mitch looked out the window. There was a slight edge in his voice as he replied.

"Did not, bro. The phone contact gave me a motel room and a time. In Anaheim. It was a good secure drop. He reserved two adjoining rooms. Papers were passed under the locked door, the one between the rooms that makes them into a suite. We talked through the door. All the people specs are here on the paper. Plus those two pictures on the back. Everything else was verbal. I was told to leave first. He could see the freeway from the room so he could tell when I was out of the area. I couldn't play any games. Was tempted to bust through the damn door and tell the asshole his cover was fucked. Figured you'd be pissed, though."

He stopped, smiled, and blew some smoke in Ram's direction.

"No doubt about it," he added. "It was our lance colonel. Same voice that was on Freddie's tapes and on the phones."

"Money?"

"One hundred and twenty-five grand. In a duffle bag. Outside his door when I left. Another one-twenty-five a week after the hit. He delivers. Luggage locker at McCarran. If he's happy, maybe a little bonus."

"How does he want it done?"

Mitch looked at Ram. "Would you believe dropped from a plane?" He grinned at Ram, who looked up.

"A plane?"

Mitch nodded.

"Over the ocean? Chains? A Triad job?"

"Over the desert. Into the Nopah Range."

Ram shook his head.

"In daylight, too," Mitch added. "Scotch on the rocks. The Happy Hour special."

"Any reason?"

"Didn't give me any. But it's probable they got some eyes out there to make sure it goes down."

"He'll go down, all right."

"They also might want to get to the body in the future for some reason. For teeth, something like that. To show the man was taken out."

"Feds? Insurance?"

"Maybe."

"Has to be a touchy situation to do it this way."

"Terrorists carry big prices."

Ram read down the paper again. He shook his head. "The military connection gets me curious, Mitch. If it's a government thing, why not use their own boys? If the CIA can go after Castro and Brother King, why use us?"

"Our flyboy has to be operating on the outside, some sort of fringe player. He needs a tight cover; if the sunlight gets too bright, he loses his commission, no retirement goodies." Mitch grinned at Ram. "Bet our boy Varki knows we're coming, too."

"Could be why he keeps some muscle." He looked back at the paper. "This Bustani guy, you heard of him?"

"Hasn't worked the Southwest. Not for anyone we know. Has to be an independent with political icing. An edge specialist. A camel-fuckin' knife-thrower."

"Do we take out all three?"

"All three."

"Probably have to hit the others to get Mr. V. anyway. Special requests? Drop them into Mount St. Helens?"

"No. Just make sure the girl and the camel-fucker are well done."

"Where do we take them?"

"Buyer says we pop them in St. George. On the Utah border. Varki and friends are supposed to meet the buyer or some of his friends near the Skypark. That's St. George's airport on the mesa top. Varki has confirmed reservations for two nights. We take them there."

"How close to the airstrip?"

"Motel is at the strip. Two hundred yards."

"Convenient."

"Piece of cake. One road in. Couldn't draw it much better, bro. St. George is winter trade, skiing at Zion, motel won't be busy. I'll fly out tomorrow, check things over. Mouse will get a working room near Varki. He'll leave a van there. With body totes. I'll check the drop coordinates on the way back, see if everything fits."

"That your boy, Mitch?" Ram asked, looking across the parking lot toward the terminal.

Mitch followed his brother's gaze. "That's my boy." He got out and walked to the terminal where a dark, solid-looking Mexican stood by the curb. The two shook hands, said a few words, then came over to the van.

"Ram, this is Pisco."

25

Boom

At 1310 on 10 August, the largest concentration of C-4 within the city limits of Fresno, California, was located along the steel I-beams that supported the ceiling in the main administrative clearing room of the IRS Service Center for the Western Region. A polite cadre of three maintenance men had cleaned and replaced many of the overhead fluorescent light fixtures during the prior week by working through the lunch hours. Routine upkeep.

Neat runs of det cord stretched between the orderly blocks of C-4 in a dependable ring-main lay-out, a system in which det cord is looped back on itself to ensure the detonation wave approaches from both ends of the line. At 1312, most of the clerks and sorters had returned from lunch and were settling into Monday afternoon routine. The Fresno processing center had received 34.6 million pieces of mail in the past twelve months. Most of the part-time employees hired during the frantic days of March, April, and May had come and gone. A dozen empty desks used during the height of the tax rush lined the east wall. Thirty-two IRS workers sat in semiprivate cubes at their computers. Most tried not to think about the fact that it was Monday. A group of four people stood at a large window overlooking Butler Avenue, two stories below. Two were drinking coffee from stained mugs with frisky sayings on the sides. All four were from the Examination Division. At the far end of the space, near the abandoned desks, two men in suits from the Criminal Investigation Division were peering through files.

At 1314, Mildred Drew bent way over in her new swivel chair so she would be down near the ventilation intake on the floor at the side of her desk. She simply had to have one more cigarette. Her last nooner. She had maneuvered damn hard to get that spot near the air duct and intended to make the most of it before that crusty bitch supervisor shuffled everybody up again. It wasn't like the old days when a body could enjoy a smoke without getting the whole damn state of California in an uproar. In two more years she could tell the lot of them to go to hell. She snapped the wheel on her lighter. It didn't catch. She snapped it again. Still no light. She shook it hard a few times. "Damn thing, you better light this time." She thumbed the wheel hard. And was blown through two floors into the loading docks.

Part of the megablast, diverted horizontally due to the initial resistance of the floor, crushed into the group of four by the window, and they went across Butler Avenue as a unit and merged with the brokerage house of Covington, McManus, and Reed. One of the two coffee cups, with its frisky saying, blitzed into the window of Mr. Reed's office and stopped two inches short of midpoint in his brain. He was talking to Philadelphia at the time. If the explosives across the street had misfired for any reason, he would have heard a muffled blast over his phone line as the Office of the IRS Regional Commissioner went up with a roar in Philadelphia, three thousand miles away.

Most of the other employees, thirty-one to be exact, were blown, in bits and fragments, down through the first and second stories into the loading docks with Mildred. The exceptions were the two well-dressed gentlemen from the Criminal Investigation Division. One of them, a Mr. Xavier Gorman, named after the Spanish Jesuit missionary (1506–1552), was plastered against the front of the filing cabinet in which he was searching for evidence to obtain a criminal fraud indictment against one Orval Orlowitz of San Jose, California. The file cabinet was chin-high, and Mr. Gorman's head, meeting no significant resistance, took leave of Mr. Gorman's body. It would have cracked to pulp against the cinderblock wall, but was cushioned by a stack of black binders and a large copy of Reconstruction Finance Corporation proceedings involving the Jahncke Service Co. of New Orleans, 1936. The wayward head rebounded off the publications and tumbled across the surface of a still splintering desktop. It spun crazily off that desk, due in large part to Mr. Gorman's thick nose, onto the top of another desk, and landed in the open metal drawer of a third desk that was balanced on one corner leg. The third desk was one of the new steel kind. The head dropped into the drawer, the desk slammed back down on its four legs, and the door whipped shut. And locked itself.

Mr. Gorman's partner in the Criminal Investigation

Division, Mr. Rufus Rostenkowski, was simply blasted through the wall, relatively intact, into the men's restroom, where he impacted Tommy Treadway, the new janitor, at approximately ninety miles per hour. Mr. Treadway was putting cocaine lumps mixed with Vaseline into an unusual part of his body at the time. He had been extra careful not to let the small lumps break up; that way they would time-release like cold capsules, and the high would last a long time. He had to use the new route because his nose was a mess. The doctor said he'd lose his septum if he kept it up.

One interesting aspect of Mildred Drew's trip to the loading dock was not lost on Ellen Barton. Ellen was the supervisor whom Mildred disliked so much. Ellen was down on the first floor at the time of the blast. Directly below Mildred, in fact. As Mildred zipped her way through the boards and beams of the second floor, her left femur was peeled bare of flesh. Devoid of its meat and muscle, and now detached from Mildred's other parts, it lanced through the top of Ellen Barton's skull, cleaned out the contents of her neck, traversed her chest cavity, and cracked into Ellen's pelvis where it stopped. Thus did Mildred end their tedious relationship.

Houston, Texas. The Texas people didn't like C-4. They were old school, the kind who crimped blasting caps with their teeth, who purchased blasting sets with four-foot instead of six-foot leg-wire leads to save thirty cents. Plastique was for foreigners.

Running vertically through the three stories of work spaces in the Houston IRS office were three structural steel cylinders of generous proportion. The columns were three feet in diameter, hollow in the centers, with two-inch steel walls. Building regulations at the time required that inspection ports be installed so the interior surfaces of the tubes could be checked for corrosion. These ports were two feet wide and one foot high, and were located on the odd-numbered floors.

Two weeks ago, Buffy Muldoon had broken a fingernail trying to pick one of the inspection port bolts out of its hole in the cover. "Damn," she said.

"Now, girl," her father Roy had replied, "don't swear . . . say a prayer."

They worked in a storage room on the fifth floor. Their cover was that they were installing insulation in the interiors of the columns for energy-saving reasons. Union. EPA stuff.

They plugged and sealed the column with an inflatable bladder and resin. The resin set quickly in the humid space, and if anyone down in the IRS offices had leaned up against or touched the bile-yellow surface they probably would have called the fire department. Because of the heat-sinking properties of the big column, the temperature was back to normal in twenty minutes. They poured in a slurry of 34-0-0 ammonium nitrate presoaked with diesel oil. It took two hours to fill the big pipe to the midway point of the third floor. They took a break for lunch. They washed up and went across the street for pizza. Pepperoni and green chili peppers. Buffy's favorite.

After lunch, Buffy watched as Roy lashed up a neat bundle of 85 percent Hy-Drive. Thirty-eight half pound sticks. Buffy only half breathed. Hy-Drive was straight nitro dynamite.

Roy took two electric blasting caps from his sawdust pouch and cleaned them off gently. Two green and yellow wire leads sprouted from the rubber plug at the end of the narrow two-inch aluminum colored tubes. He took a stick of Hy-Drive and poked a hole into one end with the wooden pick on his Dynamic dynamite tool. He put one of the caps into the hole and after it was seated ran the wires along the body of the stick and half-hitched them so they held the blasting cap tightly in the hole on the end.

"Remember, girl, you can't be wrappin' fuse cord like this else'n it's gonna cut itself off when it burns. You only wrap electrics like this."

"Gotcha, Papa."

He picked up a second stick of Hy-Drive and pushed a diagonal hole into one side about halfway down. He was careful not to push his pick all the way through the stick and out the other side. He put the remaining blasting cap into the hole and wrapped its wires around the diameter of the stick.

"Don't hurt to side-cap one, girl."

He lashed the two capped charges into the main charge with heavy twine and lowered the whole assembly through the hatch down onto the surface of the half built ammonium nitrate plug. He carefully fed out the connecting wire as he lowered the charge so it wouldn't snag any protrusions inside the column.

For the next two hours they continued to pour ammonium nitrate slurry. At four o'clock they finished the plug and sealed it over with more resin. The nitrate plug now filled the column where it traversed the third-floor office space. After the resin had hardened, Buffy helped Roy lift a tractor battery onto a makeshift shelf inside the column at the fifth-floor level where they worked. Roy spliced the timer into the free end of the connecting wire, draped insulation wool over the whole mess, and bolted up the hatch.

On Sunday 9 August, shortly after twelve noon, Roy returned to the office building, showed his pass to the security guard, and went up to the fifth floor. He opened the hatch and moved some of the insulation to one side. He tested the charge on the tractor battery with a small voltmeter, then tested the circuit resistance with his new Sears ohmmeter. He hooked the battery drop wires into the circuit. He set the timer. He replaced the insulation once again, secured the hatch, and went away.

Houston, Texas . . . 10 August, 1510 hours (local)

Greg Marinari punched the long list of option trades on the transaction tape into his computer. The numbers flowed onto his video screen like disciplined snowflakes. The Fisher account was beginning to look like a blueprint for financial disaster. The transactions scrolled out a bloodbath of option losses. Greg felt sorry for Fisher. Bad enough not to have had it, but to have had it and lost it? That must hurt. Since the IRS had gained access to complete brokerage histories, the reality of the small day-traders was becoming painfully obvious. He dumped the file and leaned back in his chair. He stretched his arms over his head and thought of the kids. Last Saturday he had taken them down to Galveston to play on the beach. A super little trip. Matt and Paul kept him going all day. They played with the football in the surf for three hours. He smiled as he touched the bruise on his left thigh. Not a bad hit for a six-year-old.

Judy Appleton looked at the wall clock. Two more hours. Two more hours and she could get over to the Pelican. She and Bobby would kiss as she sat down at the table to share the hot fudge sundae he bought for them on every workday that ended in zero. The tenth, the twentieth, the thirtieth. A silly, sweet lover's promise. The kind of small thing that made so much difference. She had never been in love before.

At 1514 Greg got up from his desk to work the twinge out of his thigh. It didn't really hurt, but he

felt like moving around. He saw Judy Appleton looking up at the clock, and he smiled at her. He knew
about the sundaes. He walked over to the center of
the office and leaned his back against the big column
to scratch an itch between his shoulder blades. The
rough plaster felt good.

On the fifth floor, the gray plastic timer slowed its
lazy turning ever so slightly as the trip tab came into
contact with the switch release. For a small part of a
second, the release absorbed the growing push of the
spring and held fast. But, as the wheel drag dropped,
the full power of the coilspring began to bear on the
release. The spring torque built, and finally the switch
kicked over. The little wheel, victorious, ticked forward. The switch, in its new position, vibrated a bit as
the circuit closed and electricity moved. The black
tractor battery silently hurled its eager power into the
connecting wire. The new excitement ripped down
into the delicate cap filaments. Only a few microseconds
had passed. Inside the caps, the tiny bridge wires
heated up like little light bulbs, only faster. The wires,
embedded tightly in the heat-sensitive primer compound, reached and surpassed a critical temperature.
A quick flash jumped through the primer compound
and raced into the Hy-Drive. All the molecules
jumped at once. Like a bursting wave speeded up a
million times, the surge propagated outward through
the nitrate lattice. Packed into the steel, and with no
air gaps to jump, the nitrate was able to commit its
incredible energy to the outside world.

**New Orleans, Louisiana . . . 10 August,
1510 hours (local)**

District Director Hector Lafayette was going to
visit the troops. Show the flag. An expansive, blustery

man, Director Lafayette was the antithesis of the ashy federal bureaucrat. He shook hands, he laughed, he explained his mission to the common folk. It was known that he partook of dark rum on occasion, that he had a magnificent stash of Havanas, and that he was not averse to risking a dime or two on the chickens. He bubbled and cackled and kidded his fellow revenuers. He sweated into his shirts on cool days and he always smelled of shrimp and tobacco ... fresh shrimp and the finest tobacco.

The Director was wrestling off the bumptious effects of a wondrous Cajun crawfish salad, all spice and full of life. His lunching ritually devoured the better part of two hours; consuming was his vocation, work his relish.

As Hector strolled through the heat toward the New Orleans District Office, he acknowledged the friendly nods and greetings of the locals. He was a familiar character to the people who worked and hustled tourists in the sin-scented city. His passage evoked smiles and not a few shakes of the head as the incongruity of his effervescent persona battled with their preconceived vision of what a man in his capacity should be. He was a refreshing reminder of the fallibility of prejudice.

Hector prepared to cross the street and enter through the big double-glass doors of his domain, doors that every day swallowed and disgorged his faithful fiscal warriors in their endless quest for truth and hidden assets. He waited on the curb while a rusty pickup truck passed by trailing an oily cloud of blue smoke. Old Guondoulette it was, hauling a load of greens to the open market by the river. He noticed that the bed wasn't covered and the greens had taken on a brown, wilted look from the noonday sun. *Probably drunk already,* he thought. *Going to lose the whole load, too. All those greens going to wind up at the mission for sure.* He waved at the truck as he caught a glimpse of the driver's hand waving to him from the cab. He shook his head and smiled. He looked at his watch as he stepped off the curb. Quarter after three. Just about right. A quick visit with the troops, then an easy stroll over to Peppers for a dash of rum and Coke. *Life was okay. Damned straight.*

Hector crossed the street and was stepping up onto the curb in front of the big doors when all the air around him seemed to suck in toward the building. The thing lasted only a moment, but it was real. He felt his body lurch forward as though he was being inhaled by something. The "forward" business reversed itself immediately. A sharp blast crushed back at him from the building and tore all the clothing on the front of his body away and back toward the street.

Hector Lafayette had a very quick mind. He had been a good baseball player in his day. Batted .453 at LSU in his senior year. It was due to his good eyes. He could make the fastballs slow down to look like balloons. That was the secret of all good hitters. They could slow things down.

And his eyes were still good. He had been leaning forward and since he was a very solid man he was still standing upright as he watched half of one of the big glass doors spin out at him like a jagged Frisbee. It wheeled at him in slow motion because of his good baseball eyes. It came in a flat arc, spinning on a horizontal plane. He actually kept his eye on the leading edge of shining glass as it impacted his skin and sliced like a cleaver through the middle of his body, severing him completely in two. In fact, his cognitive capacity was so far above average that he actually received in his brain, as his head hit the road, the bizarre image of the lower half of his body standing there without the upper half.

Tampa, Florida . . . 10 August, 1610 hours (local)

A light rain was falling over most of Central Florida, which was unusual. Tampa seemed to either broil in hot sunlight or submerge beneath thick tropical downpours. A misty rain that only wet the streets made people look up at the sky, made them look at the water stains on the rock fronts of buildings, made them look at the small silver beads of moisture that gathered on their clothing. The little rain was pretty. It slowed things down and made the world softer. Perhaps that was why there wasn't much grousing when the second fire alarm in less than ten days sounded at the IRS office complex in Tampa at 4:11 P.M., although several groans of weak protest could be heard as they filed out of the spaces.

Once outside, the employees from the central office joined with the eight members of the visiting TCMP team down from Martinsburg. They lined up dutifully for a head count under the tree at the edge of parking section B, where they had gathered only last week when the alarm also went off.

Good-natured chatter flowed between the IRS people as they stood in the soft warm drizzle. It was exactly 4:15 P.M. At least they weren't any slower than last week in getting to the muster point. They stood in four loose, easy rows while Lester Nicklaus took the roll. Lester was the office fire warden. He was officious and took all the regulations and drills seriously. Even the atomic attack drills. Fortunately, they rarely did those anymore. Even Lester didn't like getting down under the desks with the rest of them on that dirty floor.

Lester completed the muster. He had been a little

short with the electricians for not having an explanation as to why the alarm went off last week. That probably explained this week's exercise. But everything had gone smoothly as usual. The only difference today was the blue delivery van parked right there in the middle of his muster area. And the soft rain. Weak as it was, it was making his muster sheet wet. He stuffed his fire warden's clipboard up under his new Slazenger sweater.

At 4:15 and eleven seconds, the blue van vaporized. A central core of three hundred pounds of fresh plastique surrounded by sixteen five-gallon jerrycans, alternately filled with gasoline and roofing nails, all mudpacked over with patio concrete, blossomed out in all directions in a bubble of death. The front axle of the van tore through the fourteen-inch trunk of the palm tree just about at ground level, and the big tree, instantly aflame, cartwheeled like a giant torch out into and across Lois Avenue, where it blasted into the parking lot of the McDonald Center and crumpled up a silver Cadillac on the back of a flatbed. The car was being secretly readied for a fall preview showing at Sununu Motors.

Every IRS employee listed on Lester Nicklaus's damp muster sheet, plus the eight TCMP auditors written into the "others" section, were chopped to mince by the hail of nails. The great floating sheet of gasoline then settled over the shredded mass of meat, and the filmy inferno randomly cooked the remains, charring the uppermost pieces to carbon and only lending a gentle baste to the lower, more protected ones.

From all sides of the city, aid poured forth. Fire dispatch teams, paramedic squads, military and hospital disaster resource units, and Red Cross field support teams converged on the hub of the disaster. While those near the center of the holocaust were beyond help, even beyond identification, there were many injured in the outer areas. The intense shrapnel storm caused a wide cone of secondary trauma. The on-site coordination was difficult, but things were being done, being done with skill and compassion. By 4:52 P.M. there were over 168 assist professionals working the lot and the adjacent street. Three triage centers were in operation amidst the carnage. The area looked like an outtake from the last days of Dresden. But it was getting done. Tampa and St. Petersburg had done their homework in joint disaster planning.

A white paramedic vehicle, its motor still idling and its orange lights steadily blinking, was parked near the hectic center of the great rescue effort. The truck had been one of the first on the scene after the thunderous blast. It stood unmanned and ignored in the middle of the noble commotion.

At 4:58 P.M. the white truck, with orange lights winking in the soft rain and its interior packed with a munitions system identical to that of the blue van, detonated.

The Colombians always gave you that added twist, that something extra . . . what the Creoles would call a *lagniappe*.

Tampa was in trouble.

Philadelphia was founded in 1682 by William Penn. Mr. Penn, a gentle Quaker fellow, applied the praiseworthy ideals of the Golden Rule to his new city and its colonial enterprises: Do unto others as you would have them do unto you. In fact, the translation of the word "Philadelphia" means "city of brotherly love." And if one considers the many churches, benevolent groups, and charities located there it would seem an appropriate name indeed.

Varki had been in Philadelphia thirty days earlier, in July. He spoke in Fairmount Park near the little zoo.

> *The choice is coming. We either build something better, build it on the stone of Constitution, honesty, and self-reliance that stands strong under federal weed and legal trash, or, through public inertia, let cynicism boil until the people trust no one, trust no one from the President on down to the county judge. Maybe until people don't even trust one another. That is when unity dies. And when unity dies, the might of a people is done.*

> *I think I know what real courage is. Real courage is to leave that nice chair and walk into the flame of history. Real courage is to fight when there are so many places to hide, so many excuses. The halls of forever are long. Somewhere, far from this time, you may have to look into the eyes of your children once again. Somewhere, far from this time, you may have to look into the eyes of patriots. Somewhere, far from this time, you may have to look into the eyes of the young soldier who never got to hold the tiny hand of his firstborn; who took the hit for you because he knew that somewhere, somehow, in all the confusion of his youth, freedom mattered.*

And Varki had been there in Philadelphia for another reason. Jesse was a candid individual. He had informed Varki that the Philadelphia connection was "squirrely," that the people he was going to use there were dedicated but unpredictable, ingenious but definitely on a different bus.

Varki used the occasion of his speaking to follow

up on the trio of operatives. He left Philadelphia a few days later with a smile, shaking his head.

Philadelphia, Pennsylvania . . . 10 August, 1610 hours (local)

Arlo Loop peered up at the window on the fourth floor of the building directly across the street from the IRS complex that housed the Mid-Atlantic Regional Headquarters in the City of Brotherly Love. He had to shade his eyes slightly from the afternoon sun that knifed at him through the canyons of the big buildings. In the window high above Arch Street he spotted the flutter of Peashooter Magee's pink handkerchief. Arlo raised a thumbs-up signal at the window and hurried east toward the river and Delaware Avenue. Arlo Loop was excited.

Peashooter sighted carefully through the scope on his "main stick" at the ass of William Penn. He was relieved to see that the big sliding window across the street was open, as it had been all last week. He could have brought off the shot with the window closed, but it helped that the window was open. The factors of refraction and glare were thereby taken out of play. He had watched through the scope as Arlo entered the large office ten minutes ago to make sure Mr. Penn was where he was supposed to be. The molded figure was bigger than life, about eight feet tall. It had been created ten years ago for the grand celebration of Philadelphia's Tricentennial. In a move to enhance the image of public-spiritedness, a response to Internal Directive No. 446-92, District Director Winston Sherk had asked the city to take the thing out of storage. He had it placed at the counter break in the center of the large customer service area. William Penn was situated with his back to the big window so he could face the walk-in trade at the service counters. The effort was, for the most part, completely lost on the citizenry who came into the office thinking mainly of economic survival rather than history. Director Sherk had initiated an inspired Historic Clothing Competition among the employees in the District Center. Anyone with the requisite skill and motivation was encouraged to compete by designing and creating authentic colonial attire for Mr. Penn. Employee response had been about as enthusiastic as the public's increased perception of IRS humanity. But Director Sherk was not a deep and sensitive man. He continued to marvel at his management insights. His wife, Clementine, who was fornicating regularly with Zoltan Heap, the Hungarian soccer player, was careful to coo and inquire about the project every night when Winston arrived home. Director Sherk usually arrived home late, about eight, due to his dedication and tough work ethic . . . long after Zoltan had left his moist calling card on Clementine's tummy. Zoltan used the withdrawal method.

Arlo Loop had begun to work on the project as soon as he received the target info from Gene Plum. He was impressed when he beheld William Penn standing there so stoically in the customer service area. He decided how he wanted to approach the job long before Kevin showed up with the three hundred thousand in cash. In the course of a few after-hours photo sessions for the Manager magazine, to document the progress of Director Sherk's heady morale decisions, Arlo, Peashooter, and Seldom Home Jones managed to fill the hollow interior of William Penn with exactly 479 blocks of C-4. To the level of his neck. Accessible by unscrewing Mr. Penn's head.

Arlo had placed a rack of eight sticks of 70-percent-grade dynamite up against the inside of William Penn's ass. He centered it as best he could in the middle of one butt-cheek amid the blocks of C-4. The dynamite could be detonated by a rifle bullet. It would then set off the C-4. The C-4 was too stable to be lit up by a bullet.

They screwed the head back on when they finished with the loading. Then Arlo took a real picture of William Penn. It was the only time he put film in the camera all week. Arlo called Director Sherk down from his office, where he was once again working late. He had the Director pose with one arm around William. The Director had to stretch up on his toes since the figure was bigger than life. After he took the picture, Arlo noticed a metal plaque sitting atop information handouts on a nearby desk. The handouts contained information about William Penn and about the founding of Philadelphia. He took a third and final picture of Director Sherk and William Penn. He had the Director hold the plaque in front of Mr. Penn's tummy. It was the motto associated with William Penn. The plaque said: "Do unto others as you would have them do unto you." Arlo felt that said it all.

It was 1613. Peashooter peeped through the sight. A few anxious feet away, the constantly-in-motion Seldom Home studied his watch. It seemed to be stopping between seconds. Seldom and Peashooter were both nervous. Seldom, especially, fidgeted.

"How much time, Sel?"

"Under two minutes, Pea." Seldom dug his right hand into his pocket and rocked back and forth.

They waited. Peashooter kept the scope on William Penn's ass. Aimed at the right cheek. Where Arlo said.

"Jiminy Cricket!" said Peashooter.

"What?" said Seldom. He jumped visibly at the sound of the sudden words.

"That dingbat is standing in my line!"

Seldom looked up from the watch and stared

across the street. His hands were shaking. One of the IRS ladies was between William Penn and the window. Leaning on the sill and looking out.

"What do we do, Pea?"

"I dunno, Sel."

They both stared across the space at the woman.

After thirty seconds she moved away and disappeared into the office.

"Jesus," said Seldom Home. He stared out the window, turned to Peashooter, then stared out again.

"Quick, Sel. How much time?"

Seldom hurriedly looked at the watch. "It's 1613 and forty seconds," he said. "What if she comes back, Pea? You got to shoot right at 1615. Arlo says so."

"I dunno, Sel. She might come back. If I have to shoot through her, she might knock the thing over. I might not be able to hit it."

"What you gonna do?"

Peashooter thought for a few seconds. "I'm gonna shoot now."

Seldom Home looked across the street. Peashooter squeezed down.

Cruck!

The kick snapped the rifle up. The flash suppressor muffled the sound of the shot.

Nothing happened across the street.

In the scope, Peashooter could see the entry hole in William Penn's tan breeches. Right in the middle of the right cheek.

He waited only four seconds, then squeezed down again.

Cruck!

Nothing.

Peashooter could now see two holes in William Penn's right ass.

"Omigod," said Seldom Home. "Shoot him in the goddamn ass, Pea, shoot him in the goddamn ass."

"Where the hell do you think I'm shooting!"

Peashooter fired a third time. Three holes in the butt. No blast.

In the other windows they could see people starting to look out in their direction. Some were getting down under desks, some crouching near the floor, but the people were moving slowly, not quite sure what was happening.

"For God's sake, Pea," shouted Seldom, "put one up his asshole! The stuff must have moved!"

Peashooter put one directly into William Penn's seam. Bull's-eye. Nothing.

"What time, Sel?"

"Omigod. It's five seconds away. It's gonna be 1615. What's wrong, Pea? What in the name of hell is wrong?"

Peashooter frowned. He thought with all his might.

Then a broad smile split his face.

"What, Pea? What?"

"Watch this, Sel." He took aim and slowly squeezed down. The smile was still there.

Cruck!

KAAABOOM!

They were sprawled back on the floor. The rifle had been knocked from Peashooter's hands, and glass shards from their own window covered them both. Dust and plaster snowed down in a swirl from all around. Seldom Home was busy spitting flakes of paint and lath from his mouth. His friend was flat on his back bleeding from some cuts on his face, but still smiling broadly.

"What was it, Pea?"

"It was the left ass, Sel. From this side, it was the left ass." The smile got bigger.

26

Out Date

Rebeca looked down at the people by the pool. From the third-floor window of his room in the Frontier Hotel and Casino, she was close enough to see the oiled faces of the sunbathers directly below her as they basked in the sensuous afternoon heat of the sun that was closing in on the west roof of the hotel. She envied them their obvious pleasure luxuriating down there in the last sweet heat of the day. The heat chased away the dry chill that the big air-cooling units up on the roof had worked so efficiently to build on their skins inside the casino. Rebeca didn't like the dryness in her nose and around her eyes that the hotel air put on her.

She was on her knees on the sofa that backed against the window. Her elbows rested on the sofa back, and the palms of her hands pressed against the skin of her face at both cheeks, supporting her head in a lazy nonchalance as she surveyed the scene below. Like some small kid staring at the outdoors on a rainy day when she couldn't go out to play. She absentmindedly tapped the little finger of each hand on the skin of her forehead, keeping time with the hectic in-and-out of B. Ryan Pogue, who energetically pounded away at her sex from behind with his strange, four-inch, bent-to-the-right penis. She maintained an exaggerated low arch to her back so he had access to the flare of her hips. He was rolling along in fine shape. She liked the feel of his hands on her waist; they were warm against the cold on her skin, and his grasp kept her from having to worry about him popping out. She wanted to enjoy watching the people down by the pool and didn't want to worry about timing him every second. She was glad she had coaxed him into a standard doggy. The way he had been jumping around the room in her new silk panties for the last half hour made her suspect he was a Dress Dragon. She didn't want him stretching her new mini. The thing cost $12.95. She began to go over the things she needed to pick up on the way home. Bread, pickles, toothpaste, baking soda, postage stamps.

"Oh, baby, harder, harder. Don't stop," she said.

When she thought about the baking soda it made her think of the funny name of the guy who made the stuff . . . *something like Arland Hammer? . . . No, that's not right. What the hell is it?* She turned it over in her mind. *Arland? Garland? Harlon? Screw it.* She thought instead of her old friend Silverado Bush, who worked the Green Lantern up in Ely. Silverado had told her about baking soda and how it was used to remove body odors. When she was starting out, Silverado had tried to talk her into joining the Ely girls. She had seriously considered it, but the weather got cold up there, and she felt more comfortable working in Vegas. Then there was Tyrone. They were really stuck on each other.

"God, B. Ryan. I've never felt it like this. What are you doing to me?"

Things were picking up back in Sex Central. B. Ryan was about to get his wheels up. *Full flaps!*

She tightened her sex muscles and drove back on him with a squeal. Perfect timing. He blew. She noticed the lifeguard scolding a teenybopper for running through the chaise lounges.

They sat naked on the couch sharing a cigarette. She felt pretty good. *Sixty bucks. Prepaid. Fifty minutes. Plus three free drinks and a hot dog. With sauerkraut.* And the pack of cigarettes if she played her cards right.

"You got a real nice dick, B. Ryan."

"You really think so?"

"Sure do. The way it bends right there makes a girl feel real good. Believe me. Like having two pricks."

B. Ryan looked at his wizzled peter.

"You really think so?"

"Sure do."

She meant it. B. Ryan's was like Tyrone's. And B. Ryan looked like he believed her. If only Tyrone would. From her experience she had decided that kindness in a guy was inversely proportional to the size of his thinger. Bugdicks were fun and tried harder to be good . . . weird at times, but nicer. She liked to give herself to them. Horsedicks usually acted like they were doing you a big favor, and sometimes they went on ugly power trips that pissed her off. She bent down and planted a pert kiss on the shrunken pale warrior.

"Can I see you again sometime?" he asked.

"You betchum, Mr. Humping Machine. Any time."

She got up and went to the table, where she jotted her number down on the notepad by the phone. She held the note up in the air when she finished writing, then made sure he saw her place it on the desk under the edge of an ashtray. She went into the dressing area to wash up.

"What do you do, B. Ryan?" from the sink.

No reply.

"Dogcatcher?" she tried again.

"I work for the government."

Pause.

"Doing what?"

"I work for the IRS."

"IRS?"

"Yes."

She felt a slight chill. She sure didn't report all her income. She worried about that. No one in Vegas would forget the raids on the casinos a few years back when the feds selectively rousted and prosecuted dealers and pit crews for not reporting all their tokes. The government men had broken some people, people who were still trying to climb out, people with kids, cars, and mortgages. The cars and mortgages were long gone. The raids had been vicious and showy. Fear still hung in the air. So did hate.

"Gee," she said.

She felt a bit paranoid for a few seconds, then relaxed as she pictured him prancing around the room earlier in her skivvies with his thumb up his ass. She knew he would not have done that if he was investigating her and Tyrone. But she still felt uneasy. "You a big wheel?" she added.

"Pretty big. I go after some of the heavy hitters in this town. If the folks who don't pay get away with it, the rest of us have to pay their share. I don't mind getting tough with those bastards."

"Yeah."

"We try not to step on the little guy. Sometimes it happens, though. That's the way the cookie crumbles."

She jumped as she heard a shrill beeping sound. She stuck her head around the corner to watch him as he went quickly to his jacket on the chair.

"Just my pager." He waved the noisy thing at her from where he stood by the TV. He punched a button and the noise stopped. Then he went to the phone and dialed. He waited a few moments while the call went through.

"What?" he shouted.

She watched him.

"When?"

She watched him some more.

"Jesus! How long ago?"

She reflexively looked at her own watch. She wanted to get out of there. He was really worked up, his face scared her. The watch said 4:42. The calendar setting said Monday, but she didn't look at that.

He slammed down the phone. There was a strange look in his eyes. She watched, fascinated, as he dressed more quickly than she had ever seen a man dress. She stood there with her soaped crotch cooling in the air as he rushed past her. He didn't even say good-bye.

Five minutes later she stepped out of one of the two elevators that served that wing of the hotel. She noticed a crowd of agitated patrons standing around the open door of the other elevator. They were buzzing and jabbering in a confused knot. One man was off to the side, down on one knee, vomiting repeatedly onto the red and gold carpeting. Another man in blue Bermuda shorts was trying to take a picture over everybody's head with a small camera. His wife was trying to shove him around to get him in position for a clear shot. Another man was holding up a woman who had passed out in his arms. Two fat security guards were waving frantically at some casino employees who were running down the passage toward the elevators.

Rebeca stood on her tiptoes so she could look over the crowd into the other elevator. Crumpled against the back wall was B. Ryan Pogue with a hatchet buried in his face between his eyes. The hatchet was buried right up to the handle.

"Gee," she said.

27

St. George

The city of St. George spread across the valley far below the windows of the restaurant. In the clear air of the Utah desert, hundreds of lights in the houses and along the streets gave sparkling definition to the quilted geometry of the place. The great Mormon temple at the middle was awash in its robes of electricity, and it centered the eye of those who sat at the tables. The windows of the dining room were set in a graceful convex curve that allowed a sweeping view of the entire city that stretched from the base of the great cliff out to the east. The August night was warm, but it was early, and soon the chill of the dry desert night would be stealing into the deeper washes from the secret places it knew, places where it hid from the crushing indifference of the August sun. The crystalline air created a portrait of silence for the mind. The deep blue translucent dome of the desert twilight sky had gone to black transparency, and sharp stabs of starspot began to puncture the heavens. The remote distance was crisp, unreal. Time hung. The great space hovered.

Down below, the city was a stillness. Traffic lights winked in empty, unheeded repetition . . . green . . . yellow . . . red . . . and over again. Few cars moved through the clear night. At 8:00 P.M. on 10 August, St. George was watching television. As was the rest of the country. Some were awed. Others sickened. All who watched were fascinated. Even the beast that had come under attack. Things coiled and uncoiled. Darkness twisted. Power turned to look at power.

Rayburn Varki lifted a glass of port into the air. An image of the man, dimly reflecting back from the depth of the restaurant window, raised with him. The glasses of the woman and the third one came up. The fine thin rims of crystal touched. In silence they drank. The vessels, drawn off, regained the table.

The restaurant was not empty of customers, but almost so. Only four other tables were occupied and those by silent, distracted groups. Three handsome young girls moved solemnly in turn between the diners, and the two busboys of the place leaned against the salad bar, where they were not supposed to be, and talked in hushed voices full of warning and importance. The exaggeration of the young was being sorely tested.

"It has happened as you said," from Aixa.

Varki looked into her face. "It is up to the people."

She filled the glasses from the dark bottle. In the lightness of the air, the sound of the port, poured in a deep red stream, carried across the room. She turned the bottle expertly at each conclusion, spun the trailing droplets back into the depth, and moved with grace, her fingers firm, unshaking.

"And what will they do? How will they speak in this moment?" she asked.

"This is a caring and compassionate country," said Varki. "There will be great sympathy." He paused to sip the blood-red wine, then talked again. "Some will act to keep it going. Maybe only a few, but there will be some."

"Many?"

"Perhaps not. What has happened may be enough. I do not envision anarchy. The event has spoken."

The silent one drank from his glass. His eyes looked past Varki and Aixa and savaged the room. The look of the man crackled with intensity. It was a time to be aware.

Varki put his gaze into the air above the city.

"The country will not fall," he said. "That is not a possibility. Ten percent of the people could overthrow the system, bring it to the ground. But even in this land, with its rough, raw history, you'll not find such a portion of fighters."

"Will it change?"

"Yes. Our beast wants to live. We must show it that to survive it must choose a different form. It listens. It can remember." The yellow fire was in his eyes.

Aixa looked down. "You could not say this in a book?"

Varki took her hand in his. There was sadness. "Aixa, the people do not read."

The words spun into the air. And disappeared.

They dined on trout. The night drew in around the place. The other tables emptied. Varki stood.

"We must rest. Time runs quickly now. I thank you for your loyalty. I could have asked for nothing more."

The trio, Loza in the lead, moved to the door of the restaurant. Varki and Aixa paused while Loza went out onto the steps to look into the night. The Skypark Motel was located twenty yards north of the restaurant. Both buildings were built right to the edge of the three-hundred-foot cliff and faced east to take advantage of the spectacular view. The buildings stood side by side, alone on the rim of the precipice with a two-lane access road separating them from the runway of the small airport to the west. A chain-link fence guarded the runway.

Loza looked and saw all the things of the place. It was as before. The same cars were parked in the same spots behind the two-story motel. Their own Taurus was there. And the two red Broncos. The '89 Chrysler. The older Datsun wagon. And the '86 Chevy panel van. All those vehicles had been there when they checked in that afternoon. To his left, six cars were parked near the Dumpster. He had watched the employees park as they came to work for the evening shift. All those cars were accounted for. His gaze swept the flightline behind the chain-link fence. There was no visible activity. The road along the fenceline was empty. The nearest houses were eight hundred meters distant on the mesa top to the north. Nothing moved outside except his eyes.

He held the door open for Varki and Aixa. The three of them began the short walk to the motel.

The men walked with Aixa to her room. It was on the ground floor next to the one that Varki and Loza shared. The entries to the rooms were level with the designated parking spots, and the cars were able to park six feet from each door. All of the rooms had a curved balcony on the east side, opposite the parking lot. The balconies fronted the quiet city below and were separated by concrete dividers. The balconies jutted into the empty night air over the cliff edge.

And Loza missed something.

Perhaps it was because of the strong port wine. He had felt a profound obligation to drink with them when Varki raised the toasts. To them and to their success.

Or maybe it was the long drive down from the cool mountain where the flowers still held their bloom in the high country. His only pleasure was the flowers. The beautiful flowers of the mountain. Yellow ones, blue ones, and the special white ones. When his time was upon him, he wanted to meet the White Bird of Death among the white flowers. That was his secret wish.

Or maybe the big meal had made him tired. Eating the food, for him, was an effort. He had to work carefully at it because the side muscle of his tongue was gone, cut away in the time of the darkness.

But, whatever the reason, he missed something.

The Chevy panel van was parked next to the Taurus. At the first feathery touch of chill night air, a difference could be seen coming onto the cars, onto the glass of the cars. If his eyes had been sharper, if his mind had stayed clear, if the thinking of the flowers had not come in that smallest of moments, he would have seen. He would have known. On the windshield of the van was a wetness, a slight mist, a gentle condensation. It was not on the other cars. If he had seen it, he would have shifted his eyes to the metal roof and, even in the half darkness, he would have seen the telltale moisture put there by the heat of the predator.

At Aixa's door they stopped. Loza stepped forward and unlocked the door. Varki and the woman waited. Loza went into the room and turned on the lights. The spring-loaded door almost closed, but Varki put his foot against it to keep it from latching. The motel owner had put closing mechanisms on the entries to protect his air conditioners against burnout in the brutish summer sun.

Loza moved inside the room, checking. They could hear the scrape of traverse slides as he pushed back the big curtains of the balcony doors and checked the locks. They heard the snap of the shower curtain. Then it was quiet, and they waited.

Loza came back to the door. He nodded to the girl.

"Good night, my friends," she said.

She went inside and Varki let the door close. He was sleepy. The bed would feel good.

They stepped the few feet to the door of their own room. Varki paused to look up at the sky, and Loza, key in hand, paused, too. He looked up with Varki at the sharp brilliance of sparkling desert black.

"We have done it, my good friend. We have done it."

Loza nodded. Even in these moments, these rarest of moments, when he felt the ache to share, he didn't speak. The sounds that came from him were intelligible, but just barely. He sounded as the animals did. Or as some insensate rock grinding down the gravel flanks of the mountain of his brother.

Loza opened the door and stepped inside.

The tinted window in the van rolled down an inch.

Varki followed Loza in, but stayed by the door while Loza turned on the lights. He waited for Loza to cross over to the big curtains by the balcony to check the locks on the sliding glass doors. After that, he would wait for Loza to look into the closet, then into the shower. The routine was always the same. It only varied when the room was different.

As Loza crossed to the glass doors, he thought he detected the scent of corn oil, or something like it. His quiet world had sharpened his other senses. The faint aroma of the oil reminded him of Mexico, of Mexican food. The odor was pleasant, and he pictured the girls over in the restaurant carrying plates of tortillas to the tables. But he didn't remember seeing Mexican food on the menu.

Loza was a professional at the top of his vocation. There are attributes found in those special people called pros, the ones in the top one percent of their natural calling, attributes that redefine the word "excellence." The excellence at times approaches instinct, and at times the instinct approaches precognition. The "pro's pro" seems to be able to operate somewhere out front, two seconds into the future, two seconds ahead of reality. Awareness. The mind snapping a finished picture from a few starting details.

And that was how it was when Loza crossed the room through the faint scent of the oil. And that was how it was when the upper half of his visual field picked up a slight billowing in the heavy fabric covering the balcony access as an easy breeze from the valley moved through the partly open door behind the drapery.

Or that was how it should have been. The part of his brain that was supposed to receive these things received them. But the part of his brain that was supposed to interpret was compromised by the port wine and fatigue. Loza had not registered three important details in the space of three minutes.

Smith and Wesson manufactured a special nine-millimeter pistol for the Navy SEAL teams in Vietnam. With its slide lock, special suppressor, and subsonic round, the super-silent weapon was so effective that it was used to kill enemy guard dogs on raids inside VC camps. That is how the Mark 22 Model O got the nickname "Hush Puppy."

Loza closed on the doors and reached up with his right hand to grasp the plastic wand used to pull back the big curtains. As the drapes began to open, Pisco, standing on the balcony with the Hush Puppy braced by the edge of the open door, shot Loza in the right chest. He would have preferred that the bullet find Loza's heart, but in the critical microseconds of the shooting Loza again became the pro's pro. He saw, registered, and reacted. He started left and the bullet missed the heart. The 150-grain round lique-fied two ribs, and Loza continued his rolling turn, shoved along by the impact of the big projectile, and crashed into the corner. There had been no sound. Just his crashing against the wall. He knew he would die. But he was not dead now. And the seconds had started to grow pristine, beautiful, slow. His right arm was paralyzed. It would not move to the leg hol-ster on his outside right shin. It would not move. He used his good left hand to free the knife in the sheath that balanced the leg holster inside the right shin. In one graceful, sweeping motion he backhanded the heavy blade into Pisco's right side as Pisco turned through the door. The blade entered one inch below the lower border of the protective Kevlar vest that Pisco wore and sliced deeply into Pisco's liver. The hot shock of the big blade caused a reflex contraction in Pisco's arm, and the Hush Puppy spun away. Pisco watched it go and knew he should have protected it to the left.

Now the seconds became crystalline for Pisco also. A bubble of radiant purity defined their intensely private world. Silent. Weightless. Mysterious. It was a place normal people didn't go. A place where seconds turned to minutes. Where things didn't fall, but floated. Where you could see the spin on bullets. Where you almost felt love for the other man because of the magnificent place you had created for each other. Death, his green face full of admiration, waited for them both.

Pisco left the blade where it was in his side . . . there was not time for that . . . and stepped to meet Loza, who was rising from the corner at him. Each to close the thing. Loza would claim the softness of the throat of Pisco and then regain the knife, but his chest was collapsing to the right . . . inside . . . awash in broiling froths of bright red foam. He felt his right side slowly turn to wood in the majestic, floating eternity of one step. Then darkness as the right forearm of Pisco drifted toward his face and took away the light. Loza's head cracked back from the blow, and he crashed again into the wall. Pisco took him on the rebound at the temples with both hands, strong hands that smelled of the oils. He turned Loza, half carried by the big hands, and put the man into the wooden desk chair. The big hands pushed the head backward over the hard edge of the top of the seat back that pressed against the rear of Loza's neck.

Loza's neck snapped.

Pisco raised his eyes. The ice in them was melting. He looked at Mitch and Varki standing by the front door. Mitch had been hiding in the bathroom in the shower and, stepping out of the dark, now held Varki at gunpoint. Both Mitch and Varki had watched him battle Loza. The struggle had consumed twelve seconds.

"You!" Female voice.

Pisco turned back toward the open door that led

to the balcony. Framed against the blackness of the night was the beautiful woman. She stood, slightly crouched, her naked breasts and arms floodlit by the room lights. Wearing only the skirt. Pisco knew, as time began to crystallize again, that she must have heard the first crash of Loza going into the wall as she undressed. She had come over the rail of the balcony, climbing out into the night around the cement divider. Pisco had not seen such beauty. She was an elegant sight.

As was the stiletto turning in the air between them.

He watched the thing. He slowed it down. He made it float. But the lines of nerve couldn't make the call. He simply shut them down and watched it come. There was no way to move. At the last, he took his melting eyes from the thing and looked past it at her. She was a splendid sight. A killing beauty. The blade ripped into the left side of his neck and through the jugular; he wished the man Loza were there to see.

As Pisco went down, Mitch's line cleared and he put a bullet into her forehead on the midline. He saw the small blue hole it made. Aixa went backward and down on her haunches. Her naked back hit the iron railing and she bounced forward. She tried to straighten and, for a short moment, stayed up on her knees, long arms hanging at her sides, then pitched forward onto her face.

She died with her eyes on Varki.

28

Tape No. 2

10 AUG 2250 HRS./VOX. ACT. REC. SER. 39711.05

"Good evening, Mr. President."

"Come in, Link, I know you only have a few minutes. I believe you remember Mr. Nokuma and Mr. Vonnegut?"

"Yes, sir, we've talked before. Mr. Nokuma . . . Mr. Vonnegut."

"Hello again, Lieutenant Colonel Muldrow. Mr. Nokuma and I were reviewing your work this morning. You are to be commended. The Commission is impressed. Your efforts in this matter have been very efficient."

"Thank you, Mr. Vonnegut."

"Something to drink, Link?"

"No, thank you, sir."

"Well, then. Let's review where we stand. Bring us up to date, Link."

"Mr. President, gentlemen. The activist group we used proved to be extremely capable. Mr. Varki validated our estimates of him. His timing was well developed . . . they hit the IRS just as the taxpayers were facing the expiration of the extension deadline on the seventeenth. Varki and his associates perceived my role as financial only. I had no trouble maintaining my dead-end cover in this evolution. It stops with me . . . absolutely. Our security was verified through subcarrier drops placed in the Idaho residence. We also jumped on their computer feeds. They never looked in our direction. Nothing leads to this office, Mr. President."

"Good work, Link. The media package is in place. It was put together from human-interest bits out of IRS public relations stuff. Family snapshots, hometown news stories, Vietnam-vet historical clips on IRS employees. Picked out of PAO files from the various services. I've seen some of it. Great footage. There won't be any problem pulling public opinion into our camp."

"I hope it's as good as you say, Mr. President."

"Mr. Nokuma, it's Academy Award stuff."

"Thank you for your reassurance, Mr. President. But this is a sad business."

"It's survival business, Mr. Nokuma, don't lose sight of that. We got inside this damn bombing thing to control it, to anticipate them. The people started this thing. It's a tax revolt we're stopping, Mr. Nokuma, not a goddamn political rally at one of your fucking airports. Now, Link, tell me what kind of hardware they used."

"We decided to let Varki's ideas take priority on that one, sir. Plastique, C-4, nitrate, dynamite, a bit of everything in Tampa. At first we didn't like his concept of letting the cells get creative in the choice of tools. But his thought was good. The cells went with what they knew best. Different folks, different strokes. We procured some of what the cells needed. Major Evans ran the supply side like a Swiss watch through Corps Ordnance. Do we keep the Major, sir?"

"We should talk about that, Link. Mr. Nokuma?"

"No."

"Mr. Vonnegut?"

"Too dangerous to keep."

"Link?"

"I agree. He goes."

"No regrets?"

"Plenty of goddamn regrets, sir. But he goes."

"Sorry, Link. That was uncalled for on my part."

"I understand, sir. We're all wound a little tight."

"The others? No changes?"

"No changes, sir."

"Varki?"

"Right about now, sir, give or take a few hours. It was necessary to have him initiate the attacks. Now we want him out of the picture as soon as possible so we don't lose him."

"He would have made an ideal fugitive, Link. He would have focused public attention. There's no connection to us. He even sees himself as the mainspring."

"I listened to Varki talk, Mr. President. You don't take chances with a man like that. But what you just said is true, sir. If something breaks, everything points right at him. We are invisible."

"Who do you have on Varki?"

"The two brothers we talked of last time. They're right for what we need. Worked for the Calabrian people in Toronto. Some hard time. Ran weapons into Central America early on. Still move independently. A few contract hits on intergang scum. No citizens that we could find. A pilot and a gun. They have no one close; no family to ask questions when they disappear. We had to keep in front of them on one or two matters. They're active."

"Do they know you?"

"They do not."

"What about the rest of Varki's people?"

"Routine. The Major will handle it. Fish in a barrel."

"Who knows you besides Varki?"

"Only his man. And the Eurasian girl."

"What do they know you as?"

"As Zebra."

29

The Drop

Mitch flipped the contents of the small fuel tube onto the concrete runway. He stood next to the gleaming hull of the Titan 404 and rubbed an oil spot off the palm of his left hand with the gas rag. The chill air of the new day pressed fresh and clean around him.

The ritual ground checks on the oil and gas finished, he took one last swipe with the rag at his fingers. Blood residue worried him. Because of all the hype about AIDS. The fingers and nails were free of stains.

For a few moments, he let the shallow rays of morning sun warm the back of his neck as he went over the details of the cleanup. After the business of the killing ended, he had signaled Ram to come in from the van, where he had been covering the outside door in case something went wrong. They had taken Varki to the van at once and bound his wrists, secured him to the seat lock in the back. Ram stayed in the vehicle while Mitch packed the body totes. The totes were large-size hanging clothes bags. Each tote was modified by the placement of a heavy metal bar in the top section that connected to a strong outside hanging hook. The knees of the "suit" were put over the bar and the ankles lashed to the thighs. A well-muscled traveler could move the package without attracting too much attention. The bags were lined with plastic to keep the suits from leaking.

When Mitch was satisfied with his luggage, he went to the van and kept watch over Varki while Ram brought the totes out. Mitch was struck by the calmness in Varki. He scanned Varki's face. Mitch could see no shock, no malice, no fear there. Some sadness. *Who wouldn't be sad? That was a great-looking woman in there.* He began to feel better about not icing the target immediately, as the buyer had suggested. He felt a rising curiosity about the man. Enough to want to know more. What made Varki the object of so much attention? More practically, was there any threat left? Could there be a connection with all the bombings, all the excitement of yesterday's attacks on the IRS people? If there was a connection, he and Ram might be in over their heads; a feeling, a flickering warning light hardwired into his survival instinct, was trying to decide whether to come on or not.

Ram brought out the last bag, and Mitch had gone back into the room to begin the two-hour scrub-down. After he finished the mop-up, they drove the van around the fence to the plane. The plane was a twin-engined Titan, Cessna's Ambassador model, forty feet long. Six of the ten seats had been removed to make room for the cargo. In the darkness, they loaded the bodies of Aixa, Loza, and Pisco, packed in the tote bags, through the two-piece hatch in the aft port side. Then they escorted Varki into the airplane and secured him to the deck fittings. Ram stayed in the plane with him while Mitch took the van back to its spot by the motel. Mouse would arrive the following morning, pick up the van, and check out of the place. Mitch stayed in the motel for an extra hour before returning, on foot, to the Titan. He went through the rooms again to double-check. The hard part of the business in St. George was over.

Before starting the walk back to the plane, he stood on the balcony of the room the woman had occupied. He thought of her and of her beauty and of her knife. He had decided, in the moment of her death, that he would learn to throw like that.

He looked down at the white Mormon temple in the middle of the city. As he watched, the floodlights went out. A wisp of regret pulsed into him. The church was a beautiful thing. Elegant. He enjoyed looking at it.

When he returned to the plane, Ram told him he should talk with Varki. In Mitch's absence, the two had been discovering things. So Mitch listened. Asked questions of the man. Grew fascinated and excited at the scope of what he was hearing.

One phrase had stuck in his mind all night. It was what Varki had said to Ram while they waited in the plane and repeated to him after he walked back from the motel.

"If they're killing me now, they'll be killing you later."

Varki put it together in short order after Ram told

him of the contract and the trace to Nellis, after Ram described the lieutenant colonel, whom Varki recognized at once as Zebra, after Ram recapped the duty assignments, especially those in Washington. The white light of cognition clicked on in Varki's brain. First a look of surprise. Only for a moment, vivid, even in the half light of the plane. Ram could see a bolt of comprehension dart across the sharp features. Then anger was on Varki's face, quickly gone. Then a slow shake of the head, the shroud of resignation. And finally, unexpectedly, a peculiar look that Ram could only interpret as admiration. Hard to figure out. This man, this Varki, who earlier watched two close associates depart the world in a rush of violence, who was obviously in a terminal status himself, who had been double-crossed big-time by his government partner, this man seemed to be infused with a grudging respect.

Varki asked for more details, then went silent. After a few minutes, he began to tell Ram of the bombings, of the money. He talked rapidly, but with great clarity. Varki wanted Ram to look hard at the thing, to think about what they all had been drawn into. When it came to self-preservation, Ram was good. He listened. By the time Mitch returned to the plane, the game had changed.

And now it was a new day. A good day to fly. A day to make important decisions.

Mitch went to the boarding hatch and stepped up into the aircraft using the cable-supported double stair. Ram and Varki were aft, in front of the totes. Varki wore Pisco's black leather jacket and sat on the floor away from the row of windows. Spread on the deck between them was the Sectional Aeronautical Chart for the grids between Utah and the Pacific

Ocean. Mitch took the seat across from Ram and pointed to a black square he had marked on the chart. "There's the pass, gents. It cuts through the Nopah Range southwest of Pahrump. Here's where the buyer wants you to get off, Varki." He touched the map near the brown-colored line of mountains with the edge of his sunglasses. "You haven't changed your mind, have you?" He grinned at Varki.

"I like your plan better." The yellow fire was back.

"Okay, team. As soon as we're off the ground, break out Pisco. Get Varki's sport coat on him and tie those buttons shut. I want it to stay on, Ram. All the way to ground zero. Someone is going to be down there in the desert with a pair of binoculars. Get a razor from your night kit and cut his hairline back like Varki's here. Smear some toothpaste in it, make the black look gray. If someone's interested, they're not going to be close enough for a real good look, the terrain is too rough. So it doesn't have to be a great makeup job. Do what you can. After the drop, our instructions are to cross to the Goffs Vortac, seventy-five miles southeast. Right here." He indicated a two-inch blue circle on the map.

As he talked, he overdrew the route with arrows using a black marker.

"At the Goffs Vortac we are supposed to turn to one eight zero degrees and head due south. Here. You two will be off the plane by then. That turn puts me between these two Vortac corridors, the one just east of Twentynine Palms and the one that leads down to Parker. Our boy says we hold that heading until we cross a line that runs due east from the highest peak in the Old Woman range. Right here. Easy to spot. The one-eight-zero heading crosses the east-bearing line four miles east of the peak. Six miles later, over this depression, the buyer wants a long wing-waggle if it went okay. If something went wrong, he wants a couple of tight circles. Either way, after that, I'm on my own. I can head for home. Any surprises, they're going to happen along this line. You'll have the chart. Search down that track to the wigwag spot if I'm not back in twenty-four hours. I'll drop you at Jean behind the Gold Strike."

Ram looked up. He didn't like that part. "Mitch, we should break this off right here. We have enough to know it's a lousy percentage play. We screw the buyer by just letting Varki walk. Let them figure out what to do next. It doesn't make any sense going in blind."

"Hey, bro. Two things wrong with that. Number one, the buyer might be legit. Just because he smokes our buddy here doesn't guarantee that he'll do it to us. What Varki says makes sense, but there's a chance he doesn't have it quite right. We kiss off over a hundred grand if he's wrong, maybe more. And number two, you know goddamn fuckin' well no one fucks with us like this. We wouldn't sleep right for the next ten fuckin' years, bro. Not if we take a hike now. Don't forget, we got a hell of a lot more on him than he thinks we do. So he radios me down for a chat to blast me? Or maybe lays for me at Palomar? What's the big deal? I got the Kevlar, some good heat, and a wet nose. He's not going to surprise my ass, bro. Besides, I got you for backup. I can bail out of this baby if he gets lucky and he puts a round into my cables. Look, I've been chasin' this joker around for three fuckin' months now. You just get that damn chopper and trace the strip if I'm not home. If that guy does put me down, I'll be sittin' on some rocks chewin' on his bones by the time you get there."

Ram didn't reply. He was hungry for a piece of the buyer, too. If it was a cross. Mitch was right, they weren't going to get blindsided.

Varki looked hard at the brothers. "If it's money, I can beat your deal ten times over."

Mitch looked at Varki. "So maybe it's not the fuckin' money, Varki. It's how we do things. Do you fuckin' mind?"

Ram felt awkward. Because of the pride that came.

Mitch turned and went forward. He settled into the pilot's seat and belted up. His heart was going hard. He had the taste of rage, a taste sweet to him.

He took the yoke, caressed it.

Left window open. "CLEAR."

Master switch on. Mixtures rich. Throttles cracked a half inch. Fuel pumps on. Ignition switch on. Starter button down. Starboard engine, sputter, sputter, catch. Rough at first. The last two cylinders join the rioting. Now smooth. Port sequence.

Both humming.

Lights and dials glow, wiggle alive, jumping. Vacuum gauges, voltmeter, ammeter, artificial horizon, heading indicators, oil pressures. Radios up. Voices, thin and rambling. Reedy. Air talk.

The whole thing had him by the ass. Glory days!

The Titan angled across the head of the Pahrump Valley and tucked in along the eastern flank of the Nopahs. Ram had the top half of the circular hatch folded open. The roar of air and pressure changes banged at their ears.

Pisco was ready to meet the mountain.

With a gentle tenderness, Ram cradled the shoulders of the body. He had placed the legs partway out of the opening, ready to deliver Pisco to the wild winds and hot rock below. He kept his eyes on

Varki, who was forward with Mitch, waiting for the word.

Mitch throttled back to ninety-five knots. He wanted Pisco on a high peak, well up from the valley. The drop would come as near to the crest as possible, before any nosy eyes on the Death Valley side of the range could trace the buzz of the engines. Down came Varki's arm.

"Now!" yelled Varki.

Ram saw the arm drop, heard the shout. He bent his head and placed a kiss on the side of Pisco's forehead. Then pushed him into the abyss. Ram didn't look up to see if Varki had seen the kiss. He thrust his head out the open hatch and watched the body cartwheel through the air. It seemed to float away. The farther it got from the plane, the slower it seemed to fall. Then it disappeared in a puff of smoky dust. On the brown edge of a steep peak. Up near the top.

Ram did not know why he had kissed Pisco. He could sense the fading, tender shreds of a feeling, a feeling that whispered about sadness, about emptiness, of forever being alone, of love not being able to find a place in the heart because something dark already lived there.

After the drop, Mitch pushed the plane to maximum airspeed. The twin Continentals throbbed the plane through the thin air of the high desert at 250 knots. The side trip to Jean, where he would off-load Ram and Varki, was only twenty miles off the rhumb line to Goffs, but Mitch knew the buyer would probably be timing the run from the Nopahs south, timing it with the help of someone down below who watched the drop.

He came in fast and low, south of the two big casinos that straddled Route 15 at Jean, Nevada. The gear thudded onto the dirt strip. Loose gravel cracked at the hull as the nosewheel set down. Mitch braked hard and spun the plane around. Ram shoved open the hatch and Varki jumped into the swirling backwash of the port prop.

"Bro!" Mitch shouted over the noise.

Ram went forward and leaned down by his brother.

"Bro. Haul the girl up here. Get her out of the bag and strap her in this seat." He indicated the seat to his right, up in the cockpit.

Ram didn't ask questions. He did as he was told.

"Get that strap around her neck so she stays up."

Ram adjusted the strap.

"Thanks, bro. She might catch a slug for me. Toss me the other two Kevlar jackets."

Ram complied.

"Now get your ass out. Call Gorski for the chopper. They won't be flying tours to the canyon until later in the week. He can get one up. Give him the chart."

"Anything else?" shouted Ram. Mitch was already revving the engines and starting to roll.

"Yeah! Get the fuck out of my airplane!"

Ram jumped and ran a few steps alongside while he pushed up the steps and slammed the hatch. He jogged away from the tail wings and joined Varki. They stood together and watched the plane rush into the clear air.

"Your brother is a proud man," said Varki.

Ram took a last look at the plane. "Let's go, Varki. We have things to do."

Mitch intersected the track to the Goffs Vortac and lined up. Only seven minutes behind. He would carve that down on the way south. They should buy that.

Over Goffs, he turned due south and hurried through the bumpy thermals that lifted from the eastern flank of the Providence Mountains. It was 0815 hours. The arid desert ranges moved slowly beneath him. He throttled back, set the autopilot, and put on two of the Kevlar vests, one over the other. He placed the third vest under him, on the seat. He had to grant the possibility that he might be catching a round from below. He doubted it, though. If the buyer wanted their butts, he would probably radio them to set down. Maybe under the pretense of making the final payment. That would work. The buyer would figure they were both on board, that they would just as soon agree to take the payoff out here where there were no witnesses. That's how he would do it if he were the buyer and wanted to dust them off. That fucker is going to catch a faceful of 9mm parabellum if he even breathes wrong. Mitch wanted to see the look on his face when he stepped up to a muzzleful of Uzi spit.

He saw Interstate 40 glide below. Twenty miles ahead would be the Old Woman intercept point. He could see the top of the main peak ahead, slightly west of track.

He remembered from the chart that the intercept zone the buyer had designated fell within the Turtle Military Operating Area and that there were no floor restrictions in the spot where he was to give his wig-wags. The buyer wanted him right down on the deck when he flew across the depression. One hundred feet. He eased the yoke forward and began his descent.

The ground flashed beneath the wings. Even with

the throttles back to 120 knots, at ninety-five feet the perception of speed had a grand reality. He lined up to cross the depression and began to waggle the wingtips.

Before he saw it, he felt the rumble come. It rode right through the muffled throb of his own engines and thumped into his chest and gut. He didn't have to take time to figure its direction. There, directly in front of him, rising like some preternatural beast from the back of a broiled Mother Earth, lifted the squat, mean visage of his death in the form of a Harrier jump jet. Wings angled down, desert dust blasting in a rolling collar of sterile fluff, easily perverting all the laws of flight with its hovering, goggle-eyed stare, the woeful thing lifted onto his line.

Shock. *Stop! Go away!* Shock gone. Memory. *Sidewinders. Twenty-millimeter cannon. Survive. Turn. No! Don't turn! Dive. No room. Can't. Climb. No! No! Don't lose speed. Belly open! Don't climb! Distance: Four hundred meters. Memory. Sidewinder. AIM-9L. Minimum arming envelope: Three hundred meters. Full power. Accelerate! At him. Please, baby. Get inside! Please no cannon. Please not now. Please be on the missile!* "IT'S COMING." Flashing. *Baby, baby! Get inside!* "PLEASE!" *Fuck me. Past! It's past! Drop! Drop! Go under his belly.* "NO! NO!" *His down thrusters.* "OVER! GO OVER! HOLY FUCK!" *Six fuckin' feet.* Memory. *Sidewinder. 9L. Infrared. Heatseeker. All heatseeker on 9Ls. Sun! Get into the sun. Use the sun on the missile. Hot. One missile left. He'll be turning.* "CLIMB, BABY. PLEASE CLIMB!" *Why so slow? Circle, climb. Keep the sun. Get up. He can't shoot at the sun!*

Time to swallow. Time to breathe.

Where is he? Keep the sun. Got to know where he

is. Let it roll. Drop the tip. Where is he? There! Shit! He's still over the depression. Why isn't he coming up? He'll be seen. "HE DOESN'T WANT TO BE SEEN! HE WANTS TO STAY LOW!"

Swallow. Breathe.

Shit! I can't move either! I can't leave the fuckin' sun.

Breathe. Once again. *Good. Better. Ease up.*

Think, fucker! Think! Highway. Thirty miles. Get down on the highway. Over the fuckin' cars. Shit! Can't move off the sun. It's a fuckin' chess game.

Breathe. Breathe.

What does he do? Risk a sun shot? Will he? Shit! Can't climb much more. Lose sight of him. Ceiling. Got nothing left. What happens if I stay? Can I stay high? Memory. "YES!" *I got more time than him. He's in hover. He can't outlast me!*

Relax. Breathe. Relax. Breathe.

Where is he? Where is he? "JESUS! HE'S MOV-ING EAST!" *He's going to take the angle.* "FUCK IT!" *Move, baby. Stay with it.*

Breathe. Breathe.

Where is he now? I can't turn and track him. I'll lose the fucker. Lose him. Go at him. "NOW!" *Before he shoots. Make him change! Dive on him!*

Breathe. Breathe big.

Nose up. Hammerhead stall. *Big left rudder.* "HERE I COME, MOTHERFUCKER." *Go get 'im, baby. Speed. Speed. Go get 'im, baby. Speed! More.* "SHIT!" *He's off line. He's off the fuckin' line.* "NO! NO!" *More speed. Get rid of heat, engine heat. Take away target. Missile needs heat to track. Take away heat. Instinct. Engines. The cowl flaps! Pop the cowl flaps! Freeze the engines! No more cylinder-head heat.* "POP THE FUCKERS! NOW!" *Pull. New*

sound. Shutter. Stagger. *Hold on. Longer. Longer . . .*
"FLASH! THE FLASH! HERE COMES THE
OTHER ONE! BORESIGHT, YOU BASTARD! BE
COLD, BABY! PLEASE BE COLD!" *Oh, God. God!*
"IT'S PAST!" *Sweet Jesus, it's going for the sun.*

Breathe. Quick. Again.

*Going down fast. Back on his fuckin' head. Get
the engines back, fucker. Get 'im back . . .* "GOT
'IM! GOT THE FUCKERS!" *Go through his glass.
Take him out. Kill the fucker! No. We got speed now,
baby. All we can handle. Pull out! Pull out and run.
Go, baby, go for the highway! Press down, down in
the seat . . . Speed, baby. Speed. Come on, baby! Fly,
baby. Fly hard!*

Ground speeding by.

Still speeding by.

VRACK! VRACK! VRACK! VRACK! VRACK!

*What? Why this? Warm. All wet. Right leg
shouldn't be like that.* Red and red. Too much red on
the screen. *Can't see through the red. Funny leg.* Plane
rolling up. Up to the left. *Can't make the leg move.
Can't . . . the rudder . . . can't do it. Hurts so much.*

Warm.

VRACK! VRACK! VRACK! VRACK! VRACK!

Things pushing hard to the right now. *Where are
we? Where are we going?*

VRACK! VRACK! VRACK! VRACK! VRACK!
VRACK! VRACK!

*Oh, God. The yoke. Everything's broken. Please,
God. So warm. Wet. All the red. So much red. Rolling
over now. Going high. Up and over. It's all gone. Oh,
God, I should have flown into him. I should have
taken him down. Dizzy. Where is the mountain?
Look over . . . the girl. Head gone.*

"I'm sorry, girl."

Spinning over again. *If I could just see out. Oh, God, please let me see out.*

Breathe. *Try to breathe. Too hard. Too hard to breathe anymore.*

There! Out the side! The ground. The mountain so close. Coming up to us. Steep mountain. Coming up.

"Hold on, girl. Take my hand. You hold on now."

CRACK! SCREEEEEECH.

"OH! OH!" *Too much pressure. Neck. My neck.*

Dust. Not moving. No more noise.

Silence.

The rumble. Coming closer.

Louder. Now very loud.

Too loud. Hurting the chest. Hurting the ears.

Dust. *Too much dust. Can't breathe anymore.*

Right over us, girl. Hold on.

VRACK! VRACK! VRACK! VRACK! VRACK! VRACK! VRACK! VRACK!

Still roaring.

VRACK! VRACK! VRACK! VRACK! VRACK! VRACK! VRACK! VRACK!

Still roaring. *Too much dust.*

Look at you, girl. All chopped up. Gone now. Why did he have to do that? Why did he make you be chopped up like that? Just your legs. All that's left.

Rumble going away. *Getting quiet now.*

Blackness coming. *Please come get me, Ram. Please.*

Blackness.

30

Reunion

11 AUGUST, 1530 HOURS

Kevin took a quick step back behind the corner of the
Megabucks slot bank. He froze. It was her. Here in Las
Vegas . . . at the Aladdin hotel. Her back was to him as
she stood between two empty seats plinking her quarters into the slot of a video poker machine. Same damn
jeans. Same damn leather jacket. He was stunned.

He had come down to the main casino from his suite
high in the west tower. He was on his way to the casino
cage to put some playing cash into his safe-deposit box
before he left for the marina to meet with Jesse. Never,
never had he expected to see her again. Especially not
here. Was the eye dealing seconds to the brain?

His legs finally agreed to cooperate, and he
stepped backward, almost knocking into the change
girl who was camped behind him counting out silver

dollar tokens to a Chinese woman. He apologized without taking his eyes off the leather jacket and turned back toward the elevators he had left minutes before. In a daze he rode back up to the twenty-fourth floor, entered his room, and sat down on the edge of the king-sized bed. *Why? Why was she here?* He stared blankly into the quiet space of the big room. A jumble of emotions bumped around inside his brain. And in his heart. When they parted company back in Jacksonville two weeks ago, there had been none of that "see you later" stuff, no "let's get together in Vegas someday" talk. Not saying those standard things made the leaving even more poignant, more bittersweet. He realized that he wanted to give her a big hug . . . and kick her right square in the ass. He wasn't used to being this confused. He didn't like the feeling. He couldn't put it together, couldn't figure out what to do.

In their talking on the long drive, he had mentioned that he usually stayed at the Aladdin, that he liked the people there, that he liked the bright, open style of the place. After doing what she did, why would she come here? Why would she risk running into him this way? What kind of game was she playing?

He got up and made himself a gin and tonic. He took one sip, then poured the stuff into the bar sink. She was downstairs!

After thirty minutes, he left the casino by the back entrance near the theater. He drove out Boulder Highway in the direction of the marina. The traffic was heavy. He would be late, as usual.

He parked his car in the gravel lot at the head of the pier. After driving the big Lincoln across the country and up the East Coast, his BMW felt small, confining. He would have liked to keep the Lincoln.

But he had dropped it off in Pittsburgh, as instructed, where it was crushed flat in a salvage yard. Jesse's orders. They had been expecting him. The car was probably melted down to bars and slag by now. On the flight back, he felt as if he had lost a good friend. Two good friends.

Standing by the car door, he slipped into his black God coat and smoothed it around his collar. He felt the sun broil into the black fabric. He was getting tired of keeping track of what he should wear and when.

He went along the walkway, through the covered area of the shops, then back out into the heat of the sun that shone on the finger docks. Halfway down C Pier, on the way to Jesse's houseboat, he came to a spot where he had to walk around two elderly ladies who were unloading gear from one of the smaller open boats. A quick glance told him they had been out fishing, that the heat of the day had been more than they had bargained for. One of the oldsters, bent a bit from her age and the heat, sat on a medium-sized cardboard box. She looked dejected. Kevin didn't see any fish. *Skunked,* he thought. *Fish don't bite in this heat.*

He looked at the other lady. She was bending over something on the dock near the mooring cleat. He saw that she had a similar cardboard box and was trying to flatten it out, probably so it could fit into the trash bin next to her. The bin was overflowing with junk left by the weekend crowd. The dock boys were lagging again. The cans should have been emptied yesterday.

The lady wrestling with the box was sweating, and her hair was sticking to the back of her neck. Kevin saw that she had a knife in her left hand, and as he stepped past he saw her cut a circular slash in the bottom of the box. To get it to flatten. The scene jiggled his mind. It seemed to remind him of something. Something from a few weeks ago. Of two ladies. In Florida. He took three more steps and stopped.

Stopped short.

He turned back and looked. The other woman, the one sitting down, glanced up, recognized the fact that he was a priest, and smiled a weak smile.

"Good afternoon, Father," she said.

He was driving too fast. Much too fast. The traffic on the way back into the city was thin. Everybody was heading home, back out to the suburbs after the long workday. They wanted to get to the television sets, to watch the news, to see what was going to happen next. The city was buzzing and wondering and full of questions. There were pictures in the morning newspaper showing lines of armed troops fronting IRS offices in the major cities. Everyone was getting interviewed, quoted, grilled. Things were all stirred up.

He had seen disappointment on Jesse's face when he banged on the cabin side and told them he wouldn't be going out on the lake with them. Gene Plum had been there on the afterdeck nuzzling a pretty Oriental girl of, maybe, eighteen. Gene gave him a sheepish wave when he ran up . . . like he usually did when Kevin saw him with a new female. Kevin didn't stay to make small talk.

She had to be there. In the casino. She couldn't possibly be gone. He struggled to remove his priest frock as he drove, and the BMW swerved as he shook his arms out of the sleeves. He pictured the Florida ladies counting the stolen cash. They had taken the money while he sat in their car. It wasn't Mako after all! Mako never took the money! It was them! How could he have missed it?

"Please be there," he said.

And she was . . . by the craps pit . . . hands stuck in the top of her jeans as she watched the dice bounce around.

Kevin came up behind her, stopped, his new silk shirt wrinkled from the heat and the frantic pulling on in the car. He reached out and gave her a little shove.

"Hey, you," he said.

She turned. She smiled. She hugged him.

They sat in the Keno lounge. Among empty seats. Both reluctant to speak of the joy, but both so aware. They shared a one-dollar shrimp cocktail and sipped Cokes.

Later, Kevin walked her over to the bell desk, where they retrieved her backpack. They went up on the elevator to his big pie-shaped suite. She looked out through the wall of windows at the winking, chasing lights and at the dazzling sunset draped over the massive black peak of Mount Charleston. Kevin ordered the works from the room service menu.

God, it felt good to be hungry again.

As darkness settled over the still lake, Jesse turned the boat to face the western sky and eased the big engines back. The boat slowed and the small waves of the turning slapped against the white hull. It drifted to a stop in the calm waters by the great dark cliff. In the spot he liked the best.

He reached forward across the console and pressed the electric anchor release.

The boat exploded.

31

Rescue

The heat coming in.

Trying to take away the cold.

Eyes stuck shut. Can't open. Deep, deep pain.

Sound. A distant, beating throb. Far away.

It had come for him again. The roaring sound that would end the pain, that would keep out the cold.

The dust began to move.

"Christ, Ram! There he is!"

Down below, west of the ridge crest, the torn wreckage spread in a tattered line that ended at the silver hulk of the cockpit section, pointing skyward, twisted, broken. A mangled body, surrounded by shards of debris, hung in the rock one hundred feet from the cockpit section.

"Is that him, Ram?"

Ram could recognize the mutilated lump that had been Loza.

"No. That's not Mitch."

The helicopter, its two occupants searching into the swirling sand, moved back from the steep side of the hill and thrashed the air thirty feet above the slope.

"I can't set down here. No room. The blades would hit the rock."

"Put me down. On a line."

"No winch, Ram," shouted the pilot over the noise. "I can't bring you back up."

"Then take me up to the ridgeline. Drop me there. I'll work my way down."

"Think you can get across that fall? It's pretty damn steep! That's one hell of a drop between the crest and the plane. Looks like they hit up high and dropped down to that lower slide area."

"I'll make it across. Just get me on that ridge!"

The machine bucked away from the wreckage and beat its way back to the crest, two hundred yards above the Titan cockpit section. Ram dropped onto the barren rock from the swaying landing skid. The wash of the rotors blasted at his back, and he stumbled to his knees in the shale.

Mitch was conscious of the new sound. It was not the crushing roar of the thing that had come before. That different sound had moved away. It seemed to hang in the distance, beating the air into painful thumps.

The twisted aluminum at his ribs lurched as it was pulled away from his crushed left side. He wanted to scream as the support next to his body moved, but he could make no sound. A sheet of sunlight lanced into his closed eyelids, and he endured the painful red glow that suffused his brain.

The metal stopped moving.

"Mitch. Mitch, can you hear me?"

He wanted desperately to reply. No strength. He felt the press of fingers at the side of his neck. Strong fingers. Looking for the pulse in him.

"Mitch. It's Ram. Hang on, man."

He had to speak. Ram was there. He began to force the sound. It would come if he tried hard.

He felt the strong hands work at the Kevlar vest, pry at the fasteners. The hands pulled the flaps away and he could feel them begin to work on the second vest.

"Jesus Christ, Mitch."

The hands pushed the other vest open.

"Jesus Christ."

With the support of the vests gone, the pain attacked again in a searing rage. The hands began to work at his front. Doing something with his chest.

He felt soft taps on his cheek. Like drops. The wetness made the burning thirst rise up in him again.

He tried to make the words come.

"Ram," he said.

And passed out.

A lightning streak of agony ripped through him. Why didn't they just let him sleep? He felt the sharp shale dig at the pain inside. He was sliding down. Down through the terrible rock. The strong hands were still there. Then the dizziness came back and he let it take him again to where the hurt couldn't be.

The sliding stopped. He was in a place where the sun came down on him from straight above, way up in the blue middle of the pain. Cool water washed his face. He tried to will some of it onto his lips. He wanted the high, hot light to go away. The water was making his eyes open, was making him see. He could feel the pounding build in the air as he was lifted from the hot sand by two pairs of strong arms and was carried toward the thumping. The dust started to move again.

Then he was gone from the sun. His body stuttered in pain. Something shook him, vibrated and grated at the hurt. He was floating in gray air. His eyes opened.

"Ram." Too soft. "Ram." Louder.

"I'm here, Mitch. Don't try to talk."

He felt for the words. They had to come now. There was a great weakness coming into him.

"Ram, I love you."

And he passed into the dark again, away from the pain.

Ram heard the words. The answer to the question he would ask, but couldn't. Couldn't ask because the asking would have destroyed the answer.

32

Tape No. 3

13 AUG 0900 HRS./VOX. ACT. REC. SER. 54337.86

"Come in, Link. Sit down."

"Good morning, Colonel."

"We received your communication yesterday, Link. May I extend my congratulations?"

"Thank you, sir."

"You have the tapes and the gun camera film with you?"

"I do, sir. Here in this package."

"Splendid. Mr. Nokuma will take them. They will be in the Commission secure file. You've looked at them?"

"I have, Mr. President. The Major recorded the drop. Near Death Valley. They picked the right spot. No one will get to it. Not before the buzzards do."

"And your business?"

"It's all there. That pilot was a damn good one. He evaded both missiles. I had to use the twenty-millimeter to finish him. No problem. I strafed the wreckage. No one got out of there alive. It's not pretty, sir."

"That depends on your point of view, doesn't it? What about the others, the middle group?"

"The Major took care of that, sir. Propane and RDX. On the lake. As planned."

"Excellent. And the Major?"

"That business is finished, too, sir. It was quick and clean."

"Good work. Damn good work."

"How goes the situation here, sir? How is the big picture shaping up?"

"It's all working, Link. There's more than enough redundancy in the IRS system to pick up the slack. The money still comes in . . . the computer records are intact, and the media effect has been all we could have hoped for. The public is falling into line as expected. Now, how about a toast, gentlemen? To the future. To sanity. Link?"

"I could use one, sir. A big one."

"Mr. Nokuma?"

"No, thank you, Mr. President."

33

Run

"Better slow it down, priest. Last thing we need is a cop on our tail."

Kevin eased back and resumed the speed limit. For the first time in a long while he was scared.

He and Mako had been watching "Jeopardy!" in the Aladdin suite. The picture blinked away for a news bulletin. There had been an explosion aboard a boat, most likely a houseboat, on Lake Mead. It had happened in the anchorage near Canyon Point. The explosion was devastating, most probably propane. No apparent survivors, although darkness precluded a complete search. They would resume in the morning when they could get the divers out. The pictures, taken from a news helicopter, showed three small rescue boats circling in the dark with strong searchlights playing on the water and shoreline. An interview with a nervous teenager, one of the employees from the Boulder Beach Marina where the boat apparently was berthed, was on the screen. The boy was stumbling through his opinion that the boat was one that belonged to a Mr. Jesse Condrati. He had seen it leave from C Pier just before dark. He said Mr. Condrati and his party were headed for that general area. Mr. Condrati and his wife frequently took guests out there for dinner parties.

Kevin had grasped the side of the table, and the impact spilled coffee from Mako's cup.

"Hey, priest. Look what you did now."

Then she saw his face.

Two minutes later, Varki had knocked at their door. Kevin opened it and stood there with a confused, blank look. Then he realized who the man was. The look of fear was on Kevin's face. Varki looked once into Kevin's eyes, then stepped past the big man into the room.

"You've heard," said Varki. He noticed the girl and looked back at Kevin. There was a question in his eyes.

"My friend," said Kevin. He didn't explain further.

"We have to talk. Right now," said Varki.

Kevin hesitated, then turned to Mako. "Please, Mako, give us a few minutes."

She walked to the door. "I need some toothpaste. Be back in ten."

Varki had gone to the marina as soon as he was released from the apartment where the man called Mouse lived. The twenty-four-hour mark had passed with no word from Mitch, and Ram realized that Varki's presumptions were correct. Before Ram left, Varki told him of the safe house in the northern part of the state up near Elko. The ranch was in the western foothills of the Ruby Mountains. If any of their group needed a safe house, that would be it. The ranch was called Stagira.

Varki had driven quickly to the marina. He knew what was coming. Zebra had known of Jesse. But Varki had been late. The boat was out on the lake. He questioned the dockmaster. Gene Plum was aboard. And Ruth. The priest had been out on the pier, but he saw him hurry back toward the parking lot, probably to pick up something in the car. The dockmaster assumed that the priest had returned to the boat, but he had to unsnarl the lift and couldn't be sure.

Varki realized there was a chance that the priest had not returned to the boat. From his background knowledge of Kevin, gathered during the time he and Jesse had tested him, watched him, Varki knew that if he was anywhere in town he would probably be at the Aladdin. He went there.

A few twenty-dollar bills and a description of Kevin brought results. The second room service runner Varki intercepted remembered. Kevin was a heavy tipper. People remember heavy tippers.

The long reach of Highway 93 ran parallel to the north-to-south mountain ranges of the state. Kevin told Mako of the attacks as they drove. All of it. As much as he knew. For the first time since they had met, she was at a loss for words. But not for long.

"Christ, you sure know how to put your foot in it."

"They were going to do it anyway," Kevin said weakly, "with me or without me. I never thought they'd go through with it." A long pause. "The pay is good, but that's no excuse, is it?"

She made no reply, but he could feel her eyes on him. A moment passed. Then another. Finally she leaned over and kissed him on the cheek. She slid her rear across the big seat and sat next to him, took his right hand in her left, held it in the warm line where their legs pressed.

"Don't worry. When they come for you, I'll shoot you. So you won't be tortured."

The black of the desert night poured over the back of the car as it cut the air. It seemed to seal them off from the world they were leaving behind.

"What will happen?" Mako said.

"I don't know, little one. I don't know."

She thought for a moment.

"You know, it might not be so bad. You were supposed to be on that boat, weren't you?"

He only stared straight ahead.

"They could think you're dead, right? Fish food."

34

Stagira

Stagira.

Low and solid, the handsome ranch house was centered among forty acres of rich green meadow in the deep violet shadow of Ruby Mountain like some lyric dream in drover fantasy, a dream too long adrift above the ghosted breaths of great north-moving herds ... a destination for the mind ... an idea framed by adobe wall ... a strength of light and depth of shadow that finds form only in air scrubbed crystal by great distance. The ranchland spread along the foothills north to south; the buildings faced the valley west.

Behind the house, in stands of aspen mixed with fir, beside a mountain-mothered stream that carried ended leaves away, there stood a small and graceful

Doric temple that fit the spot with an excellence of harmony equaled only by its own simple lines—a rectangular stone base, twelve by twenty-four feet, with steps on all four sides, and marched around by colonnade supporting gabled roof. Inside the temple, a walled room, again of stone, intended by the Greeks for deity, but empty here. Into the frieze above the front were chiseled words of Melville:

> *Not magnitude, not lavishness*
> *But form, the site;*
> *Not innovating willfulness*
> *But reverence for the archetype.*

Ram sat on the steps and looked into the brook that turned nearby. Mako walked to where he was and sat down next to him. "Will he be all right?" she asked.

He looked up and smiled easily at her, dragged out of his thought. "He'll never be all right, I guess. But he sure is tough. He'll get by. He lost the leg below the knee, you know. They couldn't save it. Didn't even try. Leg didn't have a prayer."

"Kevin told me."

"He put antenna wire around his leg. Used vice grips and turned off the blood. He doesn't remember doing it. Saved his own damn life. Took two twenty-millimeter rounds in his chest. Must have been deflected, according to the doc. But stuck right between the Kevlar vests. Six ribs and a lung . . . can you beat that?"

Mako threw a pebble into the stream. "When can he come here?"

"Two months."

"Will he get a leg?"

"A few months after that."

"I have an artificial arm."

He looked at her and smiled. "Looks okay to me."

"Oh, not for me. Not to wear, I mean."

She explained about the arm. She spoke in earnest tones. Anxious to let him know she hadn't brought it up to be funny. But he laughed anyway.

"You're something else, girl."

He reached over and mussed up her hair. Friendly. It was the first time he had laughed since finding Mitch.

"You have a nice laugh," she said.

They watched the turnings in the water. Small yellow rafts of leaf swirled on the surface, then ventured off aboard the silver stream to cross the green straw meadow.

"Are you and your brother close?" she asked.

"Yes. My brother loves me."

After they left, Kevin came to that place. He had been walking in the leafy groves above the foothills, his soul in wonder at the beauty of the land. Varki had joked that he would have to bring a craps table out from town to keep him from jumping ship. Kevin said he didn't miss the green-felt wars. There was so much to see up here. Just to breathe the air was something new.

He went into the small temple. On an impulse, he lay down on his back on the cold stone. He looked up at the empty ceiling. Like some rut-snagged wheel, his mind tried to churn up the events of the last few weeks and run them through again, but the serenity of the stark room made the tension melt away.

Unnoticed, two red dice that were in his pocket, a pair he had purchased from the casino in case Mako wanted to shoot, slipped from his jacket onto the floor. The cold stone pressed up against his walk-heated skin, and sleepiness, like weighted waves of silk, crept through him. A delightful lethargy born of fresh air and new exercise almost put him away, but he caught the scent of sourdough drifting from the house from the oven of Marcella, who was the woman of the caretaker, Montero. The aroma carried the day against the sultry drowsiness. He found his feet. And close behind his nose, he hurried off.

Left alone, the dice claimed the temple as their own. The red translucent celluloid stood sharp in contrast against the white breast of swirl-frozen marble, and some leaves scratched through the open space.

One die showed six, the other five.

Were these the gods?

In the evening, Kevin and the girl returned to the temple. "What were you talking of with Varki?" he asked.

"After dinner? I asked him why he did it. Told him to make it simple."

"And how did he respond?"

Mako shrugged. "He said there could have been another way. It could have been turned around before it came to this, but a couple of things sort of fucked the country up."

"He used those words?"

"Look, priest, I'm trying to tell it like I remember it. So you'll understand. Give me a break. You want to get this or do you want to do your snooty act?"

"Forgive me. I lost my head."

"The country went to sleep, got careless, thought the system was good enough to run itself. 'No system runs itself,' he said."

Kevin leaned back against a column.

"Another thing is, we lost a sense of the future, began to think only in the short term." She sat down and crossed her legs. "Makes sense if you think about it—all this 'got to have it now' garbage." She laughed and lay back on the cool stone. "This too deep for you?"

"I can manage," he said.

"It starts to creep up on you, Varki says. Slowly we all get cooked. Like the little frog in a pan of cold water on the stove. He's happy, doesn't feel things warming up. Regulations, more taxes . . . next thing you know, frog leg city."

She picked up a small twig from the stone and flipped it at him; it bounced off the side of his head.

"You gettin' all this down?"

He looked at her. He thought for awhile. "Wisdom is not wise if it frightens pleasure."

She rolled over on her side and propped her head in her hand. "There you go again, trying to be deep."

He tossed a pebble at her. She caught it.

"He's thought about these things," she said. "He's got those funny eyes."

"You noticed?"

"Guys with funny eyes are trouble."

"So did Varki tell you how we fix the situation?"

Mako smiled. "He says the citizens have to vote, a vote is the only weapon we need. And we have too many laws, ten thousand new bills in Congress last year alone, can't even read that many. He mentioned other things," she said, trying to remember: "term limits, balanced budget amendments, line-item vetoes, stuff like that. He said some good things about the criminal justice system. Said we should build the prisons in the desert. Seven rings, razor wire, automatic zingers if you go over the fence. If you screw up, you go up to the next ring where the heavies live. Put 'em in tents, barracks. The army lives that way. Throw 'em our food surplus. Why give the wackos TV and private rooms? Why spend thirty thousand a year to keep a guy in the can? It's supposed to be punishment, he says. Make prison prison, he says."

She looked over at him. It was dark. The only light came from the stone.

"Hey, priest. You still awake?"

"Still awake."

"Well, what do you think?"

"I think I'm hungry."

"Christ! Have I just been talking to myself or what?"

He got to his feet and stretched. "I was listening, my dear. Maybe it's easier just to blow everything up."

"Yeah, right," she said, impatient with his cynicism.

He took her hand. "Come on. Let's go back."

But she pulled away. That surprised him. He turned and looked at her.

She scowled. "What if it doesn't stop?"

"What?" he asked, perplexed.

"The blowing up."

They sat before the great rock fireplace late into the night. Varki, Ram, Kevin, and Mako. They watched orange flame claw shadows across the other faces in the darkened room. They talked about what would happen next, what the government might do. Later, Varki appeared to gather spirit, as if he'd decided something. He was in a better mood, thought Mako, than the situation called for. It seemed to her they were all trapped. They talked some more about the prison thing, and Mako told Varki that if he wanted to make things really tough on the guys in the seventh ring, where the worst offenders were sent, he should put Kevin in the middle in a lawn chair sipping lemonade and spouting philosophy. Varki and Kevin laughed, but Ram remained quiet, lost somewhere.

Varki didn't speak.

More time passed. Finally Mako got up. "Good night, all. Let me know in the morning how the world's going to end."

Kevin smiled. "No hostile conclusions for us, child? To make us sleep on edge?"

"No, not tonight. I don't think it makes any difference what we say. I think we're being grazed by something . . . for our souls . . . or the juice in our brains. Like those cows out there that have no idea they're being raised for slaughter. Sweet dreams, guys."

She left. The three men looked at one another.

"Charming child," said Kevin finally.

Late that night, Varki sat alone in the yellow cone of light thrown down by a single small lamp over the black oak desk in the corner of the living room. Montero banked the vermilion coals with ash, moved the iron screen across the opening, and went to the back of the house to the warmth of his woman. The ground mist ghosted along the edge of the mountain into the valley; as it came, it created tiny silver beads of wet, each with its own small swimming moon, on the delicate green limbs of summer hay. Varki finished his short letter. He read it one more time.

Dear Mr. President,

I am requesting immediate contact via our respective emissaries on a mutually important matter. I will have my man meet your man in the Las Vegas Hilton on Wednesday 21 August at precisely 1630 hours. They will meet at the concierge desk in the registration lobby of the hotel. For recognition purposes, my man will carry a small white package, as will yours. In the interest of personal safety, may I suggest you send someone other than Lt. Colonel Muldrow.

Respectfully,
Rayburn Edmund Varki

He sealed the envelope and addressed it. He marked the front with the words URGENT and EYES ONLY. He'd have Montero drive to Reno and express-mail it in the morning.

35

Power

Ram watched him enter through the glass doors that opened into the main lobby. The man stood for a moment and let his eyes adjust to the subdued light, then turned to his left toward the registration area. He carried a book-sized package, wrapped in white paper, under his left arm and had a briefcase in that hand. A small travel bag hung by a strap from his right shoulder. Ram got up from the couch and assessed the man who walked toward him.

Oriental, Japanese, distinguished-looking, about sixty years old, and well dressed. Ram raised above his head the white package he carried in his right hand. The newcomer spotted him and came over.

"Good afternoon. My name is Yoshiaki Nokuma. Are you Mr. Varki's representative?"

"I am. I am Ram. Are you alone?"

A quick look of surprise jerked across the man's face. He cocked his head slightly to one side. "Ram? You are called Ram?" He regained his stolid composure, but there was a new look behind the eyes.

"Yes. I would like you to come with me, Mr. Nokuma."

Ram turned and walked in the direction of the north tower elevators. Nokuma followed. When they arrived at the bank of doors, Ram waited until a vacant elevator was available. He held the door and indicated to Nokuma that he should step inside. As they entered the compartment, Ram stopped a middle-aged couple from following them in.

"Sorry, this one's taken," he said.

The couple looked at one another, then moved off to the next station as the doors whispered shut. Ram pushed five numbers on the brass console. The elevator started up in silent, smooth acceleration. Neither man spoke. At the second stop he motioned for Nokuma to get off. The doors shut behind them, and the two men left the alcove, then turned right and proceeded down the carpeted hall. They passed along the series of white recessed doors and near the end of the passage entered an empty room.

"Please sit down, Mr. Nokuma."

They waited in the room for five minutes. Then Ram moved to the door, opened it, and looked down the hallway. The passage was empty.

"Come with me, Mr. Nokuma."

They left the room, retraced their steps, then stopped before the door of another suite close to the elevators. Ram knocked. The door opened and Varki stood to one side as they entered.

Nokuma set his things on the white dressing table. He turned and extended his hand to Varki.

"I am Yoshiaki Nokuma. I am happy to meet you, Mr. Varki."

The men shook hands. Varki smiled. "Are you?"

"Yes, I am, sir. I am happy to meet you."

"Well then, Mr. Nokuma. Welcome to Las Vegas."

Ram moved to the window and stood apart from the two.

"Mr. Nokuma, please understand my precautions in not meeting you downstairs, but I wanted to be sure we had a few moments to talk without interruptions. There should be no need for concern on either side once I have made my position clear. The President showed you my letter, I suppose?"

"Your letter created some surprise, to put it mildly."

"Yes. I can see why it might have."

Varki sat down on the edge of one of the two beds. "Mr. Nokuma, I have documented the series of meetings I had with Lieutenant Colonel Muldrow, the man called Zebra. I have tapes of some of those conversations, as I'm sure you probably do also. In addition, I have written records of the financial arrangements, when they occurred, and the names of witnesses to these meetings. I know that your people tried to eliminate my associates, and I am sure you feel secure in the belief that you have successfully done so. But now you have doubts about even that, don't you? That gentleman over there by the window was also on your list, as was I, and you can see we are still annoyingly present. Ram, whom you have met, and his brother, whom you have not, but will soon, can both support the fact of complicity. They were the ones who confirmed Zebra's identity. And there are other minor players who assisted these two in penetrating Zebra's cover. Their testimony would lend strong corroboration to the complicated events in which we find ourselves. This is especially true in light of the fact that what they saw meshes precisely with the chronology I have set forth, in detail, on paper."

Varki paused and looked up at Nokuma. Both faces were impassive. Pressure squared against pressure in the room. Nokuma said nothing, and Varki went on.

"Mr. Nokuma, I am laying my cards on the table in this simple fashion because I want to go on with my life. And I want the people remaining on my team to be able to go on with their lives. We won't run from this. I believe we speak from a position of power . . . not with as much power as you represent, perhaps, but enough to create an awkward, possibly unmanageable, situation. I have put numerous copies of my statements, chronology, and tapes in reliable hands, domestic and foreign. These documents are sealed, of course, and will remain so unless I fail to renew the security arrangements at one-year intervals. If I should fail to reaffirm on an annual basis, via code and in person, these documents will be released to appropriate end readers."

And he was silent.

Nokuma looked into his eyes for a full minute. There was great weight in the silent air. Ram had turned from the window, watching now, and said nothing. Finally Nokuma folded his arms across his chest and looked down at the floor. He appeared to be studying the carpet between his shoes.

And then he spoke.

"Mr. Varki, I wonder if you have enough. You make a bold move. What you ask tries to put some powerful forces on the defensive. You are few.

Believe me when I say I truly admire your courage. Perhaps we do not know all you have, but from what you have told me it is apparent that you have something of significance. On the other hand, there is the possibility that you may be underestimating us. We have resources you might find surprising. The unity of power at the top is saturated with self-interest. Even between those you would regard, out of hand, as odd, inherently opposite bedfellows. Shall I bluff you? I think not. The possibility surrenders itself in my words, doesn't it? Again, I am only one."

Nokuma paused and settled back to sit on the edge of the dressing table. He faced Varki and continued.

"Mr. Varki, I don't think you can do it. But it is a very close call. Do you have anything else?"

Varki looked into the eyes of Nokuma.

"No, Mr. Nokuma. I will go with what I have. I will live my life as a free man or not at all. It took many hard years to put my life in proportion to the needs of mankind, and what do you think I came to? I came to the realization that mankind prefers that I be an individual, prefers that I be free or die trying to be so; I came to the conclusion that the mighty accomplishments of the common effort must exist to let the one soul soar, the one soul each man and woman has wrestled from the dust, from chance. There is danger here and I can see that danger. But I see more than one danger. I have no other choice. My soul is too important to me."

Nokuma studied Varki as the last few words fell away into the silent fabrics of the room.

"Mr. Varki, your try is fair. You've been forthright with me. Let me be the same with you." He turned and walked slowly past Ram to the window. "I rage at the pain you've caused. Those IRS people, those poor souls in the middle. They had children, family, loves . . . everyone had someone. Have you seen what's left? The wreckage that you've done? They were only trying to make it work. That's all." Nokuma turned around. His words were thick. "And I was worse than you, my friend. I let it grow. I thought I had it right. But you . . . at least you had the soul of man in mind . . . what soul had I?"

Varki spoke. "They had choice, responsibility."

"Did they?" Nokuma went to the table and opened his briefcase. He handed a wrapped parcel to Varki.

"For your collection," he said, then turned to Ram. "I know, or think I know, what you'll do next. That was your brother in the plane?"

Ram nodded.

"I ask you this. Let the colonel live. I know you would hunt the man, but let him stay. A man like that, who serves his masters as he does, can be turned again, with ease and in the name of common good, to fast effect. It takes few words. His belief can swivel like a deck gun that takes its own captain off the bridge. We who still have souls may find it necessary to point him somewhere else. I'll say no more. The choice is yours, of course."

Nokuma shook hands with Ram, then with Varki, and went to the door. "Good-bye, gentlemen. I'll make your case. It is stronger now that you have that package. I should have tried to stop them. I am dishonored. It was wrong. We were all wrong. May our gods have mercy on us."

Nokuma left.

Ram watched as Varki unwrapped the parcel that Nokuma had handed him. There was a box inside the wrapping, and Varki pulled it open. In it were some cassette tapes and two videotapes. A white card, apparently an index card to the tapes, was attached to the inside top of the box.

Varki looked at the card.

21 MAY 1433 HRS./VOX. ACT. REC. SER. 32449.90
10 AUG 2250 HRS./VOX ACT. REC. SER. 39711.05
13 AUG 0900 HRS./VOX. ACT. REC. SER. 54337.86
VIDEO ONE . . . . SER. 2434: VARKI DROP, NOPAH
RANGE.
VIDEO TWO . . . . SER. 2655: AV-8B, GUN CAMERA/
ZEBRA.

36

Another Moth

The first punch was the one that did the damage. She didn't know it was coming. Deep in her left gut, the white and pink tissue folded on itself under the force of the hard fist, and the spleen burst along the crease. Rebeca doubled over and caught a knee that splintered three front teeth in the upper jaw. The DEA agent was quick, knew how to hurt. The IRS special agent winced as the girl's head snapped up and her knees buckled. She would have gone down but for the strong hand that grasped a handful of hair as the head was going back.

"One more time, bitch. Who paid you to set him up?"

She couldn't have replied if she had known what they wanted; the shock in her belly paralyzed her. She hung by the fist in her hair, on legs that were rubbery, useless.

Smack!

The DEA man cracked her across the face with the back of his free hand. The other man winced again. IRS agents were not so direct in their treatment of taxpayers; they preferred more artful torture, the paper kind. But time was important, and the DEA had been rolled into the IRS investigation to get results.

"Let's try it again, bitch."

Smack!

"I can do this all day, cunt. It's your call."

Smack!

Rebeca could feel pieces of tooth, previously stuck through her upper lip, rip across her cheek as they were dislodged by the new, more savage blow from the DEA man.

"Christ, Kirby, ease up a bit. We aren't down in Mexico this time." The IRS agent was getting nervous.

"Don't worry, partner. This sorry bitch makes her living gettin' pushed around. All in a day's work, right, bitch?"

Smack!

She went into a darkness, but could still hear the man's malignant voice coming through the black.

"Your telephone number was in his room, cunt. You put it there. Under the ashtray, right, cunt? It was a damn setup, wasn't it? Wasn't it?"

Smack!

"For Christ sake, Kirby, that's enough. She's not going to talk. You'll kill her. We'll have the whole mangy bunch of these sleazy bastards in this fuck-room in a few seconds. Let's get the hell out of here."

The DEA agent looked at the IRS agent with empty, vicious eyes. "We're not wearing uniforms, MacEnroe. So what if these greaseballs see us. Makes your job easier next time around, doesn't it?"

He released his grip on her hair. Rebeca crumbled to the floor. She saw the foot coming, but couldn't turn. A stab of pain momentarily displaced the deep, dangerous, surging ache of the first punch as the toe of the black shoe crunched into her stomach.

"Be seeing you," the DEA agent sang out. "Have a nice day."

After a few minutes on the floor, her head began to clear. The pain was getting worse. She was in a vise of building agony. And she was alone. No one came to help her. They were afraid of the suits. She didn't blame them. People in this neighborhood knew what these guys were all about, how the system worked down here.

She got to her knees and crawled into the bathroom. She hadn't imagined it. A wet, white lump of fur was crushed down into the toilet beneath the water. Cokey. Poor little Cokey. He looked so small when he was wet.

She vomited.

Somehow she made it out of the room and to the place where she put her money. She could only make three stairs at a time. *God, it hurts so much.* She stopped again to fight the dizziness and the rising nausea. Why in hell had she ever chosen a brokerage with a third floor office?

She saw the image of the john going big-eyed when the agents forced the door. He was about to tit-fuck her. A simple point of the finger by one of the suits had gotten the john under way. In a big hurry. Probably thought they were Vice. Scurried off like a bug, he did. Like a bug.

Nine more stairs to go.

She thought they were after the money at first. But when she saw the neckties, she knew that wasn't it. The three envelopes with last week's cash were already filled out and in the refrigerator where she always hid them before going to the brokerage where she'd opened the money market accounts.

God, it hurts.

She wished again she had set up the accounts in a bank or stock place on a first floor somewhere. She must not pass out here. People looked at her now as they went by. Probably thought she was an alky. Or on drugs. She had seen herself, white as a ghost, in the mirror downstairs by the entrance. Strange how people don't help.

She reached the top of the landing. The fire inside was coming back. At the deposit window, she began to push the three envelopes through the slot. It was taking all of her strength just to make her hands move. The hands didn't seem to belong to her anymore. First the envelope for Rita's account. Then the one for little Carlos. Then Tyrone's. Her babies.

She did it. They were all in.

She wished Tyrone were there to hold her. *Just one more time. Just one more time.*

She took three more funny steps away from the window.

She went down on her hands and knees, then onto her side. And died there on the cold, clean floor.

Alone in the small crowd.

37

Checkmate

"Priest! Hey, wait up!"

Kevin stopped and waited in a place on the path not far above the stone temple, and she caught up to him.

"Did you see him, priest? Did you see him?"

"Yes, I did, child."

"Damn, that was exciting! Never thought I'd see the President. Weren't you excited?"

"I was excited."

"Hot damn! What do you think they talked about? They were in there a long time. Man, I thought I'd seen it all till I saw him get out of that damn helicopter. It was really him, it was really him."

"Sort of scary to see him out here, wasn't it? To see the government wearing a pair of pants."

They continued down the path, Mako animated,

changing sides, bounding around Kevin like some eccentric satellite.

"Well, little one, we're either going to be shipped off to prison tomorrow, or there's some kind of standoff. Our friend Varki seemed casual about the whole business, didn't he? Could you see from where you were?"

"I saw everything. Looked like a walk in the park. Like they were going to play tennis or something."

They reached the temple where the mountain stream pooled before resuming its trek across the meadow. Kevin sat on the steps, but Mako continued to climb around as she tried to see the house down below through the trees.

"Varki made a deal. I'll bet he made a deal. What do you think?"

"I think one should never assume anything except a three percent mortgage," Kevin said.

"A whole two hours. They were in there a whole two hours. Did you see how they shook hands when he left? I think Varki got your butt out of the sling, priest. I'll bet you my right arm he got your butt out of hock."

"Which right arm?"

"Come on. Let's get down there. Let's find out."

"I prefer to enjoy my freedom for a few more minutes. It's peaceful here. At my age I don't like surprises."

She walked up to him and took his hand. "God, what am I going to do with you? One friend . . . I got one friend in this lousy world and it turns out to be you. Come on! Get your rear in gear."

Kevin let himself be pulled to his feet. He shook his head and frowned. "You young ones wouldn't be so familiar with despair if you were a bit harder to deceive."

"Priest, stow the soapbox. This is exciting stuff. Do I have to poke you in the ass with a sharp stick?"

"Ah, my dear. There you go again with your sweet reliance on the art of rational persuasion."

They walked among skeletal white trees to the house.

Varki spoke. "We can go our separate ways, but we hold to their conditions. Otherwise, we're gone; they'd take their chances and try to meet the revelations as best they could. We guard our own fate. And if they change, if they decide to come for us one day, we let each other know. You have the phone contact." His words cut the chill mountain air in the room, air laced with a hint of wood smoke afloat from the stone in the great hearth, air touched with the savory promise of Marcella's hot dark bread that swelled in the black oven.

"What will *you* do?" asked Kevin.

"I shall persist with words and reason and education. It's my intention to continue. And you, Kevin?"

"I don't know. I think I've lost my low profile."

"If you need money? There is enough. It hurts to mention Jesse and Ruth because they were special to you, but their sum is unclaimed. They would want you to have it. What do you think?"

Kevin looked down at the floor, his face averted from the gaze of the others. His voice was heavy. "They *were* my best friends. And I already have my share. I *am* right in that, aren't I?"

"Of course."

Kevin's face stayed down. He appeared slumped, out of spirit, drained. "I suppose their share was bigger than mine?"

Mako started to smile.

"Twice yours," said Varki. His voice was gentle.

"I shall never again know friendship like that in my lifetime." Kevin's voice was almost a whisper.

"We can talk another time, Kevin, if this hurts too much."

"No, it's all right."

Mako put her left hand over her mouth and squeezed her cheeks between her thumb and fingers.

"Look, Padre," said Ram, "Varki offered me Plum's share to help with Mitch. There's nothing wrong in doing what he says."

Kevin raised his head slightly and peered at Ram from the corners of half opened eyes. "Do you think so?"

"Yes, Padre, I do."

"Do you remember how Ruth laughed, Mr. Varki?" said Kevin. "How full of joyful energy she was?"

Varki looked down and nodded.

"Christ," said Mako, unable to contain herself. "I think I'm going to throw up."

Kevin looked up, a pained expression on his face. He looked from Varki to Ram and back to Varki. "My friends, I apologize for this crass child. I have instructed her on numerous occasions that those who live their lives only for money have a certain repugnance about them. The fact that your gentle consideration of my grief should be met with such a rude display offends me deeply, as I'm sure it does you."

Ram looked at Varki, who looked back, both bewildered.

Mako leaned back in her chair. "Priest, how would you like a swift kick in the ass?"

"Forgive her, gentlemen. She is devoid of feeling."

"He'll take the money, Varki," she said.

"Well, I think Kevin should . . . "

"Look. He'll take the money. Right, priest?"

Kevin looked up. A smile. Something sparkled in

his eye. It was not a tear. "Yes, by golly, yes!" he said. "I think I should take it. I know it would please God. It is how my dear friends would have wanted it."

Ram laughed first. Varki was slower.

Mako shook her head. "Nice, priest. Nice."

The two of them walked after supper. The priest and the girl. They went to the turn in the brook where the temple glowed blue in the northern desert moonlight.

"You were funny today," she said.

"And you were very rude."

"What are we going to do with the money?"

"What are WE going to do with the money?"

"Yeah."

He laughed. He mussed her hair. "What do you think we should do?"

"Don't know. Haven't thought about it."

"We should do something. Although we don't have to, I guess. Not with that much."

"Let's lie around and read for a year. Then we'll start a limo service."

"A limo service?"

"Sure."

"That's silly."

"Is not."

"I think we should buy a golf course."

"A golf course?" She stopped and looked at him. "You play golf?"

"Never have."

"Why would we want to do that?"

"Golf courses are pretty. I see them on TV. We could cut the grass."

"You need your head dipped, priest."

38

Ashes

"Well, look at you. Lying there like some goddamn candy-ass king. Bit off more than you could chew, didn't you, hotshot? That's what you get for going after a fuckin' Harrier with a fuckin' glider."

"Hey there, Abbey." His face lit up. "How's it going, girl? Haul those sexy lips over here."

She tossed her purse on the foot of the hospital bed, went to him, grabbed him roughly by the throat, and kissed him hard.

"There, you useless son of a bitch. That ought to hold your white ass for awhile. Bet that's better than you're gettin' from these goddamn cold-finger bedpan jockeys."

Mitch took her hand in his. "Lucky for you they got me wired into this shit, babe. You'd be countin' ceiling tiles by now."

He smiled up at her. He could see the wetness shine in her eyes.

"They treatin' you okay, Mitch?" She sat down on the edge of the bed. He slid his hand under her rear as she sat down. She wiggled down on it. Smiled.

"Sure could use a cold one, Abbey."

She grinned and leaned back to get her purse. She snapped it open and took out two Coronas. The golden bottles were wet and cold. With a small opener on her keychain she pried off the caps, and white foam billowed out onto the sheets from the shaking. She handed the first one to him.

"Jesus, Abbey. I think I'm fallin' in love."

They clinked the glass containers together and each took a long drink. Then they switched bottles, the old ritual.

"Thanks for coming to see me," Mitch said.

"Let me see your stump, hero." She smiled.

He looked at her for a second. Then he handed her the bottle and with his free hand, the other still under her tail, flipped back the covers. The right leg, gone from the knee down, was white against the white sheets. His hospital gown was up around his waist. He grinned at her.

"I see your dick is still on. Too bad they didn't get that, too. Would have saved a lot of girls a bad time."

He laughed. Put the covers back.

"Hell, Abbey. I'll be gettin' my plastic peg in a few months. Lookin' forward to it. Ought to be good for some laughs. Can't wait to visit a shoe store to see what the silly bastards do when I tell 'em the damn shoe don't feel right."

She laughed.

"So, how's everybody doing? Ram was here to see me yesterday. You know all the details?"

"Part of it. Know you got some kind of deal cookin'. Enough to keep your sorry buns out of hock for awhile. Your hot-stuff brother talked to Sweet William. Said you could use some company. William told me to get my ass over here. Told me to give you some grief."

"You still runnin' with that greedy bastard?"

"Business only. That son of a bitch has enough damn green. He don't need my ass anymore. He's too fuckin' busy keepin' his dusty balls clear of Terminal Island. He got himself a rack of titless bunnies. Young stuff."

"Sorry, babe."

"I bet you are."

He laughed and rustled his fingers under her.

She looked into his eyes. "Got some bad news, Mitch. You heard about Rebeca?"

"Tyrone's babe? No."

"She got busted up by the feds. Bad. She's history."

"Oh, shit."

"Yeah."

"Shit."

"Couple of suits came to her place. Seems she was doin' some guy who was IRS. He gets his face adjusted just after he left her. With an axe. The day all the tax folks joined the food chain."

"Shit, Abbey. She was a good girl. Who did it?"

"Ramon says it was a DEA guy. Saw him. She walked out afterward, said she'd be all right, didn't need no help, had to get something done. But her gut was broke."

"How's Tyrone?"

"Hurtin'. Those two had the real thing."

They sat in silence.

"There was a piece of paper," said Abbey. "She wrote down what she wanted done."

"What did she want?"

"She wrote that she wanted to be burned up. Tyrone got it done. She wanted her friends to have a little party. On the top floor of some hotel on the Strip. In a first-class suite up high. She wanted someone to say good things about her if they could. Then she wanted her ashes tossed. Off the balcony. She really liked this fuckin' town for some damn reason."

"Did it happen?"

"We're doing it tomorrow at 6:00 P.M. The Riviera. Don't know who's going to come. Maybe a few people."

"I want to be there."

"Right."

"I mean it, Abbey. I'm going."

"They won't let you go."

"They'll let me go. Or I'll bust this fuckin' place up. I can get around in a goddamn wheelchair. You come get me. I'll be ready."

Ram was there. Abbey had called and told him that Mitch was determined to be at the hotel. Ram had asked Kevin to come along, to put some religious words to the thing. Mako had come, too. Tyrone was there, and Rita, Carlos, Ramon, and three girls who worked the Strip and knew Rebeca. One of the girls had brought a boyfriend, a customer who was in love; she was a weeper and wanted him to cry on. He looked out of place, uncomfortable.

Four people who lived at the apartment showed up, two men and their wives, all four Puerto Rican, in black suits and dresses, neat and solemn. Rita covered one of the end tables with a white linen cloth. On the cloth she placed the little urn with the ashes. On one side of the urn she put a Bible, on the other

Cokey's red collar with two tags attached. The tags came in the mail two days after Rebeca died.

Mitch, in his wheelchair, talked to Ramon for a few minutes, then to Tyrone. They talked near the door, which was propped slightly open with an ashtray in case anyone should show up late and want to come in. Mitch's face was white. He was hurting. But only Ram knew how Mitch approached hard times. He could see the grit in his brother's eye under the pain, and it made him feel good; Mitch would be all right . . . he had something to fight.

Kevin spoke to Rita, then went to stand by the small altar that was the end table. The setting sun crushed a riot of color into the clear, dry sky over Mount Charleston to the west. The people stopped talking, looked to Kevin, and the room fell silent.

"Dear people," he began, "we are here to say words for Rebeca. I did not know this soul. I did not know her sorrows or her joys. I knew neither the sound of her laughter nor the softness of her tears. I knew none of these until I heard you speak of her in this room today, until I looked into your eyes as you gave me a sense of the gentle kindness she gave to you. It's sometimes difficult to gain an opinion of another when you are face to face in a world that is too fast, too mean. But when you can learn what others thought about that soul, when you can hear her described by those who knew her in the long, hard test of time . . . by those who saw the goodness . . . by those who knew the person, not just the shadow . . . by those who saw the love, not just the promise . . . then can you say, 'I knew that one.' And you have let me, a stranger to your lives, see the one we call 'Rebeca' . . . and I thank you for that gift of sharing."

And he said the words of the Lord's Prayer, and

they joined in, and each phrase lifted into the air on every separate voice. When they finished with the prayer a stillness drew the sorrow in around them.

"Would someone speak for her?" he asked.

Rita stood. They turned and looked at her as she said her words. She told of her friend and of the times they helped one another in the days when money wasn't there, when no one seemed to care, when they only had the child Carlos and each other to force away the emptiness. Tears ran down her cheeks and she pressed the boy against her leg, her hand shaking on his shoulder.

The others spoke, the Puerto Rican men who were her friends, in somber tones with dignity, with Spanish words that broke in among the English ones to give a color in one language that the other couldn't.

Tyrone tried, but he broke down, voice cracking, throat not letting words come. They saw his grief, and Kevin went to him. "It's all right," Kevin said, and with his fingers he touched Tyrone's tears so Tyrone would know they understood.

Abbey told of the laughter, of the good times they shared. She kept her words strong.

Mitch spoke, too. "Good-bye, Rebeca," was what he said. Kevin recited the Twenty-third Psalm in phrases firm and clear and from no book. He spoke the words as if they were a challenge to some other world, a world of comfort, wealth, and secret prejudice . . . almost angry words.

He finished with the psalm, then smiled and looked into each face in turn.

"I want to read something from a story by a lady named Margery Williams. A children's story. It speaks of love. How lucky Rebeca was to have had you. She will stay in your hearts. That shall be her 'forever.' "

"What is REAL?" asked the rabbit . . .

"Real isn't how you are made," said the Skin Horse. "It's a thing that happens to you. When a child loves you for a long, long time, not just to play with, but REALLY loves you, then you become Real."

"Does it hurt?" asked the Rabbit.

"Sometimes," said the Skin Horse, for he was always truthful . . .

"Does it happen all at once, like being wound up," he asked, "or bit by bit?"

"It doesn't happen all at once," said the Skin Horse. "You become. It takes a long time. That's why it doesn't often happen to people who break easily, or have sharp edges, or who have to be carefully kept. Generally, by the time you are Real, most of your hair has been loved off, and your eyes drop out, and you get loose in the joints and very shabby. But these things don't matter at all because once you are Real you can't be ugly, except to people who don't understand . . . once you are real you can't become unreal again. It lasts for always."

He stopped talking. He lifted up the urn and took it out onto the balcony, onto the edge of the new night. Each person, little Carlos and Rita first, cast a handful of her ashes to the wind. Mitch was last. He stayed on the balcony in his wheelchair looking down at the great banks of light, at the cars, at the people far below.

While they were out on the balcony, a man

stepped in through the open door of the room, a man wearing a gray suit. As the people came back into the room, they saw him there. The people were about to drink and talk, but the man's presence was alarming to those from the street and from the Harcourt Arms. They began to leave. As they passed the man who now stood by the door, they were asked their names and where they lived, and he wrote things into a red notebook. After a few minutes only Ram, Abbey, Kevin, and Mako were in the room. Mitch was still outside on the balcony.

The man asked for their names. They gave them after Ram asked the man to show some identification and he did. His name was Kirby. He was DEA. The four still there in the room wondered if this was the one who had killed Rebeca. Out on the balcony Mitch looked down at the traffic below. He didn't have to wonder. Ramon, the old man, fear in his eyes, had bent to his ear and told him as soon as he saw the man by the door.

"Who's that out there?"

"That's my brother."

"Get him in here."

Ram looked impassively at the man and didn't respond.

"I said to get him in here!"

Kevin shifted nervously. He didn't like the feeling in the air.

Ram still hadn't moved to obey the order.

"Scummy bastards," muttered the man. He crossed to the doors and went out onto the balcony.

Mitch still faced the western sky and stared into the night. Reflections from the neon river far down in the concrete canyon lit his face from below with unnatural twists of color. The wheelchair was hard up against the railing, the fronts of the wheels edged into the empty air. He set the brake locks.

"Gimme your name, pal."

"Who wants it?"

"Kirby, DEA. Let's go, asshole. I need your name."

The agent had his back against the railing so he could see Mitch's face. He had the notebook in his hand ready to write.

"Look, fucker. Give me your name! I don't have all fucking night."

"That's right," Mitch said. "You don't."

He shot his right hand forward into the agent's testicles. He grasped the soft bundle in the fabric with an iron grip and crunched in with a rage fed by the pain of the plane crash. He snapped out his left hand, gripped the black iron railing to gain a solid base, and from his sitting position drove the man over the rail into the night.

Mitch leaned forward to watch the body fall. The man was doing spectacular things with his arms and legs. He saw the dark form crash onto the tarred top of the casino marquee far below.

Ram was at his brother's side at once. "Was he the one?"

"Yes, he was," from Mitch.

"Christ."

"You know, they're right, bro."

"What's that?"

"If you get 'em by the balls, their hearts and minds do follow."

Mitch leaned over in the wheelchair, picked up the red notebook, and pushed himself back into the room.

Ram followed.

"Not a bad service, Padre," said Mitch.

39

Question

"Penny for your thoughts, priest."

"I don't think I have any thoughts, little one."

The night wind chafed at the skin on their faces as man and girl stood together. Insistent gusts of cold air shoved at them. Spilled from distant north mountains, it seemed to carry unseen crystals sharp enough to cut into skin, tiny stabbings too fine to draw out blood. They had driven back to Stagira, Kevin to get away from the worry of Las Vegas, Mako to be with him. She had seen something change in him after the killing on the balcony at the Riviera. She sensed he was uneasy about the fact that so many people knew they were in the room that night, but there seemed to be something else.

"Talk to me. What's with the face?"

He didn't reply, only reached over and rubbed the back of her neck distractedly with one of his soft hands, then slowly walked away from the house out onto the gray earth. At his step the brittle grasses crunched as though frozen. She followed him, caught up, took his hand in hers. They didn't speak for long minutes as they walked.

"I wish you'd talk to me," she said. She swung his hand gently, looked down at the ground as they moved.

"I don't know, Mako. I really don't." He gave her hand a squeeze.

She waited for awhile. Then, "You did all right. I mean, maybe it was mostly for the money, but you didn't go in without believing, right? It took guts and you were brave, that's what I think."

The big man didn't reply. He knew it wasn't guts ... more like a serious misreading of Varki's determination and ability.

"You should have heard Varki speak last night. At that Libertarian thing. It was fun. You would have felt a lot better if you heard him. You should have come with us."

Kevin smiled at her quick enthusiasm, then drifted back inside himself.

The quiet was awkward after Mako's words. She felt embarrassed when he didn't reply. She didn't like the sting of sounding foolish.

"Damn, priest."

"I'm sorry," was all he could say.

They walked some more.

The cold air shifted, came at them anew.

And a low rumble rippled through the earth and moved the ground. She squeezed his hand. "Did you feel that? Was that an earthquake?"

"Far away. The way it rolled. Probably somewhere in California."

"I never felt one before."

"It happens all the time out here."

Five silent minutes more they walked.

"Tell me it's over," she said.

"Tell you what's over?"

"The thing you started. You and Varki. The bombs and stuff."

"There weren't any more. The ones we set up, they all went off as planned. That was it."

"How can you be sure?"

"I'm sure. I made all the drops myself. What was supposed to happen, happened. It all worked. There's nothing else."

"Varki's not the only one, I'll bet. Lots of people are pissed off besides him. Then there's the wackos . . . and the Bombs and God crowd. This country's wide open. You guys don't have a patent on that bomb stuff."

"Won't happen," he said. "What Varki said is true. You've got cops and troops on every corner. There's been enough killing for everyone. Even the wackos."

Mako didn't reply.

"You've seen the TV," he reminded. "All that stuff the government is putting out about the families of those who died? There can't be anybody left who wants more killing."

She was quiet for a moment. Then she squeezed his hand again. "I think you and Varki should spend more time on the street."

He said nothing.

Another minute passed, then he sensed a change in her step, and when he looked at her he saw tears shining on her cheek. She felt his eyes on her and she turned her face away so he wouldn't see the tears.

"I wish I'd never met him. Varki. Not because of the trouble. Not that. I guess he's right about it being over. It's something else he said. The night we talked. He said we're not real—not what we think we are. I can't see what it is, it's just out of reach. But the way he said it . . . I can't push it away. I thought me was me, but now I'm not sure." She pressed her nails too hard into his soft palm, and her grip made him wince. "Damn it," she said, "Are we only pieces? Don't we matter?" Cold tears fell.

"We matter to each other, peanut. That's good enough for me."

He pulled her close to his side. She ducked under the big man's arm, locked it tight around her shoulders with both her hands as they walked.

"Is he the Devil?" she asked.

"Don't be silly. I'd know the Devil if I saw him. I'm a priest. That's my game, remember?"

He bumped her with his hip to cheer her.

"It's cold," she said. "Can we go back?"

40

End Game

"You put on the priest clothes, yes?"

Kevin looked at Marcella, who stood with a bundle of laundry she was about to wash.

"You put on the priest clothes and give me those ones you wear, yes? I do these ones and those ones, too. Then I put them on the line to dry in the sun, all the clothes. The air will make them nice. Make them smell clean like new. You do?"

Kevin nodded, patted Marcella on the head, and went to his room to change as instructed. In the hectic days just past, he had not thought, nor had he had the chance, to gather his belongings and get them to Stagira. The only garments that remained unused to him were the priestly ones. When, dressed in black, he emerged from the room, Marcella, as she had done before priests since she was a child, lowered her eyes and crossed herself.

"Bless you, my dear." Kevin smiled and handed

over the clothes that Marcella would wash. And then he went to walk the hill above the temple, to walk in the sun and mountain air. As he stepped from the porch, he passed Varki, who was coming from the workshop building. Kevin stopped. "How long will they be gone?"

Varki looked up, stopped, smiled. "On your way to give a sermon, Kevin? You've found a flock at last?" He put his hand out, brushed a summer beetle from Kevin's collar.

"Not exactly, my friend. I am merely following the orders of that pleasant housekeeper of yours, who informs me in her subtle way that I am unclean of dress."

"It's good to see you getting back to normal, or should I say, normal for you," and Varki laughed. "As for your question, no, I don't know how long they'll be gone. Ram wanted to spend some time with Mitch in the rehab unit tomorrow morning. And Montero has some things to get for me down there. I told them to take their time. Maybe three days, maybe four."

"Then, for once, I think there'll be the proper amount of food for us tonight. Those two eat too much."

"I think you'll be sated, Kevin. Marcella will see to that."

"If she values her soul. Adieu, my friend. The mountain waits."

One hour later the phone on Varki's desk rang. He crossed the room, sat in the swivel chair, picked up the receiver. From his position he looked out behind the house and saw Marcella, with Mako, hanging clothes on the clothesline. "Hello."

"Mr. Varki? Rayburn Varki?"

"Yes?"

"This is Nokuma. There is a problem."

"Yes?"

"The lieutenant colonel. Muldrow. He's gone from here. We think he may be in Las Vegas. He flew to Nellis this morning and we've lost him." Varki stiffened. "He is distraught, quite possibly dangerous," Nokuma went on. "His failure in your matter, he seems unable to digest the thing. He had been to the funeral of a friend of his. A major. The family of the Major said he broke down. We should have foreseen it. There is great danger. He has been under much pressure."

Varki said nothing.

"Can you tell me, Mr. Varki, is there a security problem with the one in Las Vegas, the one called Mitch? We have people on the way to him from Nellis, but they're not our best. Mr. Varki, are you there?"

"I'm here."

"If you have people in Las Vegas, we suggest you put them with the man Mitch. At once."

"I'll do that. Right away. Keep me informed." Varki put down the receiver. He snapped open the phone index on the desk, began to search the Vegas section. Then he stopped. He looked up from the index, quickly dialed a number.

"Elko Municipal Airport."

"My name is Rayburn Varki. Could you tell me if any commuter flights have come in from Las Vegas today?"

"One minute, sir."

Varki waited. He watched Marcella and Mako through the window. He saw the top of Marcella's skull erupt in a flashing sheet of blood, saw the woman slam back onto the ground, saw the white shirt she had just fastened to the clothesline go spotted with quick red marks.

Mako dropped flat, rolled instinctively behind the wicker clothesbasket that sat there on the grass.

As Varki cleared the porch and raced toward Mako, he saw the next round explode the ground beside the girl's head as she lay there, facedown, in back of the basket.

"Mako! Stay down! Stay down!"

He had covered half the distance to her when the next bullet came. Before he heard the shot, a murderous force cracked into his thigh, and he was hammered down, spinning onto the grass. In a cloud of swirling comprehension, he heard a fourth shot explode somewhere near the girl, and it was followed instantly by a wild, howling "NO!" drawn out, a banshee voice, a male roar that echoed from the mountain.

Kevin had almost reached the temple when he heard the first shot crack. His eyes went quickly to the sound, went to the temple columns where he saw the shape of a man in knit watch cap, camouflage coat, black pants. The barrel of the rifle gleamed darkly in the patchy light that filtered through the leaves. Kevin froze, he did not understand the thing. He moved forward, shifted left, and from there could see the ranch house and the yard. He saw the woman Marcella down, twisted. The second shot seemed to lift up the earth beneath the form of Mako, but as the yellow dust drifted, he saw her move, welding tightly to the ground. And still Kevin could not move. His eyes went back to the man. The priest was hypnotized. As in a dream, his eyes went slowly down to where the shooter aimed. Varki was moving from the house. The weapon cracked and Varki went down. Kevin looked back to the killer.

He saw the rifle shift again, ever slightly, back to center Mako.

And then he moved. Then Kevin moved.

Twenty feet, halfway there, the howling "NO!" the final surging twenty feet, the shooter turning toward the sound, rifle barrel caught by marble colonnade, distance closed, then no distance left, a thudding crash, and Kevin was upon him.

The two forms, locked by Kevin's heavy arms, impacted a standing column and rebounded to the inside of the temple. Kevin, still on his feet, still full of rage, crushed at the man, lifted him up, shook him from side to side in blind, ferocious fury. The rifle cartwheeled across the place, crashed to the marble floor. Kevin held on in anger, then in desperation. In the space of seconds the chemicals of rage had run their course. His was not a fighter's body; the softness that needed to be muscle, the moves that needed to be learned, the lungs that needed to be trained by long exertions—these things were not his. He knew it, could feel it quickly. And the one he crushed knew Kevin's weakness, too, could feel it happening in the breathless moments.

Kevin's legs gave out. But still he kept the pressure with his arms. It was Muldrow's feet that held them up now. Sagged against the man, Kevin's rushing blood screeched to the lungs for fuel. Black exhaustion swelled inside the priest.

The two crashed to the stone, the smaller man on top. Kevin's head was forced back by Muldrow's forearm, which pressed with purpose at the gasping larynx. But Kevin still resisted. Spots swam before the big man's eyes. His lower teeth pushed deep inside the flesh of his upper lip as the vicious pressure of the forearm mounted firmly against the jaw.

Yet he still pushed back.

Muldrow's palm cracked against the side of Kevin's head. The blow came unseen, fast. The priest's eardrum, ruptured by exploding air, sent a lance of stabbing pain into his brain, then threw a mute blanket on his world.

Kevin's arms quit, dropped away, numb, frozen by hard cramps, the gripping done.

Now freed of bonds, the shooter straightened up, a knee on each side of Kevin lying there. The right fist came down and split the face below the eye. It came down again in that same place, and hot blood splattered. Then the left fist came against the other side and jacked the head in a quick, snapping roll, and the marble floor began to stain with red. Kevin's eyes moved, looked up at the man, focused on the twisted face, tried to understand.

As he stared up in that moment, confused and done, he saw the man rammed forward, propelled by some quick, hard force. And wrapped around the man's face, a vision only snapped by Kevin's mind in the instant of the impact, were arms, white arms that locked across the eyes. The weight somersaulted from his chest in an instant. Kevin's lungs grabbed for air, but his muscles refused to move.

Like an alley cat ambushing a stray dog, Mako rode the man's back, his head and face locked by her arms. She had run at him from behind, smashed into him with all the wild force she could muster. And she was strong. They rolled across the marble floor. They thrashed and squirmed. She sank her teeth into the top of his head. He reached back, snarled his fingers in her hair, and tried to rip her from his shoulders. The hair tore from her scalp, and as her head bent forward, she bit half his ear away, spit it out, and screamed in what was left.

It took only a few more seconds for him to dislodge the girl. He snapped both his hands up inside her arms, forced them from his face, then rammed her hard, still on his back, into a stone column. The impact pushed all the air out of her, stunned her, and she dropped down. He crashed her with a backhand blow. Then another. Her head popped back against the stone. Blood ran down her neck.

The man Muldrow stood there. He looked at the two beaten people. He went to the place where the rifle lay and picked it up. He chambered a round. In the quiet of the temple, the shell nested in the breech with a solid, malicious click.

Muldrow raised the weapon, aimed it at the girl, took one step toward her. As his weight shifted to his forward foot, his boot heel lowered onto a small cube of red plastic. On the polished marble floor, the plastic was as ice. The leg skated hard to one side, slipped out from under him. He pitched forward, limbs splayed in an awkward split. The rifle rotated as he fell, and the black butt stock hit the marble floor. The barrel, in the press of his falling, found and punctured the soft tissues where chin met neck, then drove up through the back of the throat, found the skull hole, and spiked into his brain. The eyes went wide, all muscles frozen. His legs and the impaled weapon formed a tripod, balanced him for three seconds, then he crumbled. Near a column base ten feet away, the red die, ejected from beneath the man's foot, still spun. It was one of the dice that had fallen from Kevin's pocket days before. It spun on one corner. It gyrated ten more seconds, then hopped and clicked and came to rest.

Mako crawled to Kevin's side. The big man lay flat.

"Hey, Kevin. You okay? Still alive?" Lines of red necklaced her throat.

The big, prostrate man swallowed hard. He moved his fingers on the stone. Had he heard right? Had she used his real name? "Varki," he said, "is he all right? He went down."

"Just his leg. Saw him when I ran. After you made that crazy yell. He's okay."

Kevin didn't respond. He only breathed. The girl crawled closer, laid her head on his chest, on the black frock. She took his hand in hers. They rested quietly.

After a few moments he spoke. "I yelled?"

"Like a stuck pig."

"Don't remember."

They stayed that way, together on the floor. Finally she rolled over, propped her chin in the palm of one hand, and looked at him.

"Hey, priest."

"What?"

"You look like hell."

"You, too."

"We showed 'em, didn't we?"

"Don't bet on it."

41

Epilogue

Great swirling forms, dimly seen, moved in a sullen, usurped place. There was no way of man to measure them. They were. Each turned and coiled in viscous majesty.

Swept with new dimension beyond confinements known, they twisted at the five parameters and spiraled slowly around the axis next outrange of time. The universal eye, should one be, would discern in these dynamic macroforms two structured systems among the rest with common chains of vortices, formed distinct, cored along separate strange attractor streams. And these two moved along the paradox, proud, time still the one-way street, and though in such uncoded form, revealed themselves in thrust around a smaller, separate whorl.

In strictest opposition to supposed entropy, adjunct of the Second Law, the small whorl, shucking noise, pulsed stronger with each passing dot of time. The swirl formed, layered. Souls moved at it, were swallowed up. The small one sucked order from disorder as it began to pattern.

It was a chilling birth, a fractal dynamic wilder than those that swirled nearby.

Not a changed beast, but a new beast had come.

A new beast. Anarchy.